Noble Romance

www.nobleromance.com

Last Gasp
ISBN 978-1-60592-209-6
ALL RIGHTS RESERVED
Last Gasp Copyright 2010 Erastes, Jordan Taylor, Charlie Cochrane, Chris Smith
Cover Art by Fiona Jayde

Stories selected by Erastes

This book may not be reproduced or used in whole or in part by any existing means without written permission from the publisher. Contact Noble Romance Publishing, LLC at PO Box 467423, Atlanta, GA 31146.

This book is a work of fiction and any resemblance to persons, living or dead, or actual events is purely coincidental. The characters are products of the author's imagination and used fictitiously.

Erastes, Chris Smith, Charlie Cochrane, Jordan Taylor – Last Gasp

Last Gasp

Tributary

By Erastes

Guy had not planned to go to Italy, not in June, but his feet — or more accurately his tyres — took him through the Alps as if drawn by some magnetic force, and Guy could not be bothered to turn aside. He just went on, like his life. Countries had passed him by, one after the other, and he had hardly seen them go. They were marked only by the change in currency, by the different languages heard on the streets and seen on road signs. When he reached a split in the road, he made arbitrary decisions, first alternating the direction, left, right, straight on. He followed the sun for a while, then a flock of geese, until finally there were no turn-offs to speak of, just a slim, smoothsnake ride up, up into the hills, green and growing a little cooler with every mile.

The weariness hit him with the altitude. The higher the little car climbed, the more tired he felt, and eventually even the effort of negotiating every bend with his normal speed and precision felt forced and painful, as if he was steering some huge lorry instead of his Dusenberg. It was then, with some feeling of a place put on the hill for his convenience, some grey fatalism, a sense of a destination he was bound to reach, that he came upon the Hotel Vista in a place where there was nothing else, jealously hugging the road on the brow of the hill.

He stopped the car, letting the engine idle while he considered his options. He rather thought he had none, unless he wanted to navigate onwards until he reached a sizeable town. Milan was still some sixty kilometres away, and his petrol was low. Suddenly decisive at last, he wrenched the wheel and turned the roadster through the tall, ornate gates, scattering gravel behind his tyres as he sped around the drive and pulled up.

Guy was sure what he would find. It would be the kind of hotel where the English flocked like grey and white parrots, over-dressed in their jackets and ties and umbrellas, governed by set times for tea, dressing for dinner. Guy had seen a dozen similar hotels on his travels and if he were not so tired he'd have driven on. Europeans stayed away from places like this; even the staff would be from far flung dominions — the concierge perhaps from Scotland of all places, the owner a Swiss. But he felt tired to the bone. If the place didn't suit, he could weather it for one night then find something a little more to his taste in Milan.

The entrance hall impressed him with its opulence. Its dome arched high above him, its space green with palms, their leaves mirrored in bisected grey shadows on the cool marble floors. High in the ceiling, far too high to do more than stir the air, large white fans turned. The desk sat an inconvenient distance from the door — no doubt, thought Guy, to oppress the visitor with the luxury. The atmosphere, and the manager—stiff behind his counter of brass—fairly screamed their demand in the opulent silence: *Are you the right sort? Be off now, lest you embarrass yourself.* It was an entrance to sap all but the sturdiest of souls, but then Guy was English, and for all his thoughts that day, his self-worth wasn't something he doubted.

"Signore?"

Guy's heart gave a skip at guessing correctly. The desk-manager, correct and looking cool in dress greys, was clearly *not* from Italy. *Not Scottish, though. But more London than Lombardy if I'm any judge.*

"Good afternoon," Guy said, placing his hat on the counter. "Do you have a room—a suite, if it can be arranged."

"Certainly, Signore . . . ."

"Mason." Guy put his hand in his jacket, drew out his passport and pushed it across the counter. "I'm not sure how long I'll be staying." From the outside, he'd have said one night, but now, beguiled by this unexpected temple of cool marble, he wasn't so sure.

"That is of no mind, sir." The man opened the passport before turning the register around to face Guy. "I'm sure we can accommodate you." He snapped his fingers and a pretty, dark-haired bellhop appeared, seemingly from behind one of the columns. "Georges will show you to the Syrian Suite."

Guy signed his name—*Guy Mason, 7 Elvaston Mews, London. SW7*—under the entry for 17th June 1936, while the manager handed the pretty Georges a key with as little attention as possible.

"I will arrange for your car to be garaged and your luggage to be brought up and unpacked," the desk-manager added.

Guy nodded and followed Georges to the rear of the hotel.

"No lift here, I'm afraid, sir," Georges said, his flattened, genteel tones belying the French pronunciation given to his name. "But you are only on the first floor. All the better suites are."

He led the way, while Guy appreciated the view—not of the countryside, as the only window on the first floor was at the end of the corridor—but of Georges's pert posterior. Steady, he warned himself. *The boy's no more than sixteen and you are taking a rest from rough and pretty trade, remember?*

He found himself more than a little relieved when, having been tipped, Georges showed no further interest, and set off to find Guy's luggage. Guy grinned wryly as the young man retreated. *Not every bellhop is going to hop into bed with you, Guy.* The one or two that had in other countries, other hotels, drifted through his mind as he stepped out onto the balcony.

The landscape unrolled beneath him, taking not only his breath away but also his prurient thoughts. This side of the hotel seemed almost to hang over the side of the mountain, and below, Guy could see a large, tiled patio set out with steamer chairs and white tables. It was surrounded with a sturdy railing, much needed, for the cliff dropped away from the patio in a vertigo-inducing drop. *Yes.* Taking a huge breath of the cooling air, Guy felt both relaxed and exhilarated. *I could rest here.* It would be good to just . . . stop. He'd been driving for . . . how long now? Three months? Even the air tasted sweet here. And the view. God, the view. It was straight from Byron, straight from the gods themselves. A long, winding valley, peppered with Italian cypresses and gnarled olives. A river ran somewhere along the bottom, but only glimpses of it could be seen as it cut its way through the hills. On either side of the river, the valley formed terraces, some manmade, some little more than rocky outcrops. It was, Guy thought, on these very goat tracks that Bacchus ran, and Saturn blessed the olive trees. Yes, he thought again, pulling a cigarette from his case and tapping it against the silver surface. *I could rest here. For a while.*

Georges returned with a porter and Guy's suitcase; Guy tipped them both, ensuring Georges's further attention when needed, and handed his evening clothes and shoes over for pressing. *Too late for luncheon and too early for tea.* He didn't fancy socialising until he absolutely had to, so he took a shower and changed into a lightweight suit. Then he sat at the desk, found a telegram form and let his bank know where he was. *Stop. If not at hotel, mail to be forwarded to Milan Post Restante. Stop.* His hand hovered over the internal telephone, but then he changed his mind, popped the form into his jacket pocket, and left his room.

Downstairs in the marbled lobby, he handed his telegram to the concierge.

"I'll have it sent straight away, sir, and if you need anything else, please don't hesitate to ring and ask for John."

Guy was hardly able to repress a smile, suspecting young Georges had been boasting about his double tip.

"Any chance of some tea?" Guy asked, slipping a fifty lira note across the desk. The money disappeared as if by magic.

"I'm sure we can accommodate you, just this once," John said, his face showing nothing but somehow radiating that it was most inconvenient, all the same. "The tea room is not ready but if you'll go onto the veranda — through there, sir — I'll have some brought out to you."

Guy nodded. Another time he'd have thanked him, but he knew the type—probably a man who ruled not only the staff but some of the residents with an iron fist. Guy had met 'Johns' all over Europe; they ran rife in these kinds of hotels, and he wasn't going to be bullied by this one. *No hot water until 5:00 PM, sir, I'm afraid. No room service on a Sunday, can't be done, sir.* Politeness wrapped in bland stubbornness. The worst part of having British staff, he thought as he turned on his heel and walked toward the glass doors John had indicated. They have no sense of decent service. They should take a leaf out of the Yanks' book. Take the whole book, in fact. Now *there* was a country that knew the meaning of the word 'service'.

As Guy reached the door, a woman wearing a light blue, belted dress approached the glass from the other side and pulled the door open. Seeing Guy, her face went from shadow to sunshine in a fraction of a second.

"Ah, you must be Mr. Mason, si?"

Her accent was delightfully Italian, beautifully modulated and in the range that many men would call seductive. She held out her hand and Guy shook it, feeling gauche and English and wondering if she had meant him to kiss it instead.

"That's right," he said.

His face must have registered some confusion, for she went on before he could speak again. "I am Signora Sabbioneta, and this is my hotel. We are glad you found us."

She led the way back out onto the veranda, and sat at one of the white metal tables, indicating that he should join her. A few of the other tables were occupied, but Guy didn't expect, nor did he get, any acknowledgement or any direct attention. It confirmed his suspicion that the majority of guests were English.

Guy, unused to such familiarity with owners of hotels, hesitated for a moment, but unable to think of any good reason to bolt—he had been coming out here anyway—sat down.

"It was a little like that, Signora," he said. "The last thing I expected to find on top of the mountain." He wondered if he was about to be interviewed, and whether the owner singled out every new arrival in this way, and rather wished she'd done it in his room.

She smiled. "My grandfather's folly."

"It's certainly a beautiful view."

"It is," she said, "and while we are not exactly on the main thoroughfare, we haven't had problem with finding custom, even in these . . . difficult times. Most of our guests come back year after year, and of course, many of them are here for many months, or more. We are lucky. The English, particularly, seem to like the cool air."

Guy didn't doubt there were many permanent residents; the lira was falling daily, it seemed, and it would be a cheaper alternative for the English to a boarding house in Bognor Regis or Bournemouth. The Depression was everywhere.

The air was certainly cooler here than it would be down in the valley, but even up here it was hot enough for Guy to be glad he'd chosen a lighter suit than normal. Most of the guests were probably resting in their rooms.

"I'm afraid I won't be staying so long," he said. "But I am glad I found you. I just drove to the top of the hill and here you were."

The glass doors opened and an immaculately dressed waiter appeared with a tray holding the accoutrements for tea, followed by Georges, casually holding a cake stand in such a way that it swung from side-to-side in an alarming manner. Signora Sabbioneta gave Guy a sudden, brittle smile and stood. Guy followed suit.

"Well, I won't detain you, Mr Mason," she said. "I see you've already won over the unwinnable John. Enjoy your stay. I will see you again, at dinner perhaps?"

She held out her hand again with a challenging smile and this time Guy bent over it and touched it lightly with his lips.

"Most certainly, and thank you for the warm welcome."

Left alone with his tea, he realised how hungry he was. He'd had nothing since a sparse continental breakfast in Lugano, and the spread delivered by the Hotel Vista would not have been out of place in Fortnum's. He did it justice, too, finishing all of the tea, and demolishing all but two of the cakes.

After he had eaten his second scone, he wiped his mouth clean of jam and cream, sat back and lit a cigarette, while contemplating the view once again. He already felt relaxed. For so many weeks he'd tried hotel after hotel, and had never been able to stay in one more than a night, knowing, almost as soon as he'd entered their doors, that he wasn't ready to stop. But here—oddly enough—he'd felt almost entirely at ease from the moment he'd entered that marbled reception.

A slight breeze ruffled his hair and whipped the cigarette smoke away; the sun warmed his skin, and, if he were stretched out on one of the steamer chairs, he had no doubt he'd soon be asleep—like that portly gentleman over on the far side—and that wouldn't do. Guy could hear the gentleman's stentorian snoring from where he sat. Military, Guy guessed, looking at the man's prickly tweed and black shoes, buffed to such a gloss that they looked like patent leather. That mirror shine was not made by any servant in any hotel.

While he relaxed, he allowed his gaze to move around the veranda. At one table an elderly lady sat alone, working at some cloth in some mysterious way. At another, a middle-aged couple sat, as many middle-aged couples sat: entirely silent, absorbed with their own thoughts. Guy wondered if all marriages came to this—whether his own sister, Priscilla, about to be engaged to a young idiot back in England, would be sitting like that, in ten years or so, in some hotel somewhere with her husband, both unable to find two words to say to each other. Guy shook his head. Highly unlikely, knowing Priss's garrulousness.

That particular hell will never be reserved for me, at least.

An older woman and a younger one occupied the third table, but they rose and left the terrace almost as soon as Guy's eyes touched upon them.

What did you expect, Guy thought. He knew he would be fooling himself to expect a set of Bright Young

Things here, passing through like butterflies. There were hardly any of them left, anyway—and those that remained were either ageing flappers who refused to grow old, grotesquely out of step with the feelings of the decade, or pretenders, attempting to recreate something that never really existed, save as a glittering crystal bubble. He was as unlikely to find a companion here, some chap with whom he could comfortably sit and discourse—*and let's forget the thought of anything else, shall we?* —as he would in The British Museum.

He shook his head. But then that wasn't true, was it? That unlikely venue was where he'd come, half-drunk on a treasure hunt, of all things, held by . . . . What was her name? Stella Carstairs. Duchess of Wimborne now, wasn't she? Or Marchioness of Warminster. Something like that. And it was there, in the sterile dust, amongst the Greek and Roman statutes, where he first saw Arthur. He'd have liked it here, Guy thought. Arthur'd always wanted to visit Italy.

Guy got to his feet. What had brought Arthur back so vividly after all this time? Perhaps he nearly *had* fallen asleep. The only place to do that was in his room. So he went back into the hotel, passed the desk with a brief nod at John in acknowledgement for the tea, and took the stairs to his room. On his way up, he passed a distinguished-looking gentleman in a dark blue suit that suited him perfectly, but of course neither of them acknowledged the other.

* * * * *

Sir. Sir!

The shell lit the sky with red and white, hit the dugout behind them. His legs were trapped in the debris and mud, and the orderly was calling to him. The machine gun rattled over their heads, its rat-a-tat slow, like auditory treacle. That wasn't right. That wasn't right . . . .

He awoke to find that someone was knocking and he was tangled in his sheet.

"Sir?"

"Wait a moment, please," he said. Shaking his head to rid himself of the dream, he disentangled himself from the sheets, pulled his dressing-gown from the chair, and opened the door. He was greeted by a bellhop he'd not seen before. With a brief nod, he slid past Guy into the room, laid Guy's evening clothes on the bed, and left without a word or even the customary pause for a tip. Guy's head was still a little too full of mud and explosions to care much, but he called out before the bellhop disappeared around the corner. "What time is dinner, boy?"

"Eight o' clock, sir." The young man had nothing of the gamin charm of Georges, being rather spotty and far too thin to do justice to the frugal cut of the uniform. "They'll ring the gong fifteen minutes before, though."

Without bothering to acknowledge the information, Guy went back inside, gained the bathroom and leaned against the sink, staring at his reflection in the fan-shaped mirror. The dreams were lies. He dreamed things that had never happened — or at least, never happened to him. No doubt a quack would say they indicated some sort of buried guilt or other clap-trap. Guilt for spending the war safe and dry in England while everyone he knew died, or came back so changed they were different men. But while it was acceptable to have psychiatric treatment during the war — what would they think now? And what else would they find out about him, if he went down that route?

So bloody long ago. The world had moved on.

So why can't you?

After a quick wash and brush up, getting his hair under *Brylcreemed* control, and a change into his dinner clothes, he felt better. He enjoyed a cigarette on the balcony, and he was ready to leave when he heard the gong sounding from down below.

He took the stairs at his leisure, allowing himself time to scout out the much-changed scene below. Middle-aged ladies stood in small groups, and he caught the eye of one and was forced to nod in polite acknowledgement before he moved on. He could hear the whisper of curiosity, like a shallow seaside wave dragging the sand of gossip in its wake. John stood at the end of the reception counter.

"The bar is through here, sir," he said.

There weren't many people in the bar; most guests, it seemed, preferred to wait until the dining room opened, but there were about four or five residents dotted around. The barman asked him what he wanted, and Guy ordered a scotch and water. He was just savouring the first hit of it on the tongue when Signora Sabbioneta entered and made straight for him. He'd not even had time to look around. I hope the wretched woman isn't going to be a nuisance, he thought. She wore a wedding ring, but it was quite possible she was a hopeful widow. And damn it, he thought, I like it here.

"Mr. Mason," she said. "I'm glad I caught you before you went in for dinner. Please, allow me to introduce you to some of our guests." She caught hold of his arm and he had no choice but to follow her along the small bar to a gentleman standing on his own. "Captain Mayhew? I'd like to introduce Mr. Mason. Captain Mayhew comes here for a few weeks every summer." She drifted away to speak to the needlework lady Guy had noticed earlier.

Guy nodded and shook hands. Mayhew was about forty, and slim in that way some officers are, never seeming to fill his uniform or civvies, slightly hunched, still wearing his war-time moustache like peace-time camouflage. He was the type who never stopped calling himself Captain, although it was likely he'd not earned that title for ten years or more. The look in Mayhew's eyes though, Guy had seen time and time again—the one so many men had, and would never lose. The one Guy never saw in his own shaving glass.

"Good to meet you, Mason. Going to stay long?"

He'd mastered his stammer, Guy noticed. Nothing remained of it but the smallest of gaps here and there. Not many people would spot it, unless they'd made a career of cataloguing men like him, safe behind the shelter of a desk in Whitehall.

"Not entirely sure, to be honest. Just driving around."

"Not exactly the best time to be drifting about. Italy, I mean."

Guy gave him a sharp look. "Perhaps not. One place is much like another. Especially in these times. May I get you a drink?"

"Thank you, no. I should get in for dinner, but it was nice to meet you. Perhaps later."

He stood aside as the captain walked by, and without a pause or a comment the signora reappeared to whisk him on to another set of guests: a mother and daughter from Barnstaple, treating themselves to a year abroad. After that it was one of the ladies he'd seen sitting alone on the veranda, two old gentlemen who didn't look like they could make it into the dining room without bath chairs, and one or two others.

Guy had forgotten most of their names by the end and was grateful when the signora released him into the dining room, with the threat of more introductions after dinner. At least he was alone during the meal, alone at a small corner table where he could survey the room at his own leisure. True to her word, and as if by magic, the signora reappeared after the dessert had been cleared away and whisked him into the residents' lounge. It was a large, comfortable room, set off to one side between the veranda and the dining room and accessible from both. It was filled with comfortable chairs, a couple of chesterfields, and a few card tables under a small arch at the back. To Guy's relief, the mother and daughter he'd met earlier made a beeline for them as they entered, claiming the signora's attention.

"Ah, Signorina," said the mother.

For the life of him, Guy couldn't remember her name. The daughter flinched at her mother's faux pas.

"The tap in our room is still dripping most terribly, and the balcony door won't lock, we've just discovered," the woman continued. "I can't possibly sleep in a room where anyone could walk in; I have my daughter's well-being to think of."

Guy exchanged a sympathetic look with the daughter, and ended up smiling at her. Judging by her pinched and repressed expression, she wouldn't actually mind a night time adventure.

"Mrs Darnley," the signora said, transferring her immediate attention so smoothly, Guy couldn't help but be impressed. "I can't apologise enough. Sadly, our maintenance man comes in from Rasa de Varese in the morning, so there's nothing of a permanent nature we can do for you this evening." She took the arm of the older woman and led her away, the daughter trailing in their wake. "However, if you like . . . ."

Left alone again, Guy spotted Mayhew by the phonograph and went over to him. "Do you mind if I join you?" he asked, surprising himself. He'd not been this sociable in years, but it looked as though keeping himself to himself in the Hotel Vista was going to be rather an impossibility.

"Not at all," Mayhew answered, putting down the magazine he was reading.

"Please, don't let me disturb you," Guy said. A waiter approached and asked if Guy wanted coffee and liqueur. "Just coffee, no milk."

"You should try the local stuff," Mayhew said, indicating a small, spiral glass on the table, filled with a deep amber liquid. "Deceptively aggressive."

With a grateful smile, Guy acquiesced. "One of those, then," he ordered, "Whatever it—"

He broke off as a vision came through the door from the reception, and only his self-control, honed with years of practice, stopped him from catching his breath. Beauty personified, a Roman god brought to life. The man was not in the first flush of youth—probably ten years younger than Guy himself, but his hair made him look a little less. Blue-raven-black, and set in boyish loose curls, it reflected none of the artificial yellow light. And yet his face, serious and searching, as it scanned the room, had been what had truly attracted Guy's attention. A little long, but with high cheekbones that gave distinct shadows to his cheeks. He glanced around the room, as if looking for someone. Make it me, thought Guy hopelessly. *Make it me.* Not since Arthur had his heart leapt so at the first sight of a stranger.

Beside him, Mayhew waved across the room. "Ah, Calloway's here. He'll want to meet you, Mason; he's always keen to meet new people."

Guy felt an irrational rise of jealousy. The young man looked over at them and Guy dreaded seeing the look of connection between him and Mayhew, then mentally kicked himself for his idiocy. But he could hardly take his eyes off the young man. Calloway? What could the new arrival and the shabby, worn-out captain possibly have in common? Mayhew spoke again, dragging Guy's attention away from the newcomer by the door.

"Mason? Allow me to introduce Professor James Calloway."

It took Guy a second to realise Calloway was not, in fact, the dark-haired stranger, but another gentleman entirely, who stood by Mayhew's elbow. The real Calloway had grizzled brown hair and glasses, and was as tall as Mayhew. Broader of shoulder, he filled out his clothes in a way Mayhew never would, even if he ate pasta from now until doomsday. Even though Calloway had at least ten years on Guy, he was still handsome, and had one of those faces that has spent a lot of time smiling, the creases around his eyes giving him a look of an amiable bear. Guy, as ever, in his bitter, obsessed way, couldn't help but wonder what Calloway had done during the war, but it was one of those questions he never asked, in case someone reflected the question back upon himself. Something active, no doubt, and as Calloway stepped forward with a trace of a limp, Guy's suspicions in that direction were confirmed.

He struggled to his feet, a little disorientated. "Ah. Calloway. Not the explorer? Pretty sure he isn't a professor, and anyway, hasn't Lombardy been pretty well mapped?"

They laughed as they sat down.

"No," Calloway said, gesturing for a waiter. "That's my younger brother, Oswald. Currently in the Limpopo or somewhere equally remote. Perhaps they'll eat him. Couldn't happen to a nicer chap."

More rather brittle laughter that Guy thought wasn't entirely false. The waiter appeared with Guy's liqueur and Calloway ordered a Cointreau for himself.

"I see Mayhew's got you on the local poison," Calloway said then turned to the waiter. "Please tell Louis he needn't stay. He'll only be bored. Tell him he can take the car into Varese if he wants."

Guy tried his liqueur as Mayhew spoke.

"From the look that Miss Darnley was giving him over breakfast, I would imagine she wouldn't mind a drive into town."

The liquid was like warm almonds, burning his lips and heating him from the inside out. It made him concentrate, and helped him not turn his head to follow the waiter's progress back to the beautiful Louis.

"She can continue to want," Calloway said, shortly. "Oh, curse these baby drinks. Let's have some beer."

"You know the signora frowns on you ordering beer after dinner," Mayhew said.

"The signora can go hang. Gianni, Gianni! *Tre birre per favore*. I'm sure Mason—?"

Guy nodded. The little drink, whilst delicious, had simply made him thirsty.

The waiter hurried away, and Guy watched him go, wondering if he'd report to the signora.

"Not that the beer is . . . . Oh god, I miss Scottish beer. I'd give up six months of work for a good pint of Bellhaven right now."

"You are Scottish then, Professor Calloway?" Guy asked.

Calloway laughed. He had an infectious, avuncular laugh. "Can't you tell by the accent, laddie?"

Guy had a feeling he was going to like Calloway. Other than the fake Scots brogue the man had affected at that point, Calloway had no discernible accent, not that Guy considered himself any sort of Henry Higgins.

"No," Calloway continued. "But I studied in Edinburgh, and other than research trips, I've not left it since. I have more of an accent while I'm there, but I'm afraid I'm a bit of a magpie — another month here and I'll be sounding like Gianni."

The waiter had returned with three full glasses of golden beer, the condensation sparkling on the sides of the glass like frosted teardrops.

"And your son," Guy said, unable to resist. He was longing to learn more about the delicious Louis. "He works with you?"

A sudden silence descended upon the table. After a moment, Mayhew spoke up.

"N-no. I-In fact, young Chambers is James's . . . s-secretary."

The sudden return of Mayhew's stammer told Guy he'd managed to put his foot squarely in it. "Oh, forgive me," he said.

Calloway recovered himself faster than Mayhew. "Not at all, it's a quite natural mistake. People are always making that assumption. He is the right age, near enough, after all. I employed him in Rome out of the Embassy, and he's been with me for six months now. Cheers." He raised his glass. "You don't look the type," he said to Guy.

"What type?" Guy's heart contracted and the muscles in the backs of his legs tightened as he fought to remain calm.

"The type to sequester yourself away in Europe. I've travelled around a lot and I know 'em the minute I see 'em. Mrs. Hayes over there, with her needlework. Mr. Gossett and Mr. Muir, who are asleep more often than not. Miss Armitage, who needs the clear mountain air. Mrs. Darnley, because she's hoping to unload her daughter on a minor foreign aristocrat—they all have reasons to live away from home."

"And what's yours?" Guy knew the question was impertinent, but dash it, the man had started it.

"Work. That's the only good reason to leave Edinburgh, in my opinion."

"Calloway's studying the shrimps in the rivers," Mayhew said.

"Crayfish," Calloway said. "Crayfish. Quite a different thing."

Mayhew exchanged a glance with Guy as if to say that all edible crustaceans with legs were shrimps to him, snapped open his magazine and continued to read.

"I'm doing a paper for the university," Calloway said. "It's fascinating, though, the diversity here. I don't know whether it's the altitude or the clarity of the water, but I'm using both in my hypothesis. This far north I've found four subspecies with a well-defined geographic distribution. From a conservation viewpoint, Italy, with its high haplotype variability, may be considered a 'hot spot' . . . ." He trailed off with a wry grin. "Forgive me. Just because Louis listens to me ramble on all day about this stuff, it's easy to forget that not everyone is paid to be patient."

"It's quite all right, although I don't have a passion that I could bore you about." A lie, but that wasn't the point.

"In that case," Calloway said, finishing his beer and asking for another three, "let us talk of other things, as the Walrus said. Mayhew, put down that damnable rag and be sociable. We don't want Mason to be bored of us before his time and run away again too soon. God knows there's enough in this place to drive him away."

* * * * *

"You shouldn't have ordered beers," Louis said, pulling James's pyjamas out of a drawer. "The signora will be all frosty to us again."

James sat heavily on the bed and looked over to where Louis moved gracefully about the room, retrieving slippers and his dressing gown. Something seemed to stretch painfully, deep in his chest, like it always did when he watched Louis unobserved. Like an adulterous gift, hidden away, only to be dug up and pored over in secret. "It's an hotel, Louis. Stop worrying about me annoying the staff. I'm paying, they serve. That's rather the point." His throat felt a little dry, so he stood and made his way to the bathroom. He gargled for a moment then continued his conversation.

"Anyway," he called out, "if she really cared that much, she'd throw me out. She isn't likely to do that. I'm paying her." Over and above, too, he thought, damping his flannel. He glimpsed Louis in the mirror, giving him a sharp, brittle look at the remark about payment and service. *Damn the boy and his touchiness on his apparent position, what else did he expect?* "And I don't care if she is frosty to me tomorrow." He pulled off his tie and started to unbutton his shirt. "Tomorrow I'm planning to show Mason our research sites."

Louis entered the bathroom and laid James's pyjamas on the towel rail. "That's not like you," he said quietly.

"He's a breath of fresh air," James said. "You know what I think of Mayhew—"

"Dry stick," finished Louis.

"Exactly. And Mason's the best thing here."

"Really."

"Oh—damn it, Louis." James turned, caught Louis by the elbow and pulled him close. The boy—he still thought of him as that, even if he was in his late twenties—hesitated for a fraction of a second, then melted into his arms and rested his head on James's naked shoulder, his hair tickling him in a pleasurable way. "I didn't mean it like that, you know."

"I know," Louis murmured.

He stayed like that for a moment, stealing the still moments from Louis while he could — God knows they were rare enough; the boy was eternally restless. He rested his hand on the curve of Louis's back, that warm space that might lead to delight in a moment, if Louis kept still long enough. He felt Louis's lips against his shoulder and the flutter of love stretched again, deep in his being, for it was more poetic than saying it happened in one's belly. Stupid old man, he castigated himself. *What a predicament to find yourself in, after all these years. In love. At your age.*

Louis shifted, predictably unable to stay in one place, sliding from James's grasp. James didn't try to hold on; he couldn't force Louis to stay, not in his employ, and not in his arms. He was only grateful that he did. But Louis granted him a brief, dazzling smile before turning away into the bedroom. As James changed into his pyjamas he could hear the boy humming from the other room and it took effort not to watch him through the crack in the door.

Instead, he sat on the edge of the bath and washed his face again. As he got to his feet, he shivered. He'd been feeling a little dizzy since he took the stairs and now his joints were aching. He hadn't paid attention to them much during the evening, but they'd been complaining since before dinner. *Oh no. Not again.* Looking at his lined face in the mirror, he could not resist a grimace at the comedy of errors he was in. He knew he was obsessed. Knew he was caught in the saddest of things—an older man's fancy for something he could never keep—and he played his part. He didn't cling. Didn't go overboard. Louis had to know he could trust him to be there—so far, and no more. How Louis would shy from the truth—the truth about all of it. How he'd hate to know the depths of feeling running under the surface. He'd run from that.

James had had no idea the beer he'd drunk in Rome with the quiet, well-dressed man—Louis's father—would lead him here, to this great, and laughable, infatuation.

"I need a secretary," he'd confided to the man. "Dr Kidd said that when he was in Rome you'd recommended someone."

"My son," Chambers had said. "Yes, I believe Dr. Kidd was very pleased with his work."

"So he said."

Chambers, James had heard, had been at the Embassy in Rome for 25 years, and yet he looked like an English tobacconist. Like a Mr. Polly, transplanted by a genie-click of the fingers from a high street in Cheltenham to drinking espresso on the Via Piave. Yet his Italian was fluent and they said at the University that he was the man to approach for secretarial contacts.

James never imagined that the slim, slightly gauche young man he'd been introduced to the next day — the fidgety young man with the nervous hands who looked like a teenager but was in reality in his mid twenties — would have captured his heart so entirely in six months. Soon he'd have to leave here, and what would he do? Could he ask Louis to come with him? And as what? Take him home —

such as it was? He couldn't see Louis there, not buried away. He was too young. And they couldn't live any more openly there than they could here. Was there anywhere in this damnable world where they could? James couldn't see an end to it. *Serves you right for falling in love – damn you. You'll have to be noble, and you aren't good at that, are you? No, not exactly your strong suit, old boy.* He shivered again.

He sighed, pulled on his pyjama jacket and entered the bedroom. Louis had turned down the bed, dimmed the lights and had put James's book on the side-table, just as always. James climbed into bed, watching Louis circumspectly as he gathered up the papers from the day and put them into his briefcase.

James slid deeper into the deliciously cool sheets, something he felt he'd never get used to, pulling the cover down beside him. "Don't go yet, Louis. Please." Oh, to not have to say please. To find Louis already there, naked and welcoming. Just once.

Putting the briefcase carefully down on the table by the door, Louis gave a small smile and moved to the bed, pulling off his jacket and tie with a delightfully formal ease. James found himself wondering whether he was lying to himself. Perhaps he preferred this, the matter-of-fact but—to James—madly erotic strip-tease Louis performed when asked to spend time in James's bed. His secretary undressed with no more theatre than if he were peeling his clothes for a doctor, or for a healthy swim, but James loved it, for the very thoroughness of it was entirely Louis. He did nothing with abandon, even placing his socks carefully on top of his beautifully folded clothes—immensely efficient, for, of course, Louis always dressed socks first. Louis's formality, like their entire relationship was a pose, a lie. His movements out of bed spoke of no desire, but once he slipped in next to James and their arms went around each other, his façade slid away, like frost melting under the first glance of the northern sun, and James was grateful for the change. He could feel his very bones warming as they slid down into the bed, with those achingly familiar fidgets as their bodies sought and found the places where they fitted together. A different man gets into my bed, thought James, running his hands over the taut, smooth skin with its smattering of hair. *So correct, so controlled, but he takes off his dignity with his clothes and becomes someone entirely . . . else.*

A nasty little voice tried to poison the moment, a voice talking of duty, of pay and service. But it spoke with a butler's voice and sounded far, far away. James rolled over, propping himself above Louis, and ignored it. I don't care, he said to the voice, as he dipped down to kiss Louis's open, eager mouth. *I don't. I don't.*

Louis knew just what to do, always had; James was grateful for that. One couldn't—didn't—talk in bed. Their first time—a drunken, awkward fumbling in that sordid attic in Verona—Louis had opened James's fly and found the damage there.

"A shell," he'd warned Louis beforehand. "Surgeons did marvels. So they say. Should have killed me. Didn't." For years, James had wished it had.

But Louis had not stalled a second, bless the boy, not for a single moment. He'd continued undressing James as if nothing was scarred, nothing was wrong. As if he'd been expecting—and had found—Big Bertha, and not some ragged remnant of the Boche's intent. He'd kissed James's stomach, tickling the mass of hair there with this tongue, and moved down, slowly and gently holding the sad, soft thing in his hand and caressing it so skilfully that James could almost feel the ghost of a response, even it was only wishful thinking.

Louis didn't insist he could cure, didn't try. He just explored all other places on James's body, places James had never thought could give pleasure.

Now, lying cradled in James's arms, Louis was ever restless, his fingers working James's nipples, one hand cradling James's balls, sending sparks of delight through his loins, a bitter-sweet indulgence for it reminded him what he'd lost. Louis's mouth—oh, the sweet wonder of Louis's mouth. Opening for his kisses, wider and wilder as their love-making went on, then, never satisfied with one position, seeking out nipples to tease, balls to mouth and the tender crease between leg and thigh, a favourite with them both. At least Louis was virile, hard — and James took such pride in what he made of Louis.

When James could stand no more, when the teasing and play became too much to bear, he pushed Louis down, flat on the bed, and slid down to take Louis's length in his mouth. The heat of him there, irresistible, and in the darkness behind his closed eyes, he savoured Louis's cock, worshipping the hardness, letting it travel from his mouth, around his face and then back, back, into his mouth, deep as he could take it. Somehow it helped him forget what he no longer had, because he had this to hold, to kiss, to taste. He allowed Louis to fuck his mouth, hard as he liked. James held tight to his lover's buttocks and didn't let go until Louis came, sinking gently back from passion to passivity.

Afterwards, they lay cradled together, Louis's head resting on James's shoulder, his curls damp against James's skin. James wanted to crush Louis to him, to pull him into his arms and never let him go. Let the chambermaid find them together. Let the world go hang. Nothing in the feminine world could make him feel like this, this fierce, aggressive passion — a lion wrapping its claws around its own, roaring at the world to stay away. None of their concern. But as Louis's hair cooled on his shoulder, so did James's self-anger, and gradually, as his heart slowed, James's common sense prevailed. What good would it do? None.

As always, Louis slid away, silent — not even offering a kiss before climbing from the bed. As soon as his feet touched the floor he became that efficient man again. For all the world, James wished he could pull him back, laugh and tease him, hold him the night through — but their routine had been established early and now it was set in marble. After sex, back to normality. As if the intimacy between them never happened. James didn't know how to break that mould, and he would, if he could. He watched Louis dress with the same hunger as he had watched him undress.

"Goodnight, Louis," he said, reaching down for his pyjama bottoms, lost somewhere in the crumpled sheets. Much easier to be British in pyjamas.

"You feel a little feverish. Take some quinine before you sleep. Goodnight, James."

Dutifully, he took two pills from the bedside table and swallowed them. Then, dressed once again—*ridiculous to dress to sleep alone*—James flung himself down, pulled the covers over his head and savoured the scent of love, for it was all that he had.

* * * * *

Guy never drank his morning tea in bed, even when it was delivered to him. Wherever he was, he made a point of getting up, sitting in a comfortable chair, and drinking his tea. This he did the next morning, with the thoughts of the night before in his head. He'd really enjoyed Calloway's company. Mayhew had given up after half an hour or so and had left them to it. They'd talked of "other things," as promised. Calloway was a well-read, highly knowledgeable man, the sort of man Guy had not encountered for many years. Not only that, he was a great raconteur, and the more they drank, the more stories he remembered. Guy couldn't help but wonder why a man like that had gone into the scientific field, shutting himself away with academics, when his brother had become such an adventurer. In fact, Calloway had shared a picture of him and his brother together. Oswald Calloway, with his pudding basin hair and round glasses, looked more of a crayfish scholar than an explorer, and James looked more like a big game hunter than someone who hunted crayfish for a living.

No one had asked Guy what he'd done in the war, for which he was entirely grateful.

Once or twice throughout the evening, Guy had steered the conversation around to Louis, but Calloway seemed disinclined to speak about him in any detail, and by the time John had ushered them out of the lounge and they'd parted company in the hall—with a promise to meet at breakfast—Guy knew little more of the secretary than he had lived in Rome for much of his life, had an Italian mother and was stubborn about the pronunciation of his name.

"He won't have it said in the foreign style," Calloway had told him. "His mother insists on it, when he's at home, but he won't have it, otherwise."

All in all, it had been a pleasant evening, and Guy had agreed to meet Calloway for breakfast, with the view of spending the day together.

He took his tea onto the balcony and opened his sister's letter again. He'd read her note the day before, when he'd picked it up at the Poste Restante in Lugarno, but it needed a second reading. Priscilla was the closest of his family, and fluctuated between affection and exasperation with him. Her letters were no different.

"Oh for goodness sake, Guy."

Guy turned his attention from the letter and looked out at the view, wondering what his sister would make of the terrifying drop into the valley. She was notoriously scared of heights, and would not even mount a stepladder to help with Christmas decorations. Guy had long been of the opinion it was more of an excuse than anything. Her letter-writing had always been on the informal side, as if she'd just walked into the room and thrown her hat down on a chair before collapsing on the bed with a tirade of abuse against her older brother.

"Oh, for goodness sake, Guy," he read again, "what on earth are you playing at? Disappearing before breakfast without telling anyone what your plans are—especially when I hadn't even begun to irritate you—is most unlike you. Anyone would think you were leaving some huge scandal in your wake. Bodies in the bath, forged cheques from here to Knightsbridge, a distrait shopgirl arriving on our doorstep declaring you done her wrong. But nothing comes to haunt us, and I must say that we rather feel you left us for sheer irritation value. Mummy and Father are maddeningly calm about it all—they obviously have no imagination for your capacity for evil—but maybe it is just me who pictures you off in Buenos Aires sporting a white hat and a pencil moustache, running a white slave market with Bunty Armitage out of Clapham. Or is it Cheam? Somewhere depressing beginning with C, white slave markets are always like that.

"So as you didn't have the good sense to tell me where you've gone, I'm sending this to your bank. At least I can guarantee you'll be in touch with them at some point.

"Richard did propose; you were right. Typical of you to spoil it by not being here. Rock the size of Gibraltar; it's terribly vulgar and I know Mummy doesn't really approve, but she's not marrying him, is she? I think she feels that the family will have to do their bit to keep up with his family and that's just rot; he wouldn't expect it and his mother is a sweetie, even if his father is beyond the Pale. I intend to get his father squiffy at the wedding and push him into a closet. You will be here in September, won't you? I've waited long enough for him, so I'm not putting him off just because you've chosen to go all Livingstone on us. I've been quizzing Mummy to find out whether there are any mad relatives tucked away, drooling on their blankets; perhaps you are going that way.

"Oh, G, do let us know where you are. It's not that I'm worried or anything, but it's simply not fair of you to go off and have an adventure and at least not tell me about it.

"You are having an adventure, aren't you?

"With no love at all,

"Priss"

He touched the paper affectionately, before putting it away and leaving for breakfast. He promised himself he would write back to her as soon as he had something more interesting to tell her than "the landscape is nice, the weather continues fine." Certain liberties would have to be taken, for he hadn't even been able to tell Priss the truth about himself, and it was clear by her letter that she still had no idea her brother's lusts were even more scandalous than she had imagined.

Entering the dining room, he scanned it quickly. It was clear his new friend was not there, but Louis was sitting alone at Calloway's table. The young man had obviously been looking out for Guy, for he rose and approached him. He held out a hand for Guy to shake, and Guy, who had a secret passion for beautiful hands, could not help but admire the secretary's long, slender fingers, square-ended but pale as milk, the veins showing beneath the skin like a proof that all Englishmen had blue blood, even when diluted.

He was a little taller than Guy had thought when he'd seen him across the room, and was not that much shorter, in fact, than Guy himself. His eyes were dark blue, Guy noticed, and right now they were looking a little distracted, as if the young man had forgotten something and was in a hurry to get away.

"Mr Mason?"

"Yes, Louis, isn't it? I'm afraid Calloway didn't give me your last name."

The odd distraction dropped away from the secretary and he levelled his gaze on Guy, perhaps surprised at him knowing his name at all. A waiter brushed past them.

"Are you waiting for Calloway, too?" Guy asked.

"It's Chambers," the secretary said. "I'm afraid that James — Mr Calloway — won't be down at all today. He asked me to say he's sorry he can't make breakfast as arranged, but he's indisposed. So I hope I'll do as his replacement."

Yes, you'll do, and quite nicely, Guy thought. But out loud he said, "I am sorry to hear that. Nothing serious, I trust."

"He gets bouts of malaria, has done for years. Oh, it's all right," Chambers continued, as Guy turned a small frown towards him at this information, "he doesn't mind anyone knowing. He'd rather people knew it was malaria than suspect something worse."

"I understand." He was tempted, so tempted, to wallow in the relative intimacy of breakfast with Louis Chambers, but he made himself resist. What would be the point of it? To tease himself with the accidental touches as they passed each other the toast? 'Try and risk', a secret wickedness, and a game most queers knew well. He'd played it to death, and he was sick of it. Besides, such a pastime could be damned hazardous in this fishbowl. "Well, I'll leave you to it. Give Calloway my regards."

The secretary's face, already pale, went chalk-white and the friendly smile shut down like a trap, but Guy steeled himself against any slight he may have given and walked back to his table. As he sat down, he could see Chambers returning to his own seat, and as they were at an angle to each other, Guy found it easy to ignore him thereafter, shielding himself with the arrogance of his nationality. However, when he had finished, was in his room, trying to decide what to do with his day, a knock came at the door and he found Chambers there.

The secretary's face was still clouded, as if he had been given something to say, and had not managed to complete his task.

"Mr Chambers," Guy said. "Was there something else?"

"May I come in?"

After a moment of indecision, Guy moved to one side to let Chambers enter. Briefly he considered whether he should leave, drive on to Milan, whether the beguiling atmosphere of the hotel was not worth the temptation of this beautiful young man, who seemed to be everywhere.

"Mr Calloway says again that he apologises . . . for not being able to make your appointment."

"Yes," Guy felt a little impatient. As much as he liked Calloway, he hadn't made any definite plans with the man. "You said as much."

"He's a man who does not . . . he is a man of his word. He said he intended to spend the day with you."

"Please," Guy said, picking up his jacket. "Tell him not to concern himself. There was no arrangement. I understand entirely." It was too much; if he hadn't made friends with Calloway and if the blessed man hadn't been struck ill, he would probably have hardly seen Chambers—and now here he was, every time Guy turned around. He turned away, ostensibly to check his reflection.

Over his shoulder, he could see Chambers's face. He looked a little flustered at Guy's casual rejection. Why on earth should it matter so much? Guy caught Chambers's eyes in the mirror. "Really. Put your mind—and Calloway's, if you please—at ease. I'm not at all put out. I have no plans to spoil."

"James is insistent you not be let down. I'm to take the car, show you about—as he had planned to do."

Inwardly, Guy felt a frisson of interest. That was twice Chambers had used Calloway's Christian name, and the second time he hadn't even corrected himself. A secretary would call his boss Mr. Calloway, at least. Priss's letter came back to him. *You are having an adventure, aren't you?*

To hell with it. There was only so much temptation he could resist, after all, and if the blasted man was going to put himself plainly in Guy's way, then there wasn't much he could do about it. He buttoned his jacket, took his hat from the dresser and turned around. "All right. Consider me entirely in your hands."

* * * * *

Not until Calloway's car was driven around to the front of the hotel and Guy had a good look at it did he begin to wonder whether he'd agreed with too much haste. The car was a roomy Crossley tourer, the size, Guy assumed as the door was held open for him, necessary for whatever paraphernalia was needed to survey crayfish in their native environment. But the paintwork was less than impressive, with scratches and dents on most of the panels, and the inside — despite being relatively clean — denoted much use, the blood-red leather worn thin in places, and the handles on the doors loose. Suddenly the thought of being driven down the winding roads, the type of which he'd encountered on his drive up here, seemed less than appealing, no matter who was behind the wheel.

"Er . . . perhaps we should take my car," he suggested, but Chambers either didn't hear him or was affecting not to, and climbed into the driving seat and waited without another word.

Guy let him win the silent argument. He wasn't the sort of man who cared that much about showing his car off to others, and besides, Chambers obviously knew the area.

They set off; Chambers proved to be a calm, capable driver, and they travelled without incident down the gradually descending, winding road. It seemed a little surreal to Guy, as he watched the valley grow nearer, that he was being driven by a total — if entirely desirable — stranger to an unknown destination. The sun was warm, but the breeze tempered it, causing Guy to feel languorous, disconnected. It evoked the same feelings he'd had whilst driving through Europe, as if he had stopped controlling the threads of his life and had cast them into the wind, letting them drift where they may. Perhaps this is where I am supposed to be, Guy thought fancifully, shielding his eyes from the sun. Perhaps the whole lost feeling was meant to mean something, however ironic that was. *Perhaps I can stay lost.*

He glanced at his companion. Chambers was concentrating on the road, but he looked relaxed, for all that. To go with the simple grey suit, he wore a Panama hat, one thing Guy had not allowed himself to buy, feeling that if he did, he would be going native. And somehow he felt it was better to maintain the pose of an English gentleman, even it meant that one was hotter than one needed to be. Sitting next to Chambers, who looked cool and suited to the environment, Guy realised how stuffy and incongruous he must appear in his dark blue double-breasted serge and his black "Anthony Eden" homburg, which did nothing but make his hair wet. He pulled it off and threw it casually on the seat behind them, feeling carefree and happy.

"Are you normally silent when you drive?" Guy asked. "It's all right if you are—my sister is, in fact it's the only time when she *is* quiet." He laughed, wondering if this counted as an adventure, and doubting that it did. "The family insists that she takes the wheel whenever any of us go out with her."

To his surprise, Chambers laughed. "She sounds nice."

"Oh, she is," Guy said. Then, not wanting to burden anyone with explaining Priss, he fell silent.

He could glimpse Chambers glancing over at him, as if he had expected Guy to continue.

"Do you have much family?" Chambers asked. He slowed and stopped the car as a man with a small flock of goats appeared around the bend.

While they waited, Chambers turned, putting his arm along the back of the seat, and looked over. Guy felt a little discomfited by the sudden, intent expression on the man's face. It was hardly the time to start sharing life stories here, perched on a strange hill in a strange land with goats and a swarthy Italian peering curiously into the car.

"Just a sister," he said. "And parents, of course." *And once, I had Arthur — and he had me.* He looked sharply aside but found little to concentrate on out of his side of the car other than scrubby scree. He knew he sounded unsociable, priggish, but he couldn't help it. He felt resentful that, instead of the bluff friendship offered by Calloway, he was now forced to spend the day with this . . . temptation. He'd had enough rejections, and that was in the relative safety of England — with men whose class he trusted to be appalled, revolted, but not treacherous. One didn't peach on fellows.

Perhaps in England, in a misty country lane, I would brush my hand against his as he changed gears; perhaps, in England, as we shared a bottle of port after dinner, I would talk of Greek ideals, and perhaps — just perhaps — he'd know what I meant. And those slender blue-white fingers would curl around mine.

Erastes, Chris Smith, Charlie Cochrane, Jordan Taylor – Last Gasp

It hadn't been anything so subtle with Arthur, though, had it? Sardines in the British Museum, lying flat in the dust behind a sarcophagus and beginning to think he'd hidden too well when Arthur's blond head appeared over the top. There was an inebriated smile, a clink of a bottle and glass — Guy always wondered how and why Arthur was wandering around with a full bottle and two glasses. Arthur had slipped down into the musty space and had kissed Guy before Guy had had time to move over to make room, and that was that. Subtlety had never been Arthur's watchword — if *he'd* wanted to make moves on Louis Chambers, he just would have, and if he'd been rejected, he would have simply pouted and moved on. But Arthur lived in a world where such peccadilloes were more accepted. Arthur never lived in fear. He'd never joined the war — a weak heart — and as a precious, sickly second son, he'd never learned to be an adult. Five years they'd danced through Arthur's life and Arthur's set. And Guy learned to be brittle, to push the war down deep, to blend with the rich but to never really belong, no matter how often Arthur told him he did, late in the warm watches of the night, their skin damp from exertion, and kisses cooling on their mouths.

Then, in '27, just when Guy had been fooled into thinking that this life could last—that perhaps Arthur was right, that their relationship could indeed be hidden in plain sight—Arthur caught what seemed to be a light cold that went straight to his lungs, and he died in the house he never called home, in the loving arms of his family. Guy, unable to show the grief fitting to the occasion, and cut loose from a set of people who now seemed no more than frozen mirrors, took his pain, hid it away and became 'something' in the Home Office.

Once the edge of his need overcame the loss, he learned to read men, to notice a walk, or an inflection. He learned how to offer an invitation to an indelicacy, and although he'd got it wrong a few times, there had been several enjoyable indiscretions. And some instances Priss would certainly call adventures. Guy had found it was often easier to frequent the docks or steambaths for swift and nameless pleasure rather than to waste time in the corridors of power, hoping for a sign from gentlemen. However, the risks involved in both locations were real; Guy, unlike Arthur, was not aroused by the thrill of discovery or the amusement of exposure—or, in the case of the docklands, the threat of physical violence.

He shook his head to free his mind from Arthur, long dead now for nine years and yet still ever young, ever smiling in the memory. He turned to see Chambers looking at him with a strange expression, and was surprised to note they were still parked on the road, the goats just clearing the sides of the car.

"I'm sorry," he said with an embarrassed smile, "what did you say?"

"I asked where you were from. I never saw much of England. Just school, you know."

"In England? Really? Where?"

"Sherborne. I hated it, if you must know."

Guy wasn't surprised. Arthur had been an Old Shirburnian and he'd told Guy enough to make him glad his own father had stuck with Eton.

"College?" Guy asked.

To Guy's surprise, the young man lost his sangfroid and blushed, looking away out of the other side of the car over the ravine. "No. I didn't." He put the car into gear and moved forward. "Couldn't wait to get out. Not terribly English of me, was it? Of course, Father was terribly disappointed, not that he'd ever show it. He wanted more for me than . . . this."

"A secretary to a man like Calloway isn't that bad a thing," Guy said, feeling himself covering Chambers's embarrassment, although God knows why.

"I happen to agree. And after a few years with a couple of decent references—"

"Of course." The Old Boy's network. Something twisted in Guy's gut at the thought of that, imagining Chambers having to go, cap in hand, to some Shirburnian who would have gone up to Oxbridge and would look down his nose at Chambers for dropping out of the system and leaving behind all the good it could have done him. No wonder the man was a little prickly.

"Look," Chambers said, his voice sounding warmer than it had so far, "you aren't interested at all in crayfish, are you? I've no interest in dragging myself across half the floodplains here if there's no reason. God alone knows I see enough streams as it is. How about we drive down into Milan and luncheon there? I can cram you with the information you'll need to impress James when we get back."

"I have to say, that's a bit of a relief," Guy said. "I was dreading trying to show an interest in crayfish. I was rather strained the other night. My experience begins and ends with keeping them in jam jars."

Chambers laughed. "Me too. Before now, anyway. Why does one do that, I wonder? Yet all boys do, it seems."

"My sister hated it. Everything I ever caught, she'd set free in minutes. Drove me mad. Did you meet Calloway in Rome?"

To Guy's surprise, the sudden change of subject didn't jolt Chambers even a little. With the atmosphere lightened, the drive down into Milan seemed to take no time at all. Guy learned a lot about Chambers — who asked Guy to call him

Louis—learned about his family, his upbringing, and his affection for Rome. The sun was warm, the conversation engaging, and by the time they were seated in Savini's sharing a bottle of Chateau Montrose '34, Guy knew that the instant attraction he'd felt for Louis had deepened, and he had to know more about the young man . . . or leave the hotel, if there seemed no chance of a response. Pleasant company such as Calloway's was not going to be enough to dull what promised to be an infatuation for Louis.

Guy was aware that many men in his situation leapt from one crush to another, and scant few of those ever turned into anything. Guy was no exception in that respect. A fellow officer at the Home Office, a rough but darkly handsome sailor on leave, met in Guy's local pub, a man who passed Guy's flat each morning at eight o'clock without fail, several superior officers and going back further, teachers and fellow pupils too. It was so much easier to want from a distance. Or to seek the nameless encounter rather than go through the so-often fruitless minuet of "is he or isn't he?" that Guy had danced too many times.

"Now you've gone quiet," Louis said, breaking into Guy's reverie. He gave a small smile. "Please say I haven't bored you."

"Not at all," Guy said, returning the smile, warmth for warmth. "I was admiring the scenery, actually." Clumsy, but hidden behind innocence.

Louis handed his menu to a brilliantined waiter and ordered for them both in, what sounded to Guy, perfect Italian.

"Osso Bucco," he explained to Guy. "It's their speciality here. Stay any length of time in Lombardy and you'll be sick of it, but it's at its best here. Be grateful for the small mercy that Signora Sabbioneta doesn't inflict it on us."

The meal was, as Louis had predicted, quite excellent, and Guy loved the restaurant. Old photos covered the walls, showing the famous and the infamous who had frequented the place. He wondered how a simple secretary could eat here so regularly as to be known by name by the waiters.

"You seem well attended here," he ventured. "I wonder if they would have even given me a table, if I'd come on my own." He laughed, sipped his coffee and lit a cigarette, offering one to Louis.

Their hands touched, and Guy fought as his body betrayed him. He felt his eyelids fluttering like a nervous virgin's and his stomach flipped over in that most exquisite of pleasures.

"James comes here pretty regularly," Louis said, inhaling and veiling himself in blue-grey smoke.

He sat back in his chair, watching Guy carefully, and Guy couldn't help but think Louis was acting the part of a more experienced man, perhaps taking his cue from Calloway. The studied, relaxed pose seemed a little out of character for the charming, easygoing young man he'd been up until then.

"Where we work on the mountains is about halfway between here and the hotel, and James prefers the food here."

"I can't say I blame him. The signora tries, but I'd rather have Italian food than replacement English fare. What do you do with him all day?"

Louis's half smile slipped completely. A hungry, almost feral look replaced it, but just for a moment. "I sit and watch while he paddles. I take notes, mainly. Then type them up when we come back to the hotel, as well as deal with his correspondence, and anything else he needs."

"I know you said . . . references and your career," Guy said slowly, inching his way into an investigation that was entirely new to him. "But I think at your age I would be very bored, shut up somewhere like the Hotel Vista."

"At my age, you were probably doing something much more useful," Louis said in a bitter voice, stubbing his cigarette out in the ashtray and taking another from his own pack. He offered one to Guy, who, having one already lit, declined.

The core of Englishness holds us upright, doesn't it? he thought. *We stay polite even when offended.*

"Not really."

"Oh, come on," Louis said. "You don't still call yourself by your rank, like that mummified fool Mayhew. But you're not a conshie."

"You can tell that by looking at me, can you?" Guy tried to keep it light, but he felt he was losing whatever small ground he'd gained.

Louis looked down for a moment then straight into Guy's eyes. "I can. I can tell a lot about you just by looking. So what was your rank?"

"Captain."

"I would have guessed."

Guy felt a wave of irritation sweep over him. "Don't go getting any ideas about me. I did nothing other than dress up and push paper. Never got out of Whitehall."

"At least . . . at least you had that. I missed it."

"You were lucky."

"You think so?"

The edge of his control began to fray. "I don't think so; I know so. Too many boys of your generation have this . . . idea . . . of what it was like. Of what war was like. I blame the bloody poets."

Louis was sitting back now, his eyes hooded. "One might say that you didn't know what it was like, either."

"Then let's not talk about it," Guy snapped. Damn it, he thought. Why do I allow myself to be rattled by this so easily, after all this time?

"I apologise," Louis said quietly. "I just wish that I had had the chance."

"So do I, believe me." There. It was out.

"Then we have something in common." With that, the subtle smile that was flickering on the edge of Louis's mouth seemed to transfer itself, like the smoke of a newly extinguished candle, across the table, touching Guy's lips and making them turn upwards.

"Or perhaps," Louis added, almost too quietly to hear, "more than one something."

"So what should we do now?" Guy asked. "I mean, this afternoon."

The hidden meaning hung heavy over them both, and the eye contact lengthened without embarrassment until Guy suddenly felt his cigarette burning his fingers and had to drop the end onto the tablecloth, causing the moment to break as he hurriedly attempted to retrieve it. With quiet speed and efficiency, Louis dunked his napkin into the water jug and placed it over the smouldering spot. Beneath the cloth, Louis's fingers brushed Guy's, then moved over the back of his hand, running over the ridges of his knuckles—all this in a graceful, balanced moment, all the while signalling for a waiter with his other hand, startling Guy with his sangfroid.

Guy had to wonder, because it was entirely out of his experience, whether men and women went through this dance, and whether they felt this nerve-shattering ambivalence of sensation when a contact was made, this melange of elation and fear.

"That's rather the question, isn't it?" Louis paid the bill and they left, but now, every accidental touch was a joy, a present yet to be opened.

Later, Guy couldn't remember which gallery they went to, or which art they saw. He remembered an internal courtyard, with galleries and statues, and he remembered moving slowly from painting to painting, but no one image stayed with him, all Rembrandts and Caravaggios eclipsed by the chiaroscuro of Louis's dark curls against his cheek.

"You should see the Last Supper, of course," Louis said, as they emerged back into the street. "It's not far from here."

"No." Guy caught him by the arm, and squeezed, just a little. "No. Let's go back."

Louis nodded. It was enough.

The drive back to the hotel was silent, but Guy didn't move his hand from Louis's thigh until the very last moment, and even after he did, the feel of the warmth of the man's leg stayed with him through all the formalities of the parting and polite exchanges as they said they'd see each other before dinner. As he walked back into the hotel, aware of Louis's footsteps behind him, he was suddenly minded to compare his homosexual life with that of a swan, gliding across a lake. *So much turmoil beneath the surface, and yet . . . .*

* * * * *

They ate separately. Guy found himself irreparably attached to Mayhew in the bar, and Louis entered only briefly to inform them that James was not well enough to join them. Mayhew suggested they all eat together, but Louis coloured and looked discomfited.

"No. Thank you, but I only intend to eat quickly and then to see if Mr. Calloway needs anything," Louis answered, before leaving them both without a backward glance.

"He's a strange chap," Mayhew said, turning back to the bar. "Keeps himself to himself. Never even comes down after dinner."

Guy certainly didn't want to discuss Louis with Mayhew, so he changed the subject to the upcoming Olympics. Mayhew, it turned out, was a track and field man and was planning to go to Berlin, much to Guy's surprise. When they parted for dinner, Guy made a note not to speak of sport again. *First crayfish, then running, if it wasn't for Louis . . . .*

After dinner, Guy went out onto the veranda. He leant on the railing, and looked down into the ravine. A waiter asked him if he wanted anything and he declined, but stayed where he was, drinking up the beauty of the landscape. The sun sat on the edge of the ravine, sinking slowly into it, as if melting into the rock itself, painting the valley in golds and a red that defied description. Crickets, somewhere below him, sang in chorus, accompanying the click-click-click of Miss Hayes's needles just inside the open lounge doors. Lighting a cigarette, Guy let himself blend into the dusk, feeling, fancifully, that as the darkness encroached, the shadow crept towards him, threatening his very life — and in mere moments it would be too late to seek the safety of the light of the salon behind him.

A familiar laugh broke behind him, and the spell shattered, the sunset becoming nothing but the mundane turn of the earth. Guy spun around, surprised to see Mayhew and Louis move out onto the veranda.

"There you are," said Mayhew. "I told you I hadn't seen him go upstairs."

"I must have been mistaken." Louis's voice was quiet; the boy seemed embarrassed to be hijacked.

"How's Calloway?" Guy asked.

"He's asleep," Louis said, looking straight into Guy's eyes. "He's got some powders to help him sleep at times like this. He won't wake until morning, most likely."

Guy felt a stirring in his groin at the obvious invitation.

"Poor chap," Mayhew said. "Gets through the war unscathed and picks up malaria from God knows where. Very unfair. I found young Chambers here floating around the lobby and asked him out for a drink. I think he was avoiding Mrs. Darnley, weren't you, Chambers? The woman has been positively poisonous today. I swear if she starts talking about that bloody Simpson woman again and how England is doomed if she gets her hooks into the crown—" He broke off and fumbled in his pockets, pulling out a cigarette case. "God, women can be the devil."

"She's probably furious that Wallis queered the pitch for her daughter," Guy laughed. "How he'd ever have got to meet her, I can't imagine."

"Oh, I know," Mayhew said, accepting a light from Louis. Something twisted in Guy's gut to see the small, intimacy between them. "But one can't tell the woman that; she lives in a fantasy land. She drags that poor horse-faced girl from town to town in the hope of some Italian noble appearing, like Darcy's coincidental meeting with Lizzie at Pemberley. Will you join us in a brandy, Mason?"

Guy nodded and moved from the railing, throwing his cigarette over into the ravine with a careless gesture. Mayhew stayed for two brandies then made his excuses, leaving Guy and Louis together — if not entirely alone.

Guy watched Louis's hands as he smoked, watched the way the moonlight caught the small, dark hairs on the back of them. Inches away, but as far as the moon. Guy was painfully aware of the presence of Miss Hayes, just inside the door, although he wondered how much she could see on the unlit veranda, whether she could hear what they said.

"James wants me to go to France with him," Louis said, suddenly. "Although he's been meaning to go for weeks now and never does. Some kind of crayfish only found in the Rhone, apparently." Louis paused then, flicking the ash over the edge, and releasing another blue-grey breath.

Guy wondered if he was waiting for him to fill the silence with questions and recriminations, perhaps to do something that justified both a moon and a landscape. When Guy said nothing, trapped by the watchful stillness, Louis cut through the silence.

"I think I will."

Guy fought him, word for dispassionate word. He felt he could deflect him now. "If you think you should, then you should. It is a good opportunity for you." *Is he sophisticated enough to be hurt? Am I that petty?* It seemed so.

The wind caught the leaves of the tree beside them and the ground rippled with light and shade. Louis turned his face towards Guy, his cheekbones catching the light. Guy masked his gasp of surprise at the sudden beauty by pretending to cough. Even if Guy had owned a camera, it could not have caught the sheer self-conscious pride Louis's face showed, sure in his hold over Guy, over James.

The moment passed with the breeze.

"I've been there before," Louis said, a little defiantly, as if daring Guy to question his motives.

If we were schoolboys, he would plant his feet astride and roll up his sleeves in preparation for a challenge, a fight, a bloody nose. Instead our weapons are nothing but cigarette smoke and a feigned boredom.

"I didn't know."

"In '24. Pater was an attaché there. Then we moved to Rome the year after."

Guy tried to imagine him then. Wide-eyed he'd have been, not this brittle know-it-all holding himself against the world. He'd have been little more than a child, eating with his parents, meeting their friends. Ignored by all. An overlooked irritant in a world he'd have to grow into, as if it were a blazer bought for him, two sizes too large.

"Why do you stay with him?" The sentence tumbled from his mouth like musty air from a freshly opened tomb.

Louis didn't answer, but lit another cigarette, then stood and moved over to where the railing looked over the valley, where the shadows were deepest and no-one could see from the lounge. He turned on the railing, and looked out into the gathering dark. "I suppose you want to know if I love him."

The intimate response embarrassed Guy, and he found himself unable to answer. It wasn't what he asked, but the clarity of Louis's perception cut him down, cut through the pretence of innocent inquiry to the heart of the matter. He hadn't really known, up to that point, what Louis's role was with James, and now he did he felt like taking Louis's hand and leading him out of the hotel.

"I don't think it's relevant," Louis went on. "For people like us, I mean."

"You can't mean that."

"Why not?" Despite the need for keeping his voice down, Louis's tone trembled with a subtle fire. "I could go through life, hoping, hoping—each man I meet, even ones like y—me. That he'll be a future. A life. But it's not like that, is it?"

Guy struggled with words he'd never voiced. Louis was saying things he'd thought over and over—who didn't? But he'd never allowed himself to sink into that morass where there was no hope, no hope at all. A life where he'd settle for comfort and sex over what else might be found on the path. "I.... There was.... I can't say I altogether agree."

"You have someone?" A catch of breath, a question of surprise.

Guy turned his back to the railing. "I did."

"Oh. Forgive me. Was it the war?"

"No, no. We didn't meet until after the war. But you mustn't think.... You are too young to think.... There is happiness. There can be."

"Are you happy?"

If I were a woman, Guy thought, I might have slapped him for that. *But then, he might have already slapped me.* "Yes." He leaned in and kissed Louis quickly, chastely, and pulled back. "I think so."

Louis didn't move, and that was enough for Guy.

"I've wanted to kiss you since the moment I saw you," Guy said. It didn't matter that it wasn't strictly true. There was a warmth in Louis's eyes that lasted a moment, then a cool wariness crept in, as if he'd heard the line before.

Without further thought—for he would only hesitate and there had been enough of that—Guy leant across, took Louis's chin in his hand and gently touched their lips together again. There was no resistance. No reciprocation at first either, but no hesitation. Guy took this as further approval, moved closer, dropping his hand and snaking it around Louis's waist. With his mouth still closed, he pressed a little harder, then let his tongue slide out and softly touch Louis's mouth. He felt a surge of sensation flood through him, starting in his thighs and radiating up, and out; it took every ounce of restraint he had not to shove Louis against the shadowed wall and let his pent-up attraction loose.

Louis was quiet in Guy's arms, his eyes closed, giving no hint that the advance was objectionable. When Guy's tongue touched his lips, his mouth opened, and his fevered, ragged breath felt burning hot against Guy's skin. Guy moved his body closer, wrapping himself around the slighter man, and pressed his cock against Louis—and found himself unable to resist a smile against Louis's mouth as he found a reciprocal hardness he had hoped would be there.

Louis turned his head to one side, but his mouth rested gently against Guy's cheek, rubbing against it, leaving a warm, moisture trail. "Please. Someone will come out."

"Then let's go in." Guy didn't loosen his grip. Now he had him, he was reluctant to let him go, even though he knew he must. Damn life for forcing them to sneak about like this. "I'll go in." He moved his hips back, but slid a hand between them and let his thumb outline the delicious bulge of Louis's cock beneath the cloth. He heard Louis's breath hitch right next to his ear, and it caused a shiver that started in his ear and ended in his balls. He should break away, he knew, but something kept him close, some sticky thread between them.

"Yes." Louis's voice was hardly a whisper, less a word than a sensation, swallowed by a sigh as a subtle push of his hips pushed his cock firmly into Guy's welcoming hand. "You go in."

An invitation Guy could not refuse, but he couldn't manage buttons with one hand. He moved his empty hand to the back of Louis's head and settled for another kiss, drawing Louis's mouth back to his and driving him back against the wall. They fitted, chest to hip, and Louis's hands grasped hold of Guy's backside and gripped for dear life. Now Louis's mouth was open, the kiss built quickly, Louis's tongue teasing, darting in and out of Guy's mouth in way that surprised and delighted him. Then Guy pulled his mouth away, and they rested, both breathing heavily, forehead to forehead.

"I'm sorry," Guy said, berating himself immediately. *What did I say that for?* "No, actually, I'm really not."

Guy couldn't see Louis's face in the darkness, but heard a deep chuckle.

"A man who knows his own mind," Louis said. "But we should go in."

"We?"

"You go first," Louis said, surprising Guy once again by taking charge. "I'll have a cigarette, then check on James—"

"Don't."

"I must, if I don't—"

"If you *do*, you'll never come." He pulled Louis to him, kissing his face clumsily, punctuating his actions with words. "And you must." For the life of him he didn't know when it had become vital. "Go to him later. Say you were walking. You must come now. You know that. You know that—don't you? Don't you?"

There was a silence, painfully stretched as the night wrapped itself around them, making them part of one another. Already Louis was achingly familiar under his hands, already his scent was on his clothes, and if it was that right so soon, what did it matter who they hurt?

Louis put his head on Guy's shoulder and stayed like that for a heavy minute. Then: "Yes. Of course I do. Go." Louis pushed him away with surprising strength then shot forward for a final kiss before retreating to the shadow of the wall, disappearing into the brickwork. "Go."

* * * * *

I'm like an expectant father, Guy thought, tearing off his bow-tie and pacing around the room. Or a nervous bridegroom. The second thought was more pleasurable, but hardly suited the situation; nuptials didn't generally involve a third party lying awake and waiting in another part of a hotel. He poured himself a drink and downed it without tasting or even feeling the burn, wanting to go out on the balcony, to shout down to Louis to hurry, but part of him was too cowardly, terrified to find Louis wasn't there—that he had gone back to James's bed, already regretting the dark embrace.

Then the door opened, and he was there—no knock and oh-so-sensibly stopping to lock it behind him.

"I didn't want to wait, someone might have—"

And he was back in Guy's arms as if he'd not been gone, silenced by a kiss.

They clung together, shuffling towards the bed, their mouths melded together like they'd never part, hands scrabbling at shirts, pulling them out of trousers until they fell backwards, Guy underneath, and knocked their teeth together—and started to laugh, both like naughty schoolboys carrying tuck to their rooms. When the giggles subsided, Louis leant down and touched their lips again, his face serious. For a moment, Guy hoped—or perhaps dreaded—that Louis was going to speak, even now. That he'd pull away, change his mind, even though their cocks were lying next to each other, sharing heartbeats and heat. But instead Louis kissed him, again and again, tongue dipping leisurely into his mouth, each kiss brief but deep, until the pace slowed and suddenly urgency dissipated and now was all there was.

Guy had never experienced such leisurely lovemaking; comparisons with Arthur—all fire and haste—came crowding into his mind, before he pushed them away in shameful guilt. Louis peeled the clothes from him with an almost professional ease, then spread himself like honey over Guy's skin, his hands and mouth moving so slowly in tingling, chaste places, that Guy felt the world grind on its axis, and even a breath seemed to take a minute.

Opening his eyes, he saw Louis's dark curls as they brushed against his face, the scent of the cream on his hair washing over his senses, mixing with the heady scent of male sweat. Propping himself up, Louis took Guy's hands and held them to each side of Guy's head, and with his body, his cock, and his mouth, moved slowly and deliberately over Guy—making him writhe beneath Louis, feeling his control slipping away.

Gasping, as his cock bumped Louis's, Guy freed his hands, impatient, and flipped over. With Louis beneath him, he rested on one elbow and looked down into those teasing eyes, then moved his hand down to cover Louis's cock. As it moved in his hand, he tightened his grip, never taking his eyes from Louis, who lay still, the only movement the rise and fall of his chest, the dark flickering fire in his eyes, and the oh-so-sensual drag of his tongue against his teeth as it begged for yet another kiss.

He slid his hand over the delightful satin-smooth skin of Louis's cock, and as he teased the curls at the base with languorous fingers, it became a game between them: Guy watching for a reaction, and Louis giving none. The game prompted Guy to tighten his hand a little more, to tease the full, rounded tip with his thumb, to push apart Louis's legs even farther, giving him more access, but all Louis did was smile that satisfied, Cheshire-cat smile, taking it all as his due.

Guy weighed Louis's balls in his hand, rolling them gently one at a time, then slipped down and took one, then the other, into his mouth. This, finally, got a reaction, and Louis arched up, pushing himself nearer, gasping in pleasure. He grabbed hold of his cock, and Guy put his hand over the top, and together they stroked Louis as Guy lapped at Louis's balls, the crease between leg and thigh, and as far towards his hole as he could reach. Guy slid a gentle finger into Louis, and slowly they reached a smooth, encroaching rhythm, hands entwined, until Louis gave a small cry, almost of pain, and warm liquid spilled over Guy's fingers.

Louis lay quiet and spent, his lips turned up in a wide smile. Catching the smile, but not at all satisfied, and not wanting to stop—for who knew if he'd get this opportunity again?—Guy slid back up, kissed Louis's smug face, then moved Louis's legs up over his shoulders. Once in position, he pushed in with a sigh that felt like he'd been holding in for ten years. He stopped there for a moment, his thighs trembling with restraint, his heart thudding in his chest, savouring the tight fit, the heat, and the annoying feeling that it was all going to be over far too soon. Louis's eyes opened, as if he sensed Guy had lost his nerve, and he reached up and slid a salty finger into Guy's mouth.

"Go on. Please. You feel . . . you feel." He said nothing more, but moved against Guy, seating Guy even more firmly inside him.

Pushing down, letting Louis bend gradually under him, Guy began to move. Little motions, getting the feel of Louis, learning how far he could pull back without slipping out, and how far he could push in, loving the slap of his balls against Louis's flesh. He felt himself lengthen, his balls tighten as he worked, and by the time he was ready to burst he had Louis almost bent in half, but it meant he was kissing that beautiful mouth as he lost control, and the moment seemed to last forever as his orgasm swept through him, each contraction sweeter than the last.

He rolled away, eventually, dazzled and exhausted, his cock almost too tender to bear as it trailed across Louis's thighs. He took Louis in his arms, and his last thought before sleep was that he hoped the gong would wake him.

* * * * *

Calloway's illness continued, and Guy took full advantage, pushing any guilt to one side, and not thinking about what would happen when the man was fit and well. Louis and he slipped into a routine, breakfasting together, then Louis would spend an hour or two seeing to whatever Calloway wanted — and neither of them spoke about that — before joining Guy for lunch, and they'd take Guy's car into the mountains. They'd found a goat track of sorts, which led to a small clearing shrouded by scrubby bushes overlooking the valley floor. There was just enough room for the car and a rug, and they'd spend the afternoons talking, kissing, and, as far as Guy was concerned, falling hopelessly in love.

Louis spoke of James, and Guy didn't dissuade him. He wanted to understand why Louis stayed with him, so he let Louis talk, feeling a little, as Louis's head lay warm and heavy in his lap, like a head doctor listening to a patient. He learned of Calloway's injury, and had to bite his lip to stop himself from saying something childish and petty. Louis spoke of it with a shade of reverence, as if the man had given up something worse than his life due to the war, and all Guy could do was tell himself how stupid he was for being jealous, especially since James had not taken Louis. That was something Guy shared with Louis, something James could never have.

"He's lying, you know," Louis said once, making Guy's attention focus sharply. "He thinks I don't know, but he's not who he says he is. He thinks I don't know," he repeated, "but what kind of secretary would I be if I didn't?"

"What the devil do you mean?" Fear contracted Guy's heart. "Who the blazes is he?"

"I've said too much," Louis said. "Let's not talk of him anymore. Not today." Louis leant up and silenced Guy quite effectively with a kiss.

They did no more out in the Lombard sun that day — or any other day — for fear of discovery, but within the hotel they took their opportunities as they arose. Before dinner was ideal; Calloway assumed they were still exploring, and most of the hotel was readying itself for dinner, changing clothes or finishing siestas. Louis could therefore slip into

Guy's room unobserved, and they'd make love until the smallest movement was an effort.

Afterwards they clung together, the sweat drying on their skin, tasting each other with mouths too slack to form words.

One such time, when Guy was languid with exhaustion, Louis started to speak, and it felt to Guy like a cold draught cutting through the ill-fitting window.

"I was in a bar once, in Rome, a long time ago. I don't remember exactly why I was alone—I have friends, I don't normally go out alone."

Guy moved his thigh a little, over Louis's, about all the movement he was capable of making, but he wanted to indicate he had noted the defensive tone and was listening with sympathy.

"And this man came in, I remember it almost completely, and that's odd, because I'm not very observant, in general. But it had been raining, that hard summer rain you get, and he made a bit of a stir when he came in, shaking his umbrella all over the place, making the marble floor all wet. The manager shouted at him, but he took no notice. We never do, do we?"

"He was English?"

"Yes. He was one of those disruptive types. You know the kind. He sat down, ordered himself a drink and told the barman to get me one too."

He fell silent, not moving, and Guy waited patiently, not wanting to push. Then he said, gently. "You didn't know him?"

"No. That is, I'd seen him, seen him around. He was a little hard to miss. A society of English people in a foreign land tend to clump together, you know? Like a village. If we don't know everyone personally, we know someone who knows them, or we've heard them talked about."

Guy moved his mouth slightly, kissing the back of Louis's neck.

"I didn't like him much. At all, actually. He was . . . he was . . . ."

"Yes?"

"I don't know how to say it without sounding beastly," Louis said, finally. "He was—he was effeminate, and that's the only way I can put it. Fussy. Immediately confiding. He sat down and put my drink in front of me and started out on some story about a man he'd just left on the Piazza Navonna, as if I knew him, as if I knew his *friend*." Louis spat the word out. "He assumed. He saw something in me . . . and he was right."

"It happens," Guy said. "Some people can tell, or they say they can. Don't see it myself. Or perhaps they just say that as an excuse afterwards, perhaps they just take a chance, and say it when they are wrong."

"Have you?"

To Guy's ears, Louis sounded hopeful, in the dark. "Not until you. I'm pretty hopeless in that regard."

There was another stretching silence, and for a moment, Guy thought Louis had fallen asleep, until suddenly he said, "And I was angry. Really angry. I already had the drink, but I stood up and left because—how dare he do that? He'd ruined my chance of ever going back there; it was obvious he was making a play and everyone heard him, everyone saw him. What gave him the right to do that?"

"He was indiscreet. There are better ways . . . ."

"Of course there are. But perhaps not for him. Perhaps it comes to us all, do you think? Is that how it is? Will I be like him in twenty, thirty years' time? Chatting up pretty boys in bars, flitting from pub to pub like some kind of hopeful traveller, not knowing how much people are laughing at me? Is that what's there for us all?"

"Don't be silly," Guy said, but it was only a platitude. Louis was dragging thoughts into the light, thoughts Guy had not allowed himself to have. "Plenty of people make a life. You know that."

"A semblance of it. Playing at happy families. Husband and *wife*. A mirror of something we can't be. Pretending to be something we can't be. Why should we be like that? What's so bloody marvellous about marriage that makes it something even we want?"

Guy had no answer to that, and suddenly Louis was laughing softly, like he was laughing at the broken hearted clown.

"I wonder what he did in the war. At least he . . . ."

"Don't, Louis." Guy pulled Louis close. "He probably spent it in prison. Don't waste your time on it."

"I want to tell you all of it," Louis said. "The next day I found the fascists had picked him up, and do you know how I felt? You'll hate me. I felt *safe*. I bet you think that's caddish of me. I should have had some compassion for him. One of us."

Guy wanted to say something, but the words wouldn't come.

"I'm not going to prison," Louis said, his voice fierce. "I want to fight."

"You don't know what you are saying."

"You know I do. You of all people. I would have gone to Ethiopia only they wouldn't have taken me."

"You'd have fought for Italy?" Guy felt shocked in a way he hadn't thought he could be.

"Why not? I've spent fewer years in England than I have here. Damn good job, as I seem to be too much of a dago to fit in there. Seems at least they are prepared to fight for an Empire, while England seems content to let hers rot. Everyone's looking backwards, don't you think?"

Guy closed his eyes, let the scent of Louis wash over him, concentrated on where their skin touched, and he felt the first stirrings of warmth in his groin.

Everyone's looking backwards.

Well he couldn't deny that.

* * * * *

The whisky burned his stomach and did nothing to warm him. James poured himself another from a bottle hidden away that neither the signora nor Louis knew he had, then went into the bathroom to brush his teeth. Nothing worse than stale drink on the breath. The doctor had told him to stay off the drink when taking the pills, but what did the damned quack know? He needed something to settle his nerves; bloody quinine seemed to make him so jumpy, almost paranoid—and God alone knew he was paranoid enough without that. Pains in his legs, pains in his chest—*fuck this body. Fuck malaria.*

He grabbed the phone, levering himself with some difficulty to the edge of the bed.

"Prego."

"Calloway, Room 208. I'm going to come down for dinner tonight; tell Mr. Chambers when he comes in, will you?"

"Mr. Chambers came in an hour ago, Signore. Perhaps he is in his room? Shall I send someone up? Do you need assistance? The doctor?"

"Oh. Of course. I should have checked first. No, it's quite all right." James put the phone down and leaned on his hands before pushing himself to his feet. Automatically he washed and dressed, taking longer than he would, hoping Louis might arrive to assist. He stopped every time he thought he heard a sound in the corridor, but Louis didn't come. When he was dressed—all but his tie; he always made a pig's ear of that—he moved quietly across the room to the communicating door and stopped for a moment, his hand on the doorknob.

He knew Louis couldn't be in his room. There was something instinctive how James knew when Louis was there—it was like walking into a house and knowing, just *knowing* it was empty—but he opened the door, just in case.

He rarely went into Louis's room, but the bed was nearer than his own and his legs didn't feel they could make it all the way back, so he sank down onto the edge. Like Louis, the room was immaculate, pristine. Aside from a book on the bedside table, there was nothing to say he had even been there. The jealousy that had been tearing at him for days, since Louis had casually said he'd been continuing to see Mason since instructed to do so, bit hard into him and he had to clench his fists into the coverlet to control his emotions. *You have no hold over him.*

Like a child grieving over a lost pet, James pulled the pillow from under the sheet and clutched it to him, wallowing in Louis's scent the way he did when the man himself was in his arms. But, like the first turning of milk, like the first change in the weather when rain threatens, something was out of kilter. The pillow smelled of Louis, but—James sniffed again—not entirely. The scent of Louis's skin was unmistakable in itself, but his cologne was *Acqua di Parma*, a fanciful, and, to James, a decidedly un-English peccadillo he nevertheless enjoyed buying for him. It was rather too floral for James's taste, but on Louis it deepened until all that remained was rosemary and a touch of rose. On the pillow something else lingered like green, poisonous smoke. A hint of something else. Something subtle, but definitely something else. For a second James felt like he'd been kicked in the stomach, as if he'd found lipstick on Louis's collar, or a hotel receipt in his wallet.

He knew then, knew he was too late. The way Louis had spoken of Mason had rung warning bells with James when he first began to mention him—their shared wish that they had seen action in the last war, the way he interspersed their conversations with 'Guy said,' and 'Guy thinks'. James had gathered, impotently kept captive to the malaria, that if

Louis wasn't already attracted to Mason, then he soon would be. *Perhaps I'm not too late. God willing, please don't let me be too late.*

James had hardly closed the door between their rooms when Louis entered, and seeing James out of bed and fully dressed, he was instantly solicitous.

"God, James. You look like death. Here, let me. That's it." He helped James to the bed and sat him down, then knelt and fixed the infernal, impossible tie. "You sure you feel well enough to come down? It's not too soon?"

No. It's too late. Confirmation assaulted his nostrils. Louis's very scent was changed, and now James recognised the subtle alteration in Louis's room, the slightly tart high note he couldn't place. As Louis knelt before him, he could sense the same perfume coming from him, almost in waves. An antiseptic kind of smell, some cologne which Louis had never worn as long as James had known him, and not one that James recognised. With a sinking heart, James was certain whose it was. He would find out at dinner.

Somehow he summoned a gruff smile. "I'm ravenous, actually. Go dress; perhaps we can get to the bar before Mayhew eats all of the peanuts, and you can tell me about your day."

The signs have been there for days, James thought to himself as he picked up some notes and pretended to read as Louis got dressed. *They're there now, only I've been too bloody blind to see.*

"I've been thinking," James called out. "Something Mason said."

"Oh yes?" Maybe it was James's imagination, but was Louis's voice slightly strained?

"Yes. About France. You've been away from your family too long." James had to walk to the window, because if he had to look Louis in the face he'd never say the words. Never give him the chance to slip from his hand like a newt, slide in the stream of life and swim away. "You know I need to go to the Pyrenees, well, it will be . . . a bit awkward. Professor Sutherland hasn't met me, you see, and . . . ."

There was a sudden silence from the bedroom, as if Louis had stopped moving around, and was simply listening. James imagined he was leaning against the crack in the door, listening. "Louis?"

"I understand." Louis's voice sounded far away, drifting like a leaf on the current. "No. I do. And you are right, of course. Quite right."

"I knew you'd understand, old man," James said, forcing his smile back on his face. "I'll write when I'm settled, perhaps, and you can come."

"Of course. Whatever you think is best." Louis turned. He put his day clothes away—immaculately folded in tissue paper—then came back into the room. He had a bland look on his face, but his eyes, at least, were bright.

James tried to imagine that Louis was a little moved at their prospective separation.

"When?"

"Oh, not for a day or so. I'll drive you down to Rome . . . if you like?" James touched Louis's arm, but it was too late; Louis was far away.

"It's all right. I can take the train from Milan."

Afterwards, James wondered how he'd been so calm. Perhaps, he thought, I don't care enough. *It could be true, I suppose.*

* * * * *

The sun was already half way across the room, bright, and lemon yellow. The empty half of the bed was still warm from Louis's skin. Guy lay in bed, staring up at the ceiling, warm and comfortable, for once in his life content to stay and savour the warmth and perfection of the moment. He could still taste Louis, and the man's scent, entirely his own: semen, sweat and pomade were all around him. How would it be, he thought, if we found somewhere, somewhere together. Rooms, as it were, like Pip and Mr Pocket. Who would think anything of it?

He took a deep breath and with almost hedonistic languor, he slid a foot out from under the sheet, letting it cool in the morning air. Louis would be packed by now, and he'd have left a letter for Calloway. Perhaps Louis was already downstairs, settling his account. Guy could hardly suppress a smile. Served the lying bastard right. At least Louis didn't have the encumbrance of a car; they could drive away together.

He checked his watch. Six already. Time to end the adventure and start the rest of his life. He rose and took time getting washed and dressed, emulating slightly, with a smile, the precise, fussy manner Louis had. Folding the flannel just so, placing the toothbrush in the glass without making a sound. Doing everything carefully, so later he could remember every second of it. So he could look back and recall exactly the warmth of the air, the way the towel felt against his skin, the scent of the valley, wafting through the window. *This is the day I changed my world.*

He'd finished packing and was just looking around, checking he'd left nothing behind — not a book, not a toothbrush — when there came a loud knocking at the door.

It was far too early for tea, so he opened the door — expecting, at the least, to hear the hotel was burning down —

only to confront a dishevelled Calloway, his fist raised as if to assault the door once more. As the door opened, Calloway surged forwards, taking Guy by surprise and pushing him to one side. It was clear, from Calloway's behaviour within the room, looking around and even marching into the bathroom, he was looking for Louis.

Guy's heart sank; it had been too good to be true to hope they could have slipped out of this man's life. They should have left the night before.

Guy affected a nonchalance he did not feel, leant against the closed door and waited. He hoped that if there were to be a scene, he could contain it here, and that it would not spill down into the reception. God forbid. He wouldn't have thought it of Calloway. He had pegged the man as a good loser.

"Are you done?" he said acerbically, as Calloway came back from the bathroom. For a second Guy felt sorry for him, for Calloway was as pale as milk, running his hands through his hair. He looked like he would keel over at a moment's notice. "Or would you like to check the wardrobe? That's generally the farcical trope, isn't it?

"What the blazes have you done?" Calloway demanded, in a hoarse, almost guttural voice. "What were you thinking?

Guy's hackles rose. "Keep your bloody voice down." Although the pounding on the door had probably been enough to raise unwarranted attention. So much for slipping away unnoticed.

"Oh, yes, that's just you all over, isn't it?" Calloway's voice dropped to a more sensible level, but his anger radiated from him as if he would explode at any moment. "You're so bloody sophisticated. This . . . tortured martyr act. The man who would have fought for his country but couldn't. Oh yes. Oh yes, he told me. If that's even true."

"I advise you—" Guy felt violence welling up in him. "Not—"

"No," Calloway said. "No."

He seemed to Guy as if he was actually going to attack him, and Guy wondered if he could get the door open in time, and doubted it. Then suddenly, something changed in Calloway's demeanour. He seemed to crumple in upon himself, and Guy felt a little nauseated. *He's surely not going to cry?* But the man turned away, his hand disturbing his hair even further, and walked to the window.

"You know," he said, finally, "I thought I was doing the right thing. I saw his fascination with you. He'd not have met someone like you before, I'm sure of that. Not in Rome, and certainly not here. Just dry sticks and those put out to pasture. But I wanted him safe. I wanted to get him out of the country. It's not safe here—and getting less so."

"He'd be safe enough at the Embassy," Guy said. "You could have let him go."

Calloway was silent for such a long time Guy was struck by the peculiar polite farce of the situation. *Noel Coward wrote this scene, didn't he? No . . . but he should.* "And you couldn't take him home with you, could you?"

Calloway made no answer.

Guy pushed on. "Because you couldn't settle him in a discreet flat in Edinburgh, could you?"

"No." Calloway's voice affirmed that all the fight had gone out of him. "No, I couldn't."

"But not because you were frightened what the faculty would say." Guy knew he was getting through, as Calloway's shoulder's straightened a little. "No, I suspect the faculty wouldn't care. You couldn't take him to Edinburgh at all, could you — because you aren't James Calloway."

The man turned around. "It doesn't matter."

"You're Oswald Calloway. I should have seen it right from the start. I said you didn't look like a professor. You even showed me a photo of you and — "

"It doesn't matter," Calloway repeated. "I couldn't take him to Africa, either — could I? A boy like that?"

"I have no idea. I assume there are reasons you are masquerading as your brother?"

"Of course. It's hardly something you do on a whim, you know, ask your brother for his passport, involve him in . . . this mess. Another reason I couldn't take him — Louis — home. Africa. There was some local trouble. Bearers playing up, you know the kind of thing."

"Actually, no."

"Well, they do." Calloway turned and sat heavily on the bed. "Got a bit rough, and one of the boys was killed and . . . well, let's say I didn't want to hang around. Smallpox is rife there—despite the blasted administration assuring everyone it's under control. They'd have sent me back into the city for a hearing."

He was silent for a long moment.

I don't want to know. It's nothing to me. Be a good loser, will you? Guy thought to speak the words, but then Calloway looked up and met Guy's eyes; all the hail-fellow-well-met had dropped away and there was nothing but loss and defeat in his expression. Guy felt suddenly guilty for wanting the man to lose. Superfluous really. Calloway knew he'd lost.

"It's not easy, you know," Calloway said finally. "A man admitting he's a coward. Faced lions, rhino, mad elephants. That's different. Smallpox. For some reason I couldn't face that. So I got out. Then I met Louis and . . . I was trapped. So I stayed here with him. For as long as I could." He looked up at Guy. "You could have got him away. Back to England. If he'd found out about me, he'd have gone to Rome."

"Oh God, Calloway. Of course he knows about you. He knew who you really were," Guy found himself saying. He wanted to lie, wanted to say, *'I'm taking him anyway, and there's nothing you can do.'* But he couldn't. For all that he'd taken away from Calloway, he still liked and respected him. *Hell, everyone has something they can't face. I should know. Look at me, still trying to avoid a confrontation.* "You underestimate him. Of course he knew." For a second he considered telling him the rest, how Calloway himself had been the catalyst for Guy's success, wanted to relate to him the conversation he'd had with Louis in the middle of the night . . . .

"I want you to leave with me," Guy had told Louis. "I can't have one more day watching you light his cigarettes and pouring his wine, having dinner with him like you really are his secretary. Can't see you touching him. I can't . . . . "

He'd had a whole speech planned, but Louis moved his hand over Guy's mouth and said, "Yes. I will. I thought he needed me. He doesn't. I thought . . . ."

Whatever else Louis had thought, Guy hadn't let him say, covering his mouth with his own, opening his legs and pushing into the semen-slick hole that felt like heaven.

Perhaps, Guy thought, a crueller man would enjoy the victory, explaining how James had driven Louis away himself by keeping so much of himself back, but looking at the defeated man, he knew he couldn't. "You should have trusted him," he said, finally.

He turned back to his suitcase and fastened it, something kicking at his mind for attention. What was it that Calloway had said? No, not what he said, exactly. But the way he'd said it. He took his case in hand then stopped, turned back to Calloway. "*Could* have got him away? What the devil do you mean? What have you done?"

The anger flared back into Calloway's face. "Me? Damn you! It's you. Dazzling him with all the things you would have done if you'd been given the chance to fight.

Sitting your arse in Whitehall while the rest of us risked our bloody lives."

Guy felt the colour drain from his face. Louis should never have shared that. "You have no right—"

"No. *You* had no right filling his head with notions of 'the next war.' Surely you must have realised he's fixated on the glorious fight?"

"I never mentioned the bloody war!" Guy snarled. "It's true he's got stupid illusions about what he missed, but that's his choice, Calloway. His to make. If Germany—"

"When." Calloway's voice was bitter. "Don't fool yourself, Mason. When. He's made his choice already. Both Hitler *and* Louis, as it turns out." He put his hand into his pocket and took out a crumpled note. "Forgive me if I don't read it out. There are sentiments which would embarrass both of us."

"What . . . he was supposed . . . what the hell does he say, man?"

Calloway looked at him for a moment then looked at the suitcase. Guy had rarely been scrutinised so minutely.

"Oh. I see I've been more spectacularly stupid than I thought. How terribly embarrassing for you. You thought you were going with him. Well, you are both fools. Kill yourself in your own country's fight if you must, but for Spain?"

Guy felt the ground shift under his feet, and for a moment he seemed to have forgotten the mechanics of swallowing. "Spain? He's gone . . . . Bloody hell. Idiot! When did he leave?"

Calloway sat down again and nodded, seemingly at the end of his strength. "I don't know exactly. I went to bed early, and I awoke early because of it. Sometime during the night, perhaps. His bed wasn't even slept in. We're all fools, it seems. All three of us."

No, Louis hadn't slept in his bed, and he hadn't left in the middle of the night. Of this, Guy was sure. If he hurried, perhaps he wouldn't be too late. Guy grabbed his case and left Calloway there.

* * * * *

Afterwards, Guy wondered about the ride down to Varese station. He remembered very little of it, and knew he was lucky to not have been killed. He ran onto the platform, his heart in his mouth, dreading that the train had gone, because he knew, once Louis got to Milan, it would be impossible for Guy to catch up with him. But the trains had not reached the town yet; wagons stood in the carpark with their goods, and one or two men waited, leaning lazily against the wrought iron lampposts.

His heart gave a lurch of relief as he spotted the unmistakable form of Louis sitting on one of the benches. On the platform, Louis seemed smaller, but as Guy got nearer, he could see it was because he was half dozing, slumped down, his great coat over him like a blanket. A light dusting of stubble lay on the man's cheeks, and he looked, to Guy, ridiculously young and vulnerable. Guy sat down beside him, thinking how to wake him without attracting more attention than they already were to the few early morning travellers. But he needn't have worried; the mere movement of the bench was enough to jostle Louis into wakefulness, and he stretched a moment before jolting himself to complete consciousness.

"Guy." Louis's eyes looked wary, for all the world like Priss the day she'd been caught sneaking back into the house after stealing and crashing the car. "Oh God, Guy. I'm sorry."

"Sorry you got caught, or sorry you left me behind?"

"It was . . . . I can't explain. I was just writing to James, the way we'd planned, and I realised I had to do this."

"You could have left *me* a letter on my pillow," Guy said. He hadn't meant to sound bitchy, but it was difficult; he wondered if he'd ever lose the jealousy.

"I couldn't. I don't expect you to understand. I wanted to come and tell you myself. But . . . ."

"Louis, you are an idiot." Exasperated, Guy wanted to hit him, or kiss him, and only one would be socially acceptable. "What did you think I was going to do? Just drive off to England and forget about the last week?"

"I-I suppose so. You know where I am going. It's not something one can ask—"

"For God's sake, Louis," Guy said, trying to keep his voice under control, "it's *exactly* the kind of thing one can ask. It's what people have been asking of each other since war was invented."

Words failed them both after that. Louis's eyes were sparkling bright, and Guy saw that he was struggling to contain his feelings. A muscle worked hard in Louis's cheek, making it almost impossible for Guy to keep his hands to himself.

The train slid into the platform and the station sprang to life as passengers boarded and goods were laden. As all attention was focussed on the great steaming monster, Guy reached under the coat on the bench and took hold of Louis's hand.

"Then if you are intent on going," he said, "I'm coming with you. You knew that. That's why you left."

"I couldn't ask you."

"You don't have to." Guy felt Louis's blue-white fingers curl around his and then nothing mattered. Not Calloway, not Franco, not Priss. And England could go hang. This was his family—all he wanted, and for as long as it lasted.

He smiled. "Let's go then," he said. And picking up Louis's case, with the feeling of his lover's fingers imprinted on his own, he led the way to the car and to Spain.

~The End~

About the Author

Erastes is the director of the Erotic Authors' Association and a member of the Historical Novel Society. Her work has appeared in many anthologies such as Ultimate Gay Erotica and Best Gay Stories, Treasure Trail and Fastballs. Her first novel, Standish, was nominated for a Lambda Award, and her second novel, Transgressions, was part of Running Press' launch of their gay romance line. Her website can be found at www.erastes.com.

The White Empire

By Chris Smith

Prologue

As I readied myself to fuck the boy, my gaze fixed on a piece of graffiti. JACK WAS HERE. The words were carved deeply into the wooden wall, and, for a moment, I wondered who Jack was, why he'd been here, and how on earth he had felt proud enough to leave this mark.

Under cover of night, I had arrived, wrapped in a stinking, salt-stained greatcoat, a hat pulled low over my head. I wore a scarf and knew I looked ridiculous, but spring in Hong Kong was misty and damp. Better the ridicule, better the untempered mirth at my garb than the boundless problems sure to befall me if the Superintendant discovered Edgar Vaughan lurking about in dens of ill repute.

I placed my hand over the graffiti and leant forward; whoever Jack was, he was of no importance to me. I would rather concentrate on the boy beneath me. Warm, soft, nubile, and with those inscrutable Chinese eyes. I had ascertained that he'd not taken opium beforehand . . . well, I believe I'd asked for one who hadn't. It definitely would not do for one of us British Missionaries to be found sporting with a boy under the very influence of that which we'd been sent here to eradicate. That the superintendant—Charles Elliot—had been looking for a reason to get rid of us, send us back to Mother England, would only make matters worse. According to expatriate gossip, the Trade Delegation had its fingers so deep into the opium pot it could well drown in it. I wished the Delegation--*especially Tarrant*--would do so and wondered what our new Queen would think of this behaviour promulgated in her name.

The light in the room was dim and the boy's pupils were large. Maybe he had taken opium before I arrived — maybe I should care more about this. But it had taken my last ounce of courage to come here tonight and I was glad the lights were hazy, the room dark and smoky. No one would recognize me in the flickering light, and as long as I didn't think on precisely what I may be inhaling — on how much more relaxed I felt — maybe I'd be able to enjoy myself.

I watched him spread himself open for my delectation; his arse ripe and those slit eyes completely black. He looked alien, different — unknown and unknowable. I should want him, or someone like him; my flock made no secret of the way we *gwailo* loved satiating ourselves on oriental flesh. This boy was the perfect mannequin on which to vent my lusts. I unbuttoned my trousers and reached inside to rub my member. *I should be hard!* He was an older boy, though, and I couldn't quite remember — *did I ask for an older one?* Whoever he was, whatever I'd asked for, he looked at me as if to say, 'Get on with it'.

I had to stop looking at him, stop staring into those judgemental eyes. I glanced around the room. All manner of dissipated, disaffected Europeans lolled indolently on worn silk chaise-longues or stiffly embroidered bolsters. All serviced by the inscrutable native, be it a pipe tray — jade bowls for the most part — or a mouth around a cock. In this house, it seemed we would receive precisely what we paid for.

My gaze swept the room. For the most part, the other men — drunk on lust and drugs — seemed to ignore me, though one caught my eye. The cut of his peacock coloured waistcoat was far superior to my own drab brown, and while he sucked on a pipe his attention moved from face to face — seeming to stop and take note. He sported dark brown hair and I fancied that behind the smoke his eyes were green. I thought he smiled my way, but his gaze jumped ever onwards . . . . I resumed fisting my recalcitrant member. *Surely, after all this time . . . .*

Then that green stare was back, and he licked his lips. I could not break his gaze, could not look away as he put his pipe down, pushed his pipe bearer to the side, pulled across a nubile whore, and pressed his face into the boy's lap. I felt myself harden—felt myself fully extend—more than I ever had under my own private ministrations. Without a word, I pushed myself into my whore. But the whore was only a vessel—a mannequin—and though it was his body I used, I was rutting with the man in the peacock waistcoat.

Gradually, the sensations enveloping my member became too much for me to ignore and I shut my eyes in rapture. I pushed on and on, remembering those green eyes fixed on mine, the feeling of being trapped in a prison of amber, being mercilessly catalogued by a natural scientist. I welcomed it and hated it, all at once.

When the moment overwhelmed me, I kept my eyes closed for one last, brief second.

There had been no need to hesitate. The man in the peacock waistcoat was gone.

Chapter One

I had been in this city since the spring of the year of our Lord 1839 coming as far as Bombay on the *Hugh Lindsay*—a small steamer—and then from Bombay to Hong Kong on the fast clipper *Ardesir*. The first leg of the journey was tolerable—the steam made for a fast transit—but aboard the *Ardesir*, the reek of raw tea pervaded the very timbers of the ship, which required me to spend the last weeks of the journey heartily ill in my cabin. To my good fortune though, other than the captain and the more senior members of the crew, I was the only white man on board. I believed it was due to it being spring—the merest threat of a monsoon had my brethren scurrying for the hills, to Peshawar and the Kashmir.

As a missionary, I was expected to take whatever passage was booked for me, however much a hill stay may have appealed. As it was presumed that I'd shun the more raucous and rambunctious goings on aboard the ship, I saw no need for anyone other than the manservant assigned to me — an old gnarled man — to observe my frequent and vocal regurgitation. By the time we'd reached Hong Kong, my clothes were loose-fitting and my voice barely a whisper of its former self.

*****

I'd disembarked, making damn sure not to cast my eye over the lithe natives unloading that stinking tea. I had come here to escape my predilections; come here to escape those furtive fumbles in Hyde Park. Been lucky, I knew that. I'd never been caught, never charged, never gaoled. But the last time had been close. I'd almost accosted a young man by the name of Mudd who attended my Bible Study group every Tuesday. He'd smelt of lilies as I'd bent over him in the bare room—that same whiff alerted me in the park. *Ah, Mudd. I remember you fondly.*

Of course, I could not stay in London, not after that. I approached my vicar and begged—like a Roman facing Cromwell himself—to be sent abroad as a missionary. "I've heard the call." "I want to go and spread God's word."

My vicar was a fusty old man, a certain Betteridge, who believed in helping those at home before one travelled to the outer-reaches of civilisation and preached to the pagan. Over port, I'd often heard him holding forth on the "native problem" and on how one should not bother to reach the uneducated as it was unlikely they would be able to comprehend enough of God to gain salvation. Better to spend one's time in England, amongst those who already had a basic understanding of mother-English. *They*, at least, had the advantage of comprehension and therefore of more probable salvation.

I must have pled my case well, or maybe the old vicar

realised more than I knew. Since becoming a missionary, I'd always dressed in good, sombre garb but admittedly, with a little bit of *savoir-faire* in my method of compiling it. I chose good, solid stuff for my suits—I was careful to do so— though my jackets may have erred closer to the silks of a dandy than I had previously presumed. Maybe it was my employment of a Cumberland-Corset that roused his suspicions. Or it could have been his Thomas Beckett moment— at least *this* turbulent priest now chose to absent himself rather than face the sword.

Whatever the reason, Betteridge gifted me with a letter of introduction to The Pious Brethren of St. Jude, a small group of High Church missionaries who were as close to the Roman mendicant brothers as good Anglicans could be. At first, I found their bells and their smells distasteful, though the lulling cadence of the chants soon became more soothing than the Book of Common Prayer.

After a quarter-year of bustling back and forth between my responsibilities for Betteridge, my avoidance of Mudd, and the Pious Brethren, they finally accepted me into their ranks.

* * * * *

At least the Pious Brethren allowed me the comfort of a fast passage—I presume they were sponsored by some of the Ton—for they were lavish both in the speed and in the quality of their procured accommodations.

On reaching the docks, I had eyes only for the odd wooden buildings that dotted the shore and crept like the pox up the looming hill. I'm sure that some would call them quaint, but to me they looked rickety and alien: a fire hazard if I'd ever seen one.

I was distracted from my musings by the booming voice issuing from quite the most spherical man I have ever had the pleasure of meeting.

"Vaughan, Vaughan old chap! How wonderful you could make it!"

I presumed by his informal mode of address—rather as if we were attending a country-house-shoot or a game of cricket than embarking upon a Mission in this strange land — that this was to be my superior, a Reginald Humphries, complete with the lavish moustache I'd been told to expect. His presumption and lack of etiquette was a disgrace, but I felt it my Christian duty to forgive the man. It was most obvious from the cut of his tail-coat and the fall of his trousers, the man had near enough gone native as made no difference. His attire was at least three seasons out of style and would be laughed at by any reputable London tailor!

 I carefully extended my hand and felt it subsumed within his meaty grasp as he vigorously pumped it. He was one of those athletic types — probably involved in boating where he schooled but who didn't quite make the grade for a Blue at University. I matched my grip to his own and clamped down hard, noting with a slight shudder of pleasure how quickly he let go. I, of course, had received my own Blue.

 He gestured to a porter, who picked up my bags as Humphries hailed a strange open carriage. I looked around for a mule or horse or suchlike, hoping our journey could be undertaken with some alacrity and I could soon remove myself from the oppressive heat. I have to acknowledge, after my initial surprise, the speed of the native who undertook to pull the cart was tolerable and I soon found myself standing next to Humphries in front of a building of the local style.

"Sorry old chap, needs must here, and getting the coolies to erect buildings is a lot easier if you leave them to their own devices." Humphries gestured lackadaisically. "It's not much but its home."

I made the usual deprecating noises as I took the structure in. It showed a certain rudimentary appreciation of symmetry but instead of being a single cohesive edifice it was broken up into a collection of little boxes, tacked together. It looked like a child's toy.

I stepped through the doorway and saw my trunk placed on the bare wooden floor. *This is now my home. From this strange series of timber boxes, I can change my life, my needs, and my wants.*

I followed Humphries to my room and sat down on my bed. The mattress was beautifully boxed and it felt like sinking into a cloud as I loosened my brown-silk stock. I'd never felt so alone.

Chapter Two

Humphries insisted I dine with him that first evening. I had included some quite reasonable wines within my baggage... which he made short work of appropriating. There were five of us at table that evening: Humphries, myself, a Mr. Smythe, a Mr. Collins, and much to my consternation, a Miss Gloria Cooke who had joined the mission at the request of her uncle, a certain Maximilian Tarrant; an undersecretary to Charles Elliot who was the Chief Superintendant of Trade in China. I wished I'd had more time to prepare myself; a few hours of rest in a foreign land is not long enough to regain one's scintillating wit prior to dining with those of influence. At least I had a freshly laundered suit, which smelt faintly of camphor, and a respectably starched shirt and waistcoat. Thinking on it now, it would be the same waistcoat in which I first met Lord Runfold, though I must not get away from the narrative.

Dinner was acceptable. The soup was warm, the fish course quite adequate and nicely paired with a dry white. The pork — while gamey — was enhanced substantially by the addition of a Burgundy, compliments of my collection. There were dried apples stewed in cinnamon and cloves and a bowl of distinctly odd fruits, which I was told the natives referred to as lay-cheese. They looked like moist eyeballs and no matter how much both Humphries and the Cooke woman entreated, I could not be prevailed upon to attempt them. Quite frankly, the sight of a young woman tucking into those dripping orbs with fanatical gusto turned my stomach. I had to make my excuses — I pled travel — and go to bed, forfeiting a glass of my own fine Port and a cigar.

* * * * *

On rising, I was met with a quandary: it seemed Humphries had neglected to assign me a valet. I made do, as one does, pulling out my looking glass and balancing it precariously on the dressing table, which was ornately carved and more suited to a feminine chamber. *Ah yes, Miss Cooke.* I wondered if this was her room, if she'd been delegated another less pleasant chamber on my arrival. I found that I did not care; for a woman to make such a show, to presume acquaintance with a gentleman she's just been introduced to, was completely beyond the pale. I decided to acknowledge her as little as possible; even with her familial connections she seemed as ill-bred as a cabby's nag.

I stumbled to breakfast—nodded at Smythe and Collins—and piled the kedgeree high on my plate. As I was raising my first forkful, I had to stand and bow stiffly as Miss Cooke entered the room. I hoped she'd take the hint but instead, she sat herself to my right and smiled as if to engage me in conversation. I focused on my plate, lifting the first forkful of bliss to my mouth. I almost was unable to swallow. While the haddock and eggs were unexceptional, the rice was of a strange texture and the butter was lacking. This, more than anything else, brought home how foreign a country I was in.

I looked up and could not avoid Miss Cooke's smile.

"Good morning, Mr. Vaughan. I trust the accommodations were to your satisfaction."

I attempted a smile. "Why thank you, Miss Cooke. They were quite adequate." *I'll be damned if I'm going to ask if I discommoded you.* "It is most refreshing to wake in foreign climes, don't you think?"

The moue of irritation on her lips amused me. I would have to find out more; I could not see how an unwilling woman could have been prevailed upon to make the journey to China for anything less than a substantial reward. *Well, her uncle is well-connected. I'm sure he has his eye on some young man doing his bit for Queen and for Country. Poor chap, whoever he is. She really is most forward.*

Her response knocked me out of my reverie. "I am sure that it is, Mr. Vaughan. I hope you will not be too disappointed, but Mr. Humphries has been called away to converse with my uncle. Matters of trade, I believe."

Her trilling laugh rang false to my ears and I turned to give her my full attention. "I trust that your uncle will not keep the good Mr. Humphries long. I was assured I would be visiting the Mission today. It is really quite galling that—"

She interrupted me, a trait I abhor in men and women alike. "Oh no, you silly, I will take you down to the mission myself."

I schooled my features into an amiable cast and nodded pleasantly. "An honour and a privilege, I'm sure."

She smiled beatifically and turned to her plate. It was obvious from her deportment that she was no lady and I could see why she'd have been shipped here to find a suitable match. However, something about her—be it the baby-talk or the false laughter—had caused my hackles to rise. I would keep an eye on her. A man in my position could ill-afford to do otherwise.

* * * * *

The mission was situated down by the docks, near a collection of filthy streets and ramshackle buildings. People shuffled aside as our native-drawn carriage passed, their eyes fixed firmly on our countenances. I thought I saw flashes of hope in some faces, fear in others, but for the most part, the mire of blank visages staring at us caused me to feel unwelcome. I wished to leave.

We alighted by a well-maintained doorway; the Pious Brethren were not letting the side down by ministering from a sub-standard building. A manservant opened the door, and I made a mental note to accost Humphries on his return about a valet. It was intolerable to have to dress oneself, especially in such a hot clime. At least I'd had the good sense to leave the Cumberland-Corset off today; the air was oppressive enough without my waist being cinched, and I was not quite sure I could fasten the damn thing unaided.

Miss Cooke took me through to the main courtyard, wherein stood an incongruous crucifix on a low table.

"It's the natives, you see. This is where they'd

normally put their idols. Mr. Humphries felt it better to place the crucifix here and put paid to their strange habits. We had to hack off the ends of the roof structures and refinish the doorframes when we took this building over. They were *covered* in graven images."

My mind leapt onto the salient information. "So, you've been here a while then?" I asked, schooling my voice to its most charming.

"Why yes, Mr. Vaughan. When my uncle came out in '36, he sent for me within a few months. I have been with the Pious Brethren of St. Jude since I arrived."

"I trust you had a good passage," I said, covering my thoughts. *She's been here since '37 then? At the very latest. This must be one fat prize her Uncle wishes her to net.*

"It was most reasonable, I assure you." Her smile did not quite make it to her eyes. "Most reasonable. If you'd follow me?"

Without waiting for my acquiescence, she strode across the courtyard and pushed open a door. I followed, intrigued. Miss Cooke was obviously a woman of strong passions and I felt toying with her could soon be my most interesting diversion. If nothing else, it would keep my mind on the straight, narrow, and assuredly female path that was required of it.

My thoughts were cut short as I entered the room. I know I am not a good man—not a kind man at times—but the sight that met my eyes would have been enough to break the heart of Satan himself. Emaciated wretches were lying in various states of undress on filthy palettes that lined the room. They were male—barely clothed—and their ribs stretched like miles of bent willow fencing. Some were puling and crying—which was to be expected from their vile condition—but even more disturbing was that some of them seemed at ease, enshrined in a beatific peace that made their faces shine like diamonds against the mockery of their bodies. I felt my gorge rise and had to leave the room.

As I stood in the courtyard—my back to that room—I heard the patter of Miss Cooke's slippered feet. When I was sure she was standing close, I turned on my heel—quick as a whisper—hoping to startle her. Her face held the ghost of a smile and it was all I could do not to reach out and wrap my hands around her delicate neck. Whatever fun I had assumed, whatever sport I would have had with such a lady, died its death in that courtyard. For anyone who could look at those poor wretches and not feel compassion, such a person could not have a human heart beating within their chest. I marshalled my dignity. *This chit will not discommode me!*

"I presume those are some of the flock?"

She appeared nonplussed by my lack of confrontation and I smiled inwardly. *One point for Mr. Vaughan, my dear.*

"Yes, Mr. Vaughan." She dropped her eyes, her hands fidgeting with the ruffs on her sleeves. I seemed to have temporarily cowed her.

"I have not heard of any food shortages. Are we not in a position to aide them in their hunger?"

Miss Cooke smiled at me, eyes wide with delight. "Oh, they're not hungry, Mr. Vaughan. Or if they are, they won't tell the likes of us. What they want is opium. Brought in by the English from the Indies. Mr. Humphries swears that is why they patronize our English mission. They hope for an easier supply, you see?"

I kept my eyes focused straight ahead. "And do they receive such?" I strove to keep my voice level.

"No, they don't." I fancied she stamped her foot under the masses of crinolines. "Mr. Humphries does not believe that opium is of any use other than the purely medicinal. But *all* the coolies use it for recreation."

I was at a loss as to what to say. Whatever happened, this woman knew influential people and I was fresh off the boat. A public falling out with the Undersecretary to the Chief Superintendent of Trade would be a disaster and to offer a woman the cut-direct was unthinkable. There was no other recourse, so I proffered my arm and smiled. I would have to bide my time. But one thing I knew—knew here and knew now—was that I had been sent with my myriad faults to this country for a reason. Whatever the cost, I would stand against the recreational use of opium.

Chapter Three

On returning to the mission, I spent the afternoon indoors, contemplating what I'd just seen. Someone — I think it may well have been Mr. Collins from the deep squeak of the treads on the wooden boards — placed a tray of soup, some cold pork, a slice of fruit tart — from which I removed those benighted lay-cheese — and some rather dry cheddar. An acceptable repast, and more than I had been expecting in China, but my stomach still turned at the thought of the mission.

In hindsight, the idea of a revelation was absurd, almost Catholic in its connotations. However, I could not help realize, I was now moved as I'd never been before. And for the first time, for someone other than myself.

*****

Perhaps I should stop here and explain how I became a Vicar. I am the second son of Baron Vaughan, a title my brother inherited two years past. As he was now healthy, married, and with a wife well on the way to producing what I could only presume was the first of many heirs, I felt no need to remain in Mother England.

I had been adequately schooled in case Maurice was taken in war — or some other odious fracas — and I had gone up and come down from Oxford at the usual times. My dear father was all for me joining one of the services; he had gone as far as to investigate a commission.

But my own thoughts lay in another direction. I could not see why — if Maurice was too precious to sacrifice on the altar of Mars — I should be any less valued. I hit upon the most perfect solution: the clergy would keep me — other than a few further lectures at the Alma Mater—out of Pater's pocket, out of harm's way, and with a sufficient income if Maurice should not do the decent thing and persist on inheriting. The clergy seemed the least self-sacrificing calling one could have—presuming one counts laying down one's life as a sacrifice, not an honour—and so, I explained to my father I'd been called. Spiritually. It was most amusing to watch the choler suffuse his face; between that and the apoplectic seizures from which his brother had died allowing the title to pass to our branch, I was quite sure my brother would soon be the Baron Vaughan.

To my private amusement, within two months of my going up to Oxford—honing my theology by listening to the Regius Professor of Divinity blather on about the Thirty-Nine Articles and the Greek New Testament—I was proven correct.

After catching the last lecture, I hopped into our waiting carriage and promptly fell asleep, leaving Benton to push the horses back along the road to London. We stopped the night at High Wycombe and arrived at our London house the following day. The final preparations were being made for the funerary arrangements. My brother welcomed me at the door, looked me up and down, then nodded.

"A curacy then, Edgar?" He looked down his nose. "I'm sure I can prevail upon one of the parishes in my gift to accept you."

I utilised a laconic leer I'd recently acquired by dint of studious practice. "Why no, brother. I already have a most particular invitation to spend my curacy in a parish on the Isle of Dogs. The docks, as you know, are thriving. I'm sure I'll be able to expand my horizons."

My brother blanched and stepped backwards into the dreary womb-like protection of the entrance hall. "But Edgar," he entreated, "Do remember school! That little misunderstanding. You know how much it cost Pater to hush it up! The Isle is full of degenerates, you'll be—"

"Tempted? Oh, not on the Isle. After all the scandal, you should understand precisely how much in the Ton my proclivities used to lie. Of course, such a thing would be unthinkable now. I'm to be a Vicar."

My brother was always exceptionally thick-headed, so, from his expression and the way he stepped aside to let me into the hall, I believe he felt genuine relief at what he had taken as the truth. Well, it was part true at any rate. I've never felt the lure of the dockhand or sailor, the farmer's son, or the blacksmith; I am too fastidious for lice or the pox. What pleasures I have allowed myself—few and far between—have been partaken of men of my own social class. Except for a few sojourns in Hyde Park. And Mudd.

* * * * *

Enough of these digressions; I believe I have adequately illustrated that I am neither required nor wanted in London. That I became a vicar more through circumstance than through calling. And that the vehemence of my repugnance and pity for those poor souls in the mission took me by complete surprise.

My views on the mission must have been more apparent to Miss Cooke than I realised, for on his return,

Humphries took it upon himself to knock on the door of my room. He let himself in—on my acknowledgement at least—and leapt into the breach without any of the presumed social niceties.

"I believe Miss Cooke took you on a tour of the mission this morning?"

I stood and closed the door, vaguely uncomfortable at the thought of our conversation being overheard. Sitting on the bed, I felt distinctly edgy, as I had in school when the House-master inspected my cubicle for contraband.

"Yes, she did. It was most illuminating." I made a concerted effort not to fiddle with the counterpane. "I must say, I found her attitude towards the souls who reside there quite unfeminine."

"Miss Cooke has very definite opinions. Many of them formed by her uncle, Maximilian Tarrant. His views on opium are very well known in expatriate circles."

"Is there anything we can do for the poor wretches?" I felt it politic to change the subject, but Humphries forestalled me.

"Yes. But please take heed. Miss Cooke has great influence. And while it appears the tide is turning against the odious brown paste and its white smoke with the advent of our new Chinese governor—"

"A new governor?" I wished that someone had bothered to explain the current political situation. *It's ridiculous, expecting me to navigate the shoals of a new country without even the most basic of maps.*

"Lin Zexu. The Emperor has charged him with stamping out the opium trade. He is known for his pointed methods of dealing with this sort of problem." Humphries stood and paced the room. I thanked God that our building was on a single level; there could be no one in the rooms below mulling over his worried tread. "However, until his arrival, it is neither here nor there. Right now, we exist at the sufferance of Her Majesty. Oh, not directly of course, but if Tarrant took up against us, I'd not place a wager on a favourable outcome."

I felt a tinge of sorrow towards Humphries. His obvious restraint in the face of Miss Cooke's provocation said more to me than an illustrated guide to Hong Kong politics. "She seems very personable. I am surprised she's not married."

I am convinced to this day that under his lush moustache, Humphries smiled. "Oh, you don't know that we are graced in Hong Kong by a certain eligible personage? A Marquess, no less."

"I've not had the pleasure of the gentleman's acquaintance." I relaxed back onto the bed, immeasurably cheered. In Humphries I may not have an ally-direct, but after his pointed warning, I was sure he'd keep Miss Cooke and me apart.

"Lord Runfold, the son of His Grace the Duke of Greenhithe's first born. He is Tarrant's secretary. Been sent out into the world to aid a career in Politics before he takes his father's seat in the Upper House. Tarrant's procurement of a passage for her was almost indecently hasty after he was appraised of Lord Runfold's presence."

"And has she been encouraged in her expectations?" I wondered if that was what made her so insufferable—the encouragement of a marriage so far above her station. *If this Runfold cannot see her for what she is, he is a fool!*

"By her uncle. As far as the rumour mill goes, Lord Runfold is completely obsessed with his work, wishing to understand all that the Anglo-Indo-China trade route offers."

I felt slightly more sympathetic to the man. He was probably one of those earnest Cambridge chaps—nose in a book—never a thought for anything other than work. It spoke well of him, I felt, that even in his position he could show such dedication. I'd enquire a bit further about her stay in Hong Kong. If she had her eyes firmly fixed on this Runfold, it is unlikely she'd cause me a particular concern. *Just in case, I'd do well to be prepared.* "Has she been with the Pious Brethren since her arrival?"

"Yes." At this, I was sure Humphries smiled. I was warming to the old chap. "It has been a most illuminating experience."

"I can see how it must have been." I let my eyes light up with pleasure and smiled. A rare occurrence. I stood to see him out, and then recollected my affairs-du-toilette. "One more thing," I asked as Humphries started to stand. "I hate to bother you, but I had to dress unaided this morning. How does one go about procuring a valet?"

"Oh, that was entirely my fault, Mr. Vaughan. I shall assign you someone from the mission, but be warned, they are not always the most reliable of fellows. I would keep my valuables under lock and key if I were you. And *always* keep your spirits secured."

"I brought a tantalus, so that will not be a problem." I tried not to show it, but I was perturbed. *Not to trust my valet? An unthinkable scenario.* But the only other choice was to dress myself and while I was sure certain people were accustomed to it, it was something I was glad to have left behind at school. I would just have to keep a close eye on my possessions.

Chapter Four

The following week did indeed see the level of my spirits sink, both those locked away in the tantalus and those in my head. The former had much to do with the latter, for I had taken Humphries advice and kept the key secreted on my person with that of my trunk. Their inscrutable faces made me feel less of a cad. After all, the natives had not been raised to our English standards and as such should not have temptation offered to them. It was my Christian duty to keep those items that may cause the men to stray out of harm's way.

It was all astoundingly similar to ministering back in

London. When one spoke of the mysteries of the Indies back home, one pictured the enticing smokes and strange little houses. While I had those aplenty, I was certain the matrons in their dining rooms in Belgravia had not the faintest inkling of the drudgery that came with said enticing foreign climes.

At least Humphries had kept Miss Cooke and me apart. Her duties seemed to include a sort of fashionable begging among the English residents around both the bay and the interior port of Canton. I have no doubt Humphries was exploiting her connections for the sake of the mission and when I pressed him on such, he tapped his right hand to the side of his nose and winked.

Due to the blessed lack of Miss Cooke, my days were filled with the hefty Mr. Collins and the almost emaciated and rather be-dandruffed Mr. Smythe. Mr. Collins—apart from an unfortunate skin condition which caused much flaking—was a rather jovial sort, and I found his company most tolerable if only I ensured to sit but one chair away. Mr. Smythe—in stark contrast—was a horrible little rat of a man who kept peering at me over his quarterly reviews and smiling in a sickening fashion. He would place himself next to me at every available opportunity and agree with everything I said. It was intolerable and much compounded my misery.

* * * * *

My days progressed as follows: I would rise, dress with the assistance of the valet assigned to me, and make my way to breakfast where I studiously ignored Miss Cooke and Smythe and attempted a jovial conversation with Collins and Humphries if they were present. We—Smythe, Collins and myself—would then take a rickety cart to the mission where I would read from the Bible and minister to the men who lay suppurating on the string beds. Anyone who believes mission work is all tea and scones and sing-a-longs should try wiping the effluent off a convulsing opium addict on a floor now formed of mud because the rain had been lapping at the door for the past three days.

After luncheon—which was most often held at the residence—I would carry out any correspondence required of me and then go for a short walk down to the harbour before washing and dressing for dinner. Humphries was rather eccentric in the position of his guests; he would seat us according to his whim and though I did not find myself opposite Miss Cooke, Smythe often loomed at me—ingratiating grin firmly in place—over the potatoes.

I would beg off the after-dinner snifters and retire to my room where I would pour myself tumbler after tumbler and lie down on my bed with my collar and cuffs strewn across the floor. Reading and re-reading my bible, looking for some sort of anchor that could bind me to this place, this *normal* life I had chosen to live.

* * * * *

After that moment of perfect clarity—wherein I knew I had been sent here to save these people from themselves, from opium—I languished in a stupor of indecision. *I can* continue to minister, to tackle the end result, or I can find the source and dam it there.

The arrival of the new governor brought this matter to a head. Lin Zexu proclaimed all opium be surrendered to the Chinese authorities and all foreign traders sign a "non-opium-trading" bond, the breaking of which would result in death.

This put me in a more jovial mood and spurred my mind to action. Having overheard Miss Cooke parroting her uncle at the table – even if one wished to avoid the dulcet tones of said harpy, one would have to emigrate to the Antipodes before such a happy occurrence could ensue – it was quite apparent that the opium trade would not be put paid to by a mere proclamation from a Chinaman, however important his Emperor deemed him.

I was, therefore, still in a position where I could only aid and abet the removal of this odious substance by virtue of subterfuge. *Bringing the ongoing trade to the notice of Lin Zexu would be sure to make an example of said traders.*

I must confess a small part of me wished Tarrant to be

implicit; if his politics were even half as abhorrent as those of his dear niece, the Empire would do well to have one less representative.

I spent a few days after this proclamation idling around the residence at Humphries' insistence. The conversation leading to this, though, was rather odd — in tone, in timing, and in content. To the best of my ability to recollect, the incident occurred as follows:

With only a cursory knock, Humphries arrived in my room on the Sunday night. He looked agitated; his hair was in a state of disarray and one stud was missing from his collar, causing it to hang lopsided. He pulled up the armchair without even a by-your-leave and looked pointedly at the tantalus. I slipped the key off my watch chain and unlocked it, pulling out a crystal tumbler and a decanter half full of scotch. I poured Humphries a heavy measure. The man was obviously on the brink of something momentous to so flagrantly disregard basic etiquette.

He took a gulp, even while I was pouring myself a smaller measure, and then he pulled his collar off completely. A second stud ricocheted off his glass with a ping and came to rest forlornly at my feet.

I took it upon myself to break the ice.

"It's twenty-year old single malt, you know. Oak-aged. From one of my brother's distilleries across the border."

Humphries started at the sound of my voice and recollected himself, putting the tumbler carefully on the small wooden table.

"Thank you, Mr. Vaughan. It is very pleasant."

"Just call me Vaughan. Most people do," I said, trying to put him at his ease and hoping to gather why he had so rudely invaded my privacy this evening.

"Vaughan." He smiled quickly then assumed a serious mien. "Vaughan, this new governor is going to cause a lot of friction between us and the natives. Collins, Smythe, and even Miss Cooke are known at the mission; their purpose is easily fathomed. While you've been of great help this past week, I would take it as a personal favour if you'd consent to spending a few days indoors. I do not wish to attract the attention of this Lin Zexu and anything out of the ordinary — even, begging your pardon, your presence — may well be cause for a disgruntled former parishioner to set some rumours on winged feet to the very ears we wish to avoid."

My face must have shown my disappointment, for Humphries continued.

"Your zeal does you credit, old chap. But could you trust an old man's judgement?"

The tone of his voice was imploring and very at odds with his usual gruff manner. "Certainly, Mr. Humphries. It will be a wrench, but I will accede to your request." The relief on Humphries face made him look a good decade younger, and a grey pallor receded from his skin. "I apologise if I am being intrusive, but are such informants common among our parishioners?"

Humphries sighed and leant back into the armchair. "Unfortunately yes, Vaughan. Opium is a vicious substance; it is rare for one of our flock to leave its cloudy delights even for the prospect of salvation. More often, they maintain a place in our mission and skulk away at night to one of the myriad dens by the harbour. Lin Zexu has promised a reward, which, with the new embargo and subsequent rise in price, is incentive enough for one of the more disaffected to implicate us on the grounds that we are *gwailo*. And *gwailo* are always found guilty."

"*gwailo?*" I asked, the word rolling strangely off my tongue.

"White foreign devils. Sometimes I think it a very accurate observation."

A plan began to form but I would need more time to process this information and arrive at a satisfactory conclusion. I uncoiled myself, aware I'd been wound so tight my limbs ached. Thankful for the information, I smiled pleasantly as Humphries made his goodbyes, my mind ticking over the possibilities his information had laid open. It had not occurred to me our very flock was the key I sought into the opium underworld. I hoped to gain entrance and learn as much as I could about this substance—from whence it came and how it was distributed. From there, I could ponder what to do with my findings—be it a quiet word with Charles Elliot or offering them to Lin Zexu as a gesture of good faith. Whatever the answer, I could not let the Empire herself be implicit in such a malignant and suppurating trade.

Chapter Five

After the conversation with Humphries, a plan began to coagulate in my head. *I must get to the source*, I thought. *I can find out who is importing opium, and from that, curry both the favour of Lin Zexu and possibly set myself up in some sort of trade monopoly.* Dear Brother Maurice was hale and hearty; it made sense for me to look to my own future. And with the departure of Father, nothing was stopping me from living the life to which I was accustomed. If that meant dipping my little finger into the murky waters of trade, well, just look at Tarrant. His association with trade had not managed to make him less of a gentleman; to my mind, his family was a more than adequate disincentive.

    The following morning, I took it upon myself to effect an introduction to the Ministry of Trade. Digging out the letters of introduction Maurice had prepared for me, I found—stuck between one for the Dowager Lady Pennington and another to Admiral Chapman—two letters, which were the cause of great pleasure: one to a *Mr. Maximilian Tarrant* and one to *The Most Honble. Marquess of Halifax*. I placed both of them on top of the clothes in my trunk and locked it—going back to check it was firmly fastened before I left the room. I would have to think carefully on whom I should procure my initial meeting with.

    As I walked into the breakfast room, I noted that Mr. Smythe and Mr. Collins were both absent and I was graced with the lone presence of Miss Cooke. She was attired in something rather akin to one of those maudlin shepherdesses produced for the mantelpieces of pretentious middle-class matrons. Her ringlets only served to emphasise her weak chin, while the ribbons that erupted both from her sleeves and her neckline made her looked more be-weeded than bedecked. It was the sort of ensemble that would look best on a child just out of the cot and I stifled a smirk as I sat down opposite her, helping myself to some eggs and kidneys.

After having three forkfuls in uninterrupted bliss, I came to the realisation that—pleasant as it was—it was most uncharacteristic of Miss Cooke to be anything other than cloyingly ebullient in the morning. I placed my cutlery on the table and relaxed back into my chair to observe the lady concerned.

Miss Cooke poked petulantly at a sausage, her scowl amusingly at odds with her ribbons and curls. It was quite obvious that something was rotten in the state of Cooke. As I had nothing better to amuse myself with—being summarily confined to pseudo-house-arrest thanks to Humphries—I thought discovering what irked the lady would prove an interesting diversion.

"And how are you this morning, Miss Cooke?" I drawled, purposely relaxing back even farther in a louche parody of the manner-less. It was amusing to see her mouth pucker as if she had ingested lemon juice as she noted my posture.

"Most well." She bit out, stabbing the unfortunate sausage.

"Is the breakfast not to your taste?" I asked, indicating the pile of macerated food strewn around her plate.

"It is most agreeable!" She took another stab at the sausage, missed it, and managed to slide it down the front of her bodice, leaving a grease-stained streak.

For a moment, we sat in silence, both our gazes fixed firmly on the front of her dress. Then—to my complete lack of surprise—she burst into tears.

I was at a loss; other than a cleaner at school who soon left under a cloud, I had never been in such close proximity to a woman in this state. I got to my feet, cringing at the scrape of the chair against the floorboards, and turned my back towards her, hoping to afford her a measure of privacy. After a time, the voluminous weeping stuttered to a close and I turned back to see her dabbing her eyes with a damp handkerchief.

"May I be of service?" I asked, somewhat unsure of what to do. I moved around the table and offered up my freshly laundered handkerchief, watching with distaste as hers was deposited on the table in a wet lump.

She dabbed her eyes for a few seconds more and then turned her red-rimmed gaze on me in what I'm sure she hoped was a limpid and alluring look. It made me want to smack her with a wet kipper, but mindful of Humphries' advice, I fixed a look of concern firmly in place.

"May I take you into my confidence, Mr. Vaughan?" she said, batting her eyelashes. I tried to damp down my elation; hopefully, whatever she was about to disclose would help me move forward in stunting the opium trade. However, I dared not risk she think me an adequate substitute for Lord Runfold; at the best, she was a puppet of her uncle, but at the worst she'd have designs upon me herself.

"Why certainly, Miss Cooke. Whatever you say will not pass outside these walls." I pulled up a chair and sat, close enough to invite confidence but far away enough to not seem improper if Smythe or Collins entered.

"I was at my uncle's last night and . . . he has rescinded his funding for the mission! Because of that new governor's proclamation, he says he has no money to indulge in fripperies! I was only here for . . . ." She broke off, raised a hand to her mouth at her near-indiscretion. "I may have to return to England!"

I obliged her with the requisite indignant response, my mind tumbling in circles behind it. *The Governor's proclamation has the Trade Delegation that concerned!* "What! I presume he has previously assured you of his commitment to the mission?" Unlike Miss Cooke, I was not boorish enough to refer directly to her uncle's pecuniary interests.

"I've already told Mr. Humphries the money would be forthcoming; under that impression, he has extended our lease. If it does not come through, what reason do I have to stay? Uncle Maximilian is already making noises about finding a berth for me on the next suitable boat—apparently I am now a drain on his resources and Hong Kong will soon become too unsafe for ladies."

"Would you not like to return to the comforts of England?" I enquired, most curious as to what she'd say. She coloured in a blotchy fashion, the contrast with her blonde ringlets and pale skin making her look rather like a mouldy strawberry.

"No. I would rather remain here. I feel I can accomplish much more."

The blotchy colouring extended to the neckline of her dress. Ill-mannered as she was, it did appear she had some measure of decent comportment.

"Would you like me to intercede?"

"You? I did not realize you knew my uncle!" Her voice turned up at the end, like a querulous parakeet.

"I believe your uncle belongs to the same club as my brother, Lord Vaughan. Maurice has given me a letter of introduction." I watched as she composed herself, the calculating wench. Her interest in me had obviously increased and I shifted back in the chair, trying to ensure my lack-thereof was quite apparent.

"If you have a letter of introduction, I'm sure he'll be

more than happy to receive you. But could you not mention my . . . concern? Regarding the ship, of course."

"I will not breathe a single word." I got to my feet and slid the chair back under the table, trying to ensure it did not look out of place. "I will call on him today, assuming he is available."

"I believe he should be," she said, making no mention of how busy she'd previously stated he was. "And I am sure he will make time to receive Lord Vaughan's brother."

"I do hope so and I will keep you apprised of the results. Good day, Miss Cooke." I bowed stiffly and left the room, my mind already mulling over how best to tackle Maximilian Tarrant. All thought of Lord Runfold, Marquess of Halifax, was banished.

Chapter Six

I tied my stock and peered into the mirror, staring querulously at the reflection. Damn the lack of a good valet! *It simply is not possible to get a decent knot from a stock that is not adequately pressed.* If his niece was anything to go by, Mr. Tarrant would be more impressed by a well-starched collar and crisply creased trousers than a well-placed argument.

I pulled a jacket out of my wardrobe and wrinkled my nose at the noisome native smell that had permeated the cloth. I donned it and took one last look in the mirror. The best of a bad job, I thought as I left the residence.

I hailed a rickshaw, taking care not to step in any

effluent and ruin my shoes. As I collapsed on the wooden seat, I breathed a sigh of relief and asked the runner to take me to the British Trade Mission.

My gaze meandered from shack to shack along the route and I was surprised when the vehicle stopped in front of yet another unprepossessing building and bid me to alight. So, taken aback by the dull and decrepit facade, I stepped straight into a pile of unmentionable and proceeded to make a spectacle by hopping from foot to foot and cursing vociferously. *This better be the damned mission!*

A liveried native met me at the door and I was ushered into the anteroom where an English manservant took my card and offered me a drink. "Gin and tonic," I replied, glancing at my pocket-watch and noting the sun was firmly over the yardarm. I settled in an opulent leather armchair. *Ah, good, solid English craftsmanship.* I was about to lean even farther back into the chair and sink into a blissful reverie of good old Brittania—where tea and crumpets constantly beckoned and clotted cream flashed an ankle at me whenever I looked away—when the manservant returned and informed me that the exceptionally busy Maximilian Tarrant would be able to slip me into his schedule a few minutes hence. I nodded my assent and looked around at the empty hall. Either Tarrant was cloistered with other servants of the Crown, trying to understand the implications of Lin Zexu's proclamation, or he was purposely leaving me waiting to make himself seem more important. From the derisive look the manservant had shot me as he departed, I assumed the latter.

Having already got to my feet, I decided to prop myself up against a wooden column. It was intricately carved with heathen symbols and an image suddenly came to me of what our mission would have looked like in an unadulterated state. It must have been an impressive building.

At this, I pushed myself off the column and undertook a closer inspection of the room, noting that while this was self-evidently a native building, it was most certainly one of high quality. Even my unappreciative eye could see the quality of the carving and the tightness of the joints. My portrait of Tarrant was given another pigment; presuming he had procured or agreed the procurement of this building, and unlike his niece, he had an appreciation for subtle beauty. I had to hide a smile as the manservant returned and left me in the anteroom of Tarrant's office, where I was made to wait once more and where the fixtures and fittings served to confirm my previous judgement. *This is a man to watch.*

On eventually being ushered into Tarrant's office, I was most amused at how he'd positioned himself just at the point of convergence. Every line in the room—the ceiling, the floor, the edges of the paintings ornamenting the walls—led to him. In such understated surrounds, the size and finery of the man—now *here* were the *latest* fashions—shone brighter than a comet.

His face was leonine, and his hair swept backwards in a style that was to become fashionable twenty years later, but then only served to bring out the cragginess of his cheekbones. His nose was strong and mottled with the faint tracery of much wine and that webbing extended to his cheeks, which were smooth-shaven and beautifully kept. His mouth was narrow and pursed into a moue of disapproval as he took in my own appearance. He did not seem impressed but perfunctorily extended a hand to accept my letter of introduction, skimming it while sinking back into his chair. Quite frankly, he had the most appalling manners and I could not understand *why* the crown would place such a man in such a sensitive post. *Unless they want to provoke a war?*

The thought stopped me in my tracks. *To provoke a war with China?* We had power on our side—that was a certainty—but to provoke a war? Opium was admittedly a very lucrative trade, but surely it could only be a small fraction of what the East India Company must transport in a single year. *What is it? Is opium a link in the chain that can't be removed? Is there nothing else we could offer China in its stead?*

Tarrant brought me to reality by the tinny ringing of a pewter bell on his desk. It was an incongruous object, slightly dulled and very worn. The manservant entered with a tray of tea, a parsimonious pot of sugar, and a tarnished jug of milk. A studied insult, especially as compared to the finesse of the rest of the building and the appointments of Tarrant himself.

"So *you're* Vaughan's brother." His tone of voice indicated censure so severe that I had to assume he'd heard about me through the hushed-voiced whisperings that had accompanied my disgrace at school. "I was at College with him, you know."

Ah, definitely knows about my peccadilloes then. And does not approve.

I relaxed my posture until I was as slack as a sailor on shore leave and let an enticing smile rise to my lips. He looked at me — dumbfounded — and started, spilling tea onto the sage-green leather blotter. I was intrigued by this reaction; still waters run deep.

It dawned on me I probably was not going to achieve my aims by getting him so incensed that he had me summarily removed from his office. I stood and ineffectually helped him blot the tea, wincing as I noted how far it had penetrated into the leather. After a few moments, he seemed to give it up as a bad job and sat once more.

"My thanks for receiving me at such short notice." I assayed, hoping to recoup my losses and put him somewhat at his ease. This return to formality had him sitting up straighter in his chair, his composure returning, his spine stiffening with every breath. I could see his thoughts as they passed over his face, the moment when he realized he was in control, when he realized I was at best an inferior and at worst an equal, and when he realized we were six-thousand miles from the drawing rooms of Belgravia and that his cutting me would be unlikely to make the least bit of difference as it was my dear brother who was titled, not I.

He smiled at me then, and I was put in mind of a tiger or a shark—all grace and beauty but a fearful lack of conscious beneath. Yes, her Majesty's government must surely be aware of *what* they'd sent. *No wonder he decided to stop funding the mission. With Lin Zexu here it makes little sense to placate the man with missions and help for the disenfranchised if Tarrant's brief was to promote a pivot-point for hostilities.*

All of this passed through my mind in the time it took

for him to reply with a brief pleasantry. He then continued . . . .

"Of course, much as I appreciate this social call, I must continue with my work. Time waits for no man, etcetera . . . ."

"A social call? Did your man not mention I was here about the mission? Miss Cooke mentioned to me in passing, over breakfast, you know, that there was talk of its funding being removed."

Besides dropping the manservant into it from a great height—which amused me to no end—I could see Tarrant re-cataloguing me under the class, genus and specie of "Suitor, Untitled, Money-Grubbing." The fact that I had breakfasted with his niece had cast a slight green pallor over his features. Imagine if his bloodline was to be sullied with my peculiar taint! It would be most unbecoming. A rictus-like smile affixed itself to his features as he weighed up my implied price. One could almost see his lips move as he balanced further funding for the mission versus my possible entanglement with his niece and the impact that would have on his plans to wed her to Lord Runfold.

"It was a slip of the tongue. I only meant that some of the funding could be delayed. She must have misinterpreted; I would never let such a worthy cause fall into disrepair."

"I can then assure Miss Cooke that the promised funds will be available in a timely manner? And possibly it will be known that the Superintendant of Trade is behind the mission?"

His face dropped, but he nodded his assent. "Certainly. Now if you would excuse me?" He bent over his desk and began to shuffle papers. With one last smile, hoping he could see my reflection in the pewter bell, I left the room. I had found out what sort of a man Maximilian Tarrant was. *If I am going to help the people in the mission, I will have to stop a war.* The thought made my blood sing.

Chapter Seven

My mind was whirring when I returned to the mission. For the Empire to tacitly provoke a war was beyond the pale, but to do so over such a noxious substance was a most egregious abuse of power. I pondered on what to do: should I go above Tarrant? No, even with my brother's name it would be foolish to accuse not just him but the entirety of Her Majesty's Government of trying to provoke a war based on mere observation. Should I talk to Humphries? A moment's reflection rendered that option less than useless.

I stumbled through the door and almost fell over Miss Cooke. She had donned her bonnet and was slipping on her cloak, primping and fussing in the hall mirror. She turned her big blue eyes on me and I felt like I was drowning in a loch. A deeply unpleasant sensation.

I smiled at her perfunctorily and told her the funds would be forthcoming. She vibrated with gratitude in the most unbecoming manner. Even though I was repulsed, I made an effort to smile before pushing past her. I had to stop and think, and having Miss Cooke trailing after me like a sick dog was unlikely to aid that.

I placed my boots outside my door in hope that someone would remove the drying unmentionable. I unbuttoned my collar and cuffs and lay down on the bed. The tantalus beckoned me, but I concentrated on not getting up and pouring a measure or three. *This is no time for clouded thinking . . . ! What a fool I'm being!* Only days before, I'd thought of using the mission as the starting point for my investigation. Surely, someone there would know where the opium was actually sold?

A clatter in the corridor made me jump. I opened the door and found Smythe in an ignominious heap. It looked as though he'd tripped over my boots, the poor sod. I reached out and extended a hand, somewhat repulsed at the look of gratitude that suffused his features. However, the brief contact seemed to have rendered him amenable to conversation; to my good fortune, the smell of him indicated he'd just been to the mission.

Surely, Smythe will have some knowledge of the opium dens? He could not have been in Hong Kong for two years without having a vague idea of where they could be found.

"A drink?" I asked, wedging the door of my room open in invitation. He leapt to his feet, brushing his threadbare jacket and adjusting his poorly tied stock in a hopeless attempt to make himself more presentable. I stifled a smile. Really, if he were to keep himself better — rid himself of the dandruff — he would be an almost passable specimen of man.

I gestured to an arm-chair and he sank down happily, gently fluttering flakes of skin on the carved wood. At least the chair was most assiduous; his residue would not rest there for long.

"So, Smythe," I said, handing him a drink. "What brings you here in the middle of the day? Collins and you rarely return before nightfall." I raised my glass towards him in a toast and downed the scotch, feeling the grateful burn run down the back of my throat.

"S-s-some of the Ch-Chinese Governor's troops came to the m-mission. They s-s-strongly s-s-suggested we leave."

"And you just left?" I was astounded. "What of the poor wretches? Did you leave them there at the mercy of Lin Zexu?"

"What do you take us for? We ushered them out as soon as we received word. I presume they will go back to whatever dens they crawled out of in the first place." Smythe took a mincing sip of his whiskey and grimaced. I noticed the beverage had put a stop to his stutter.

"So they've gone back to the dens that spawned them. But surely if we know from whence they came we could close them down?" I decided to play the ingénue in the hope of luring some more information out of Smythe.

"British policy would not allow for that, old chap."

He chortled, eyes lighting with a secret glee. "Not with the amount of money in contention."

"So we're to just tacitly accept that it occurs?"

"We have no choice, Vaughan. The Trade Delegation will force us to close down if we don't turn a blind eye to the source."

"Have you been there, though? Have you seen the opium?" I asked, seeking to drag the location out of him. "It may be that the opium is not ours."

Smythe's chortle turned into a full-blown roar of laughter. "Oh, Vaughan." He stood and placed a hand on my shoulder. "*All* the opium that comes into China is brought in by the East India Company!"

I kept my composure even though my heart was fluttering a mile a minute. "Forgive my ignorance." I sought to alleviate my nervous energy by leaning from side to side. "And if—hypothetically speaking—someone would like to see this first hand?"

Smythe's look turned conspiratorial. "I would think that one could—hypothetically—do worse than the Floating

Lotus. It is located by the docks and is a hot-house of many of the more *unusual* unnatural vices."

I returned his confidential gaze. With a squeeze, he let my shoulder go, downed the rest of his whiskey, and left my room with a spring in his step. I wondered just what I'd agreed to venture into.

* * * * *

After dinner, I wrapped up warmly, pulling my greatcoat about me even though it was early summer and it made me look a complete fool. I could feel the sweat dripping down my back as I hailed a rickshaw and asked the runner to take me to the Floating Lotus. We passed the mission on the way and I ducked low. It would not do for news of my travels to be broadcast abroad.

Upon arrival, I noted that it was in a dank location; a miasma creeping up from the ground — the stench of the mission multiplied a hundredfold. I tried to make myself inconspicuous — difficult as I was a good half-foot taller than the natives—as I approached the den. The door was beautifully carved and oiled, incongruous in such a derelict edifice. At my knock, the door opened and I was granted the merest glimpse of the treasures within. The fug of poppy hit me, a delightfully sweet and pungent scent. My gaze was drawn towards the back room where I could just see yards of unclothed flesh parading for the delectation of those customers sober enough to appreciate their ambivalent charms.

The doorman took my coat and hat and I loosened my stock. I was in luck; the steamy atmosphere meant there was little chance of my damp shirt and waistcoat being considered anything other than the norm. He ushered me through into the main room. As my eyes adjusted to the murky light, I discerned that the servants and wares—all completely naked—were male.

I must have stood rock-still for a moment, my gaze lurching around the room from form to form. The hazy purpled light made each boy look like a dream-creature—an enchanted paradigm of flickering flesh. I was completely enraptured.

The doorman's tug on my shirt-sleeve made me recoil, though it had the required effect of recollecting me to the present. I accepted the proffered gin and tonic, finding the bubbles and the sharp taste of quinine a welcome alternative to the cloying smell of the opium. A selection of pipes was brought to me but I waved it away, noting the intricately carved stems and bowls, crenulated with writhing figures.

How had Smythe known? The thought struck me as I downed the last of my G&T, a drip running down my chin, my throat, the hollow at the base of my neck. The iced liquid mirrored the frost of my blood. *Smythe knew. Dear Jesus! How?* I cast my mind back through our conversations. *Had I ever given him an inkling of such untoward desires?* I waved for another drink and yet another in near-instant succession. *What shall I do?* I stood, nearly tipping the stool over as I bolted towards the internal courtyard. I pushed through the gentlemen enjoying their pipes and the attentive natives at their sides, unthinkingly stepping on both fingers and toes. *Air! I need air before I am ill!*

The courtyard captured only the faintest of breezes, but even that trace was welcome in my fraught state. My head was reeling, my palms sweaty and shaking. *Smythe!* I sat down on a stone bench and put my head between my knees, feeling my chest heave.

I felt a touch on my shoulder and a manservant — this one clothed, thank God — passed me a glass of water. I drank it unthinkingly; the flux seemed of little import in comparison. He indicated I should follow him and led me into a small room across the courtyard.

There was less of a fug here which enabled me to clearly see the array of boys on offer, all lined against the wall. *It's time for me to choose my paramour for the evening!* I thought, suppressing a hysterical giggle. *It's not as if restraining myself from the use of the facilities will ally the suspicion in Smythe's mind. There's no way he'll know what transpired tonight. All he knows is that I've come here. I may as well revel in the situation and deal with any consequences on the morrow.* I could sense the manservant getting impatient and so gestured at random; a not-particularly-attractive-boy stepped forward. He was slightly older than the rest and his pockmarked skin shone greasily in the candlelight. I must impress upon you, while my inclinations may be base and vile, I've never stooped to those who'd be out of limits if they were possessed of female characteristics. My proclivities have never lain there and so my relief at gaining a whore of an older mien did not require counterfeiting.

We were ushered through into a windowless room where I was unceremoniously deposited near a pile of cushions. I sat down and began to perfunctorily unfasten my trousers. *Six thousand miles from Hyde Park and it's the very same process.* The thought brought a cynical smirk to my face. The man whom I had chosen began to mirror me in my undress so rather than feast on the unprepossessing sight I glanced around the room. My eyes fell on the man in the peacock waistcoat about whom I'd commenced this narrative.

Having previously graced you with the prurient details I see no need to reiterate. Suffice to say, whatsoever I placed on the page can only be a mere fraction of the pleasure that surged through both my body and my mind at his performance. There was also no counterfeit in my anguish when I noticed he'd left; I was as bereft as I'd been in the courtyard only minutes before. The man in the peacock waistcoat had brought me to the greatest pinnacle of pleasure and pulled me to the deepest nadir of despair that I had ever felt.

Mired in that despair, I hastily approximated an appropriate standard of dress, pushed some money at the doorman—more than enough judging from the avaricious gleam in his eyes—and walked towards the docks, my thoughts roiling. I hailed the first rickshaw I saw, stuttering the destination several times before it was understood. I was silent on the ride home, wishing I was able to coherently contemplate the situation, but in reality, feeling egregiously blank. It had all been too much for me. On arrival, I pushed past the intelligible words of Humphries, Collins, and Miss Cooke—noting the concealed smirk on Smythe's face for later measures—and made my way to my room. I fell asleep fully clothed.

Chapter Eight

As I was mooching around the residence—bored senseless with my lack of employ—Humphries sidled up to me. We had spoken, both at breakfast and at luncheon, so I was somewhat perplexed to see him skulking around and gesturing to me as if we were characters in a women's novella planning an assignation. I glanced from side to side, cursing myself for a fool as I let Humphries' delusions overcome my good breeding. *Whatever is causing Humphries to behave like such a dolt could be the very thing to push me out of the doldrums!*

Since patronising The Floating Lotus, I had tried to

keep to the common areas when Smythe was about. I will confess to being unsure of how well this stratagem was working, for in the intervening two days, his secret smile had moved — to my mind — from prurient through obscene and was now verging on the downright malicious. At least I had availed myself of the presented wares, as it was most evident that Smythe took the presence for the deed.

A coil of concern still writhed in my belly though. *How had Smythe known?* On thinking it over, I could only come to the conclusion that my beloved brother had played fast and loose enough with my proclivities for six thousand miles to be little barrier. I guessed Tarrant had dropped a word to the wise and Smythe had taken full advantage of the situation. *Maybe my use of Miss Cooke as a pawn was too impulsive?*

Humphries' waggling eyebrows — like two joined-up caterpillars — pulled me back down to earth. He darted into the drawing room, beckoned to me, and then quickly shut the door behind us. I winced as he eased the shutters closed, as I was not sure the prolonged creak did anything to disabuse passers-by of our presence. Walking to the sideboard, he lit a single taper. This was the first sign of a reasoned mind; one would rather not have the chandelier radiating heat in the oppressive Hong Kong summer.

My curiosity was now baying at the gates. I sat on a chair, crossed my ankles, and attempted to portray casual interest. *I'm almost as intrigued as I am with peacock waistcoat!*

Humphries' perched on a neighbouring chair, his eyes alight with pleasure. "Vaughan?" he whispered.

I leant forward on my chair, my nose a hairsbreadth from the taper and maybe four inches from Humphries' face. I could smell the candle wax and the sweet singe of hair. "Yes, Mr. Humphries?" I mimicked his tone.

"I have a favour to ask of you."

The bottom dropped out of my world. Surely, this mutton-chop of a man had not pulled me into the drawing room for a nice game of hide-the-sausage? *Even in Belgravia such rumours would not spread so very fast! Tarrant must be dropping my indiscretions into every conversation!*

I felt my skin become clammy, my palms sliding up

and down the rough twill of my trousers. "A favour?" I returned, pleased that I was able to keep my voice so steady.

"Nothing onerous, old chap. I would think this is just up your street."

Oh damn! Well, there was only one way forward. *Maybe it had not been Tarrant: maybe one of the parishioners had been at the Floating Lotus. Or maybe Humphries had seen me there himself!* The thought drew the cold sweat down my back, and I sat up straighter so as not to stain my shirt. "If I can be of service?" My voice broke on service.

Humphries gave me an odd look before continuing. "I told you old chap. Nothing onerous. I have been informed that Miss Cooke requires an escort for the ball being held this evening at the Trade Delegation. Due to circumstances apparently beyond her control, her uncle was unable to ensure the presence of Lord Runfold on her arm. However, it would not do for her to turn up alone. I am rather too old for these jaunts and we do get so very much of our funding from subscriptions at these events. It would be a great favour."

As the old man's sentimental prattling drew to a close, I felt my heart slow to a more normal pace. *Escort Miss Cooke to a ball? A ball where all the beautiful, influential young things in Hong Kong will be present. A chance to find out the identity of the man in the peacock waistcoat? How could I refuse?* The smile must have suffused my face rather too enthusiastically, for Mr. Humphries cast me a knowing grin. "Ah lad, I was sure you'd come around. She's a rather pert lass, but the best you'll find this side of India, I'd warrant."

I was about to contradict him and then thought the better of it. With Smythe and Tarrant both seemingly apprised of my personal peccadilloes, it would not be unintelligent to push the rumour mill in the opposite direction. I smiled in what I hoped was a discreet manner. "It would be my pleasure to escort Miss Cooke, Mr. Humphries."

"Excellent, excellent!" His booming laugh was the closest I'd come to hearing someone guffaw. He rose, slapped me on the shoulder in what I presume he meant as a paternal fashion and threw open the shutters, letting a blessed breeze enter the room. "I will have a rickshaw ready to take you both at seven."

"That would be most kind of you, sir."

"No Vaughan, it is most kind of you. One of these balls can keep our mission open for a quarter if approached correctly. And I'm sure that you will be a most attentive escort. Just let Miss Cooke work her usual magic."

"I will endeavour to rise to the situation," I replied, piling it on a bit thick even for my own liking.

"I'm sure you will. I'm sure you will." He smiled paternally and left the room, still mumbling happily to himself, while I collapsed once more into the chair. I hoped to God that I knew what I'd done.

* * * * *

It was a quarter hour later when a double-rap knock on the doorframe alerted me to Smythe's presence. *Damn! I do not need this right now!* "Mr. Smythe" I blandly enquired. "Is there anything I can do for you?"

Smythe entered the room and sat on the chair recently vacated by Mr. Humphries. "My dear Vaughan," he began, the benign twinkle in his eye ramping swiftly towards prurient. "I had begun to think you were avoiding me!"

His lack of manners startled me; addressing my behaviour so bluntly was not the mark of a true gentleman. It behoved a response in kind. "Certainly not, Mr. Smythe. It has been a rather busy couple of days."

From his expression, it was obvious that he did not believe my lackadaisical explanation, but was willing to let it lie for the time being. "I trust that you enjoyed your sojourn two nights previous?"

It was certainly not the mark of a gentleman to refer to something so delicate so directly. Nausea roiled in my stomach, the smell of candle-wax turning to rancid fat. *How on earth did I end up in a position where I am conversing with such a cad about something so very delicate? I must be a fool!* But cad or not, Smythe believed he knew about my predilections and Tarrant could back those up with my brother's own words. *Angering Smythe could mean my destruction!* "It was most . . . educational," I replied, carefully emphasising the latter word.

To my brief amusement, Smythe looked slightly confused, as if he were at a loss as to what education one could receive in a house of ill repute. As a meaning dawned on him, I could see his face mirror mine in glee and then pity. It dawned on me, I had suggested an inexperienced virginity, and in indulging in the first rut of my life. I coloured in shame.

"I presume you found what you were looking for," Smythe said, a slight sting in the tail of his words.

I kept my composure—just—my fingernails digging into my palms. "It was most informative. Though I should say, I found the dress of the servants rather exceptional."

"But they don't wear any—" Smythe broke off.

I'd trapped him, he'd been there himself, I was sure of it! I breathed a sigh of relief that he'd chosen not to grace the Floating Lotus with his presence that evening. The image of Smythe in a state of dishabille was something I could well do without.

"My thanks though, Mr. Smythe. I found out much about what we'd been speaking." A blatant lie. I'd been much too interested in peacock-waistcoat to worry about such trifling business as international warfare.

"I am pleased to have been of service. If you ever require an escort . . . ." He finished hopefully.

"I will be sure to enquire." I felt jubilant, with Smythe on the back-foot, and a ball where I could well be formally introduced to peacock-waistcoat, it seemed like this could be a fascinating night indeed.

Chapter Nine

I pushed my pearl studs through the front of my dress shirt, thankful for the newfangled placket as one had been chipped in transit. I must write to Maurice for a replacement set, I thought, slipping the matching pair into my cuffs. At least these were whole. I tied my stock, and smoothed my white silk waistcoat into place. Finally, I donned my tailcoat, pleased at how the laundry-wallah had pressed them so flat without them accruing the cheap sheen of worn cloth. I dropped a hint of scent on my handkerchief and tucked it into my coat-pocket. While this was ostensibly an English ball, I was unsure if the natives would be *personae non-gratae* and I would rather have a handkerchief to lift to my nose than commit a social faux pas.

In the hall, I met Miss Cooke, who for once was suitably attired in a gown of deep blue silk, off the shoulders and ruffled to make the most of her assets. The decoration was surprisingly modest and while the colour was too deep for her skin tone—bringing out the pink once more—the lack of ornamental fripperies made her look almost innocent. No doubt a look she intended most clearly.

I proffered my arm and under the burbling thanks of Humphries lifted her into the rickshaw. My hands almost encircled her tightly-corseted waist and I knew that any red-blooded man would have felt a thrill of pleasure at having such a delicate flower within his grasp. I merely pondered on how one could both eat and breathe in such a ridiculous get-up.

I kept up the usual patter of pleasantries on the way to the ball but underneath my calm demeanour, my mind was a seething mash of contradictions. On the one hand I was afire to find out who the mystery-man had been. I had not been able to get his languid smile out of my head, nor the sense of intense playfulness with which he participated in that little game. However, the feeling of emptiness had not left me and I was half-worried that peacock-waistcoat had been a figment of my imagination. Unlike a love-struck chit at a cotillion, I could not simper and swoon to my friends about how *Mr. D.* had graced me with three dances and had only danced at most two with everyone else. How he had attended upon me above all others and how we were feted by all the matrons to be engaged a fortnight hence! Rather, I was left to ponder the physical reality of my sordid interest and concern myself with all problems that could occur if he were anything less than a gentleman of the finest calibre. For anything else would leave me — in the nautical parlance — high, dry, and thoroughly exposed to a blackmail broadside.

We alighted in front of the mission and I was pleased to note the street had been cleaned since my previous visit. The outside of the building was covered in tiny candles which were constantly being replaced by a servant stationed there for the sole purpose. The flickering light so close to the wood gave me brief cause for concern, but in looking around I noted everyone else seemed to take it in their stride. I lifted Miss Cooke out of the coach and handed my card to the doorman, who announced us to a general disregard. On escorting Miss Cooke to our hosts, I made my pleasantries while smirking at the glare on Mr. Tarrant's face. Apparently, I had been promoted to Suitor, Untitled, Money-Grubbing, Rather-More-Intelligent-Than-Previously-Assumed. My presence was obviously not to his taste, for while Miss Cooke was waxing rapturous about the rather mediocre decorations, Tarrant excused himself with a short bow in my direction, much to the disgust of the women. I took the opportunity to bow deeply to Mrs. Tarrant and Miss Cooke and made my escape.

I have always hated balls. They seem to me to be a puerile waste of time, with simpering women eyeing up sotted men and often the reverse. If I danced with the girls on offer, my politeness was taken as a near-proposal of marriage. If I decided to absent myself from the floor, a matronly battleship—normally draped in either moth-eaten-velvet or corseted so tightly the creaking-timbers were audible even above the background noise—would accost me and demand, *positively demand,* I take some homely wallflower out onto the floor. If I acquiesced, it was yet another hopeful looking for a foot into the Vaughan family name. If I declined, I was spoken of as a bounder and a cad. It was a no-win situation and frankly, I would rather play cards at my club or sit at home with a book.

 Seeing a motherly battleship bearing down on me, I swiftly retreated to a small alcove wherein I found—to my great surprise and unparalleled pleasure—a servant bearing a tray of mixed drinks. After surreptitiously knocking back two scotches in sweet succession, I took a long glass of G&T and leant back against the carved column, just out of view of the rest of the room, better to observe if my quarry was present. I needn't have bothered, for at this point, the doorman raised his voice to announce the presence of "The most Honourable, The Marquess of Halifax, Lord Runfold."

 Oh, for all the . . . ! I looked around, panicked. *Thank*

God! All eyes on the bloody Marquess! No one's looking at me! Not wishing to tempt fate, I darted back into the alcove. *Lord Runfold was the man in the peacock waistcoat!*

* * * * *

I would love to say, in that moment, I was more amused at the hopelessness of Miss Cooke's aspirations than I was of anything else, but all I can remember is a feeling of absolute cold suffuse my body. Though I was standing in a pressed-bodied room of people—all rubbing and squeezing between one another—I felt as if I were standing on the peak of Ben Nevis in a gale, all noise drowned out in the dense patter of the snow swirling around me.

It was then I realised how lucky I was to be leaning against the column—my knees gave way and I jammed my fingers into the crenulations between the carvings, feeling the sinew and bone strained to the breaking point as I kept myself up by willpower alone. Well, I'd wished for a gentleman, but the Duke of Greenhithe's son was more than even I'd expected.

At this point, the servant returned, bearing with him yet more sweet sustenance. This time, I ignored the scotch, settling on a light elderflower cordial that almost made the servant drop the tray. Apparently, *gwailo* were not supposed to indulge in anything other than hard alcohol.

Knowing it was Lord Runfold with whom I'd indulged myself put a different complexion on the situation. If it had been another mere gentleman, I would have been able to affably find someone who'd be able to effect introductions. Runfold was a peer in his own right and therefore I could not presume acquaintance with him. Though, at least I had been able to hide my shock in the bodies of the crowd. *Imagine if I'd blithely gone to his office after my visit to the Floating Lotus and presented my letter of introduction! And then had to spend the appointment trying to keep a straight face!* It was much better this way; I could keep to the margins of the party and out of the sphere of the battleships and pray that Miss Cooke quickly lost interest so we could return to the residence. I could have yet another night of quiet contemplation.

* * * * *

A half hour later, my plan lay in ruins. After a fourth elderflower, I was beset by an urge to utilise the facilities. Not knowing where they were, I'd ambled into the path of a velvet-matron and her dog-faced offspring — attired in something more suited to a nunnery — and was coerced into a dance. We lined up as for a country-dance. I glanced to my right and noted the gentleman was a rotund old fellow, unmarried, with a twinkle in his eye for the pretty girl before him. In front of me was the basset-hound. To her right was Miss Cooke, who smiled approvingly at me. And in front of her — to my left — was Lord Runfold.

It would give me great pleasure to blame my dancing incompetence on my pressing physical requirements. But I can't say that stumbling mince-footed through the dance in a horrific parody of a clockwork soldier could be blamed on anything other than the presence of Lord Runfold. As we stepped and circled — around and counter-clockwise — my gaze kept catching his, my steps stuttering as a result. I kept dragging my gaze back to the basset-hound, but in all honesty, even the presence of Venus de Milo herself would have been hard put to capture my interest.

After an initial flash of mutual recognition — in which I tried to communicate a lack of hostility through my gaze — Lord Runfold seemed to relax into the dance and his eyes sparkled with mirth every time I nearly tripped over my own feet. I was causing a public spectacle and at the end of the dance could do nothing more but bow perfunctorily towards my partner and make a bolt for it, stopping only to ask a servant where the facilities were housed.

At his answer, I made my way out into the courtyard toward an ornately carved cabin in which I found two cubicles in the English style. I managed to unfasten my trousers and relieved myself, throwing my head back as the twin feelings of bodily pleasure and complete humiliation warred within.

I part-registered the creaking open of the door; with

two cubicles, another person in need of relief was no concern of mine. On fastening my trousers and exiting the cubicle, concern swiftly became a priority though, as there stood Lord Runfold, larger than life. I was rendered mute. All I could focus on was against all convention; his waistcoat, shirt and stock, rather than being the standard white, were the most beautiful shade of pale duck-egg-blue. The colour brought out the deep tones of his skin and served to enhance the jade-green of his eyes.

    I would suggest my looks served to please him as well, for he placed a hand over my mouth and drew me back into the cubicle I'd so recently vacated. It should have been a sordid experience, rutting up against the walls of the Trade Mission, stopping as and when the door creaked open, stifling our breathing against each other's necks and then continuing when the coast was clear. We wrapped our hands around each other's members and his laconic pulling and pushing caused me to near-bite-through my lip while stifling my moans. When I risked a look at his face, his eyes were almost black with pleasure and there was a sheen of sweat across his brow. But most wonderful of all, I could see the tip of his pink tongue poke out between his white teeth. And though I could fool myself that we were only taking a base pleasure in each other, a treacherous part of my mind wanted to pull his head to mine and stifle our moans in a kiss.

Chapter Ten

I have no recollection of what occurred after the sojourn in the facilities. I vaguely remember Miss Cooke prattling on about her uncle's inadequacies during the ride home and as the man himself was not at my door to demand satisfaction the following morning, I assumed I'd done a good enough job so as not to embarrass her or cast aspersions upon Tarrant himself.

It took me a good week to decide what to do with regards to Runfold. We'd not exchanged a word and even I recognised anonymity could well be the better part of valour. If I chose to formally present myself, it seemed likely

I would appear to be a blackmailer or a lout and could even possibly be given the cut-direct, which would intrigue Tarrant were he to hear of it. On the other hand, Runfold did seem to be a bit of a risk-taker and I did wonder what such a man would have made of Maximilian Tarrant.

Fortunately, for my peace of mind, a brace of native soldiers came to our door on Monday and informed us that as the mission had been deemed to be free of opium, we could recommence our work. This time Humphries asked me to serve with Smythe and while this involved me waking at an unconscionable hour, it did provide a much needed distraction.

Smythe was most amenable and attentive, as long as I was sure to smile favourably on the thought of a trip to the Floating Lotus at some undetermined time in the future. On observing his work at the mission, it was obvious that Smythe was one of those most kindly but feminine of men, more suited to the role of a nursemaid or tutor than to the harsh labour of mucking out the opium-addict's pallets and restraining them through their wracking seizures. The addicts could get violent and vicious, and often I found myself standing between Smythe and a knife-wielding native intent on procuring more opium. I still have no idea what in my calm demeanour placated them, and at times I wonder if it was my complete contempt that made them relinquish their weapons and curl up on their pallets once more.

By the Friday, I'd decided I could not sit idly by; whatever the consequences of my formally introducing myself to Lord Runfold, it would be extremely remiss of me to not attempt to stop a war because I was concerned about a personal humiliation brought on by my own base desires. It would not be the mark of a gentleman to shirk this duty.

I duly dressed myself in my finest day-wear and pulled Maurice's letter of introduction out of my case. I hailed a rickshaw for the Trade Delegation and repeated the journey that had landed me in this situation.

At the door, the same sneering manservant took my card and ushered me into the hall, this time, with no offer of a drink. I remained standing; creased as my trousers were from the journey I did not wish to exacerbate the situation. After what seemed like an interminable eon a po-faced secretary ushered me once more up the stairs—this time, turning left instead of right—and into an office that was almost the diametric opposite of Tarrant's.

The walls were obscured by paper—files and piles lined the room from floor to ceiling—with only a narrow column bereft of such around the window. The desk was piled high with folders, arranged in an arcane order, which I was quite sure no mortal man could fathom. And behind the desk, peering at me from behind a pair of Oxford-spectacles, sat Lord Runfold.

His stock was loosened; his jacket was lying idly over a chair. His hair was mussed as if he'd been running his hands through it, like any clerk trying to get the books to tally. He looked up and smiled in vague recognition, then started and almost toppled backwards onto the floor.

I stood quietly in front of the desk, not wanting to presume, though it must be said that my first instinct was to rush around and help him to his feet. I kept my mind fixed on a higher purpose and smiled as I extended the letter of introduction.

Re-aligning the spectacles on his nose, Runfold peered at Maurice's crabbed handwriting. After what seemed like a decent interval watching Runfold attempt to decipher the scrawl, I decided to take the bull by the horns.

"Lord Runfold. It is a pleasure to finally meet you."

He looked up askance, as I continued. "It has been my great pleasure to have been apprised of you by Miss Cooke. She spoke of little else after the ball."

His gaze scoured my face and I made sure my mien was amiable and discreet. I tried to communicate the need for a reserved demeanour within this building and after a few seconds of very obvious confusion the same seemed to occur to him.

"It is indeed my pleasure, Mr. Vaughan." It may have been my imagination but I fancied he placed a little too much emphasis on pleasure. "Ah yes, the ball. Were you in attendance?"

I laughed, realising the depths of his duplicity. "You

must have only had eyes for Miss Cooke, I warrant, for I was dancing next to you."

Lord Runfold smiled broadly, his eyes crinkling up at the corners in a most becoming fashion. "It is true . . . when someone piques my interest, I find it very hard to let go."

I felt myself respond to his subtle emphasis on the word 'hard'. It was most inappropriate and so without invitation—and after removing yet another stack of papers—I sank into a chair. Better to be considered a boor than to be humiliated. All I could manage in return was a feeble, "I understand that to be the case."

I must have shown adequate signs of discomfort to elicit his concern, for without further ado he removed the Oxford's from his nose and summoned some tea. We sat in silence until the beverage was delivered and then Runfold closed the door with strict instructions that he was not to be disturbed.

"It's still not safe," he said. "Tarrant believes that this office is his personal fife and comes and goes as he pleases. However there is a creaky board outside which will give us at least a second or two's notice of any impending entrance. Now . . . ." He sat back behind his desk, shoving his glasses back in place. In time I would come to know that gesture for what it was; in a social situation it tended to be a barrier or defence. Archie was not keen on people reading his eyes. "I will do you the courtesy of assuming you're not here to blackmail or blackball me. It would be a no-win situation for either of us, and with your brother—"

"What on earth does Maurice have to do with my behaviour?" I interjected.

"Your brother is less discreet than the most fripperous drab in Southwark. He was most vocal about your schoolboy indiscretions at the club. I feel he intended to differentiate himself from you, to draw a clear line between you and him. However, he only succeeded in making himself appear a complete fool. Which is why I would be extremely surprised if someone in your position were to try blackmail anyone. Though to set my mind at ease, would you please give me your assurance, as a gentleman, on this point? As I said, it would little benefit you or me to create a public scandal."

I stared at him, mouth agape. "That is very well thought out. I can certainly give you my assurance on that score. However, I am surprised at your frankness m'lord, if you do not mind the observation."

Runfold smiled and got to his feet. "Thank you, Vaughan. And my forthrightness is a facet of my employ — working with numbers one soon learns to abhor the byzantine and the convoluted. It is, I have found, much easier to deal with things directly. Which may well be why I've been sent to darkest China." He smiled wryly and perched on the edge of the desk. "But I must admit to some curiosity; while I had no idea of your identity, you have admitted to having known mine prior to your proffering this letter of introduction. It would interest me greatly to find out why you chose, knowing that until you showed me this you could choose to pretend a complete lack of personal acquaintance, to come here and introduce yourself."

I swallowed and thought to give him the half-truth, for while I could not confess to anything untoward, it would be possible to raise my suspicions with regards to Tarrant. I intended to insinuate this in a most subtle manner but the words that fell from my lips were: "I've come to stop a war."

His teacup clattered to the floor and shattered. Apparently the servants were well trained enough to leave one alone behind a closed door — even in a domestic emergency — and so we both stared at the broken china and the spilt tea. Runfold looked around as if the walls had ears.

"But how did you know?" He whispered, running his hand through his hair and mussing it even further.

"I've had the pleasure of meeting Maximilian Tarrant. And I am employed by the Pious Brethren of St Jude to minister to the opium addicts. It appears that this Lin Zexu is taking opium importation most seriously. That, coupled with the political acumen of Mr. Tarrant, would suggest that a war — whether desired or not — is the most likely outcome."

"I know." Runfold sank back against the desk, and I couldn't help but focus on the crinkles of his waistcoat just above his midriff. I wanted to run my hand across them, smooth them out, straighten him up. "Look, this is probably not the best place to have this conversation. Would it be possible to meet elsewhere? Unfortunately, I'm stationed in one of the rooms here."

"And I'm berthed in the Mission's residence. Neither place is conducive to a forthright conversation. It is a pity there are no clubs here."

"No clubs. Though I have been reliably informed that it is possible to acquire the use of a private room at the Floating Lotus. I'd not like to presume and it would mean that any conversation is conducted in the most rudimentary of settings, but could you see your way to joining me there?"

I smiled at this as my heart was suffused with gladness. For all his swagger and directness, it was obvious that some questions were still considered too precious to ask outright. "Yes m'lord—"

His exasperated sigh cut through my reply. "Please stop calling me that. My name is Archie. If that is too familiar or if you consider our acquaintance too short to presume upon such, you may address me as Runfold. However 'm'lord' makes me sound quite ancient and I'd rather forgo the experience."

"Certainly. Though if I may, I will stick to Runfold. It would be less questionable if anyone were to overhear us." He nodded at this, so I continued. "Meeting at the Floating Lotus does seem like the best possible solution. And I will not presume anything other than a conversation."

It seemed to me that Runfold appeared disappointed—but only for a fraction of a second—before his game face returned. "Certainly, Mr. Vaughan."

"I would, if it suits, like you to return the courtesy, Runfold. My given name is Edgar, but most people call me Vaughan."

At this Runfold stood and almost landed foot first in the broken crockery. I nodded at his lack of composure, filing it away.

"Tonight then?" I asked, trying to regain at least part of the upper hand.

"Tonight. It will be after nine though. Tarrant will have my head in a vice if I don't complete this month's books on time."

"After nine. It was, I must say, a pleasure to be formally introduced to you, Runfold." I bowed and made to leave the room.

"And I, you. Please give my warmest regards to Miss Coo—" He burst out laughing, presumably at the look on my face. "I jest. See you tonight."

"Yes, your lordship." I mocked, bowing low as I exited the paper-piled office.

Chapter Eleven

I arrived at the Floating Lotus just after a quarter past nine and made my way to the bar. It had been exceptionally unintelligent of me not to *enquire* what the procedures around privacy were and as a result I did not want to risk procuring a room of my own, only to find that Runfold had procured another. It would be a fine comedy of errors to have us both ensconced in separate rooms, each waiting for the other.

At half past the hour and on my ordering a second G&T, Runfold slid onto the adjoining stool. I nodded coolly in his direction, mindful that Smythe or someone from the

Trade Delegation could well be watching and saw him understand my action with a not-undue haste. He ordered a scotch, without ice. This made me smile; the thought of Runfold with the flux—especially in an intimate situation— was more amusing than something to be pitied. He downed it in one and I followed suit, then matched him step for step as he walked across the courtyard, through a maze of corridors and finally into a small room that contained nothing but a bed, a stool and a chair. Not wishing to presume anything, I sat upon the stool and noted he, in return, took the chair. The bed leered at us from across the room, tempting in its clean sheets and laundered softness. However, we were meant to be conducting a business discussion. It would not do to begin rutting at the first opportunity, no matter how our acquaintance had commenced.

    I found myself looking anywhere else than at him. Unfortunately, the highly rusticated finish of the walls, floors, and ceilings provided little purchase for my gaze. Out of the corner of my eye I noted Runfold, staring assiduously at the bedclothes. I felt that under the circumstances, it was up to me to break the ice.

"Thank you for joining me, Runfold." I assayed, looking him full in the face. "I appreciate your time."

"My apologies for being late." He got to his feet, walked towards the bed, seemed to realise what he was doing and scuttled back to the chair.

I bit my lip, feeling laughter rise up inside me. "Come now, Runfold. You can't tell me an inanimate upholstered furnishing"—I flung my hand towards the bed—"has you so discommoded."

Runfold looked at me askance, and then burst into laughter. I could not help but join in and soon enough we were guffawing like two schoolboys peering through the cracks in the boards of the Master's showers.

After a few minutes of this ridiculous behaviour, I managed to school myself into something approximating dignity. I resituated myself upon the stool and Runfold did likewise. We lapsed once more into silence but this time, it felt distinctly comfortable—something to which I admit feeling a degree of scepticism.

I was just about to recommence our conversation — for even a pleasant pause can draw out too long — when Runfold began.

"Thank you for coming to the Trade Delegation." He pulled his Oxford spectacles out of his jacket pocket and placed them on the bridge of his nose.

I was pleased to see a startling flash of peacock blue as he withdrew some parchment from his breast pocket. He stared at it for a few long moments, going paler with each lengthening minute. I began to fear for his health, and got to my feet to summon a servant. He waved a hand imperiously at me, indicating that I should remain seated. For a second I was reminded of the difference in our station. It was most discomfiting; few men had ever dared treat me with such disdain.

He looked up and must have caught my moue of disapproval for he smiled and said, "I'm sorry. It's just . . . . Well. Take a look at this, would you?"

He handed me a well-worn piece of paper, with

columns of carefully annotated figures. I stared at it complete incomprehension. It looked extremely well thought out and extremely cleverly put together, but for the life of me, I could not figure out what it meant. My lack of understanding must have shown on my face, for Runfold came and crouched by the side of the stool, stretching across me until he could reach the paper.

The smell of him overwhelmed me. I was unprepared for the viscous feelings that it stirred in me; all of a sudden the bed loomed large in my thoughts.

I leant forward, trying to disguise my obvious physical reaction. It left me weak—unstable—and I rocked forward more than I intended, like a poorly weighted ship on a rough sea. I fell against his outstretched arm. He braced it, and much to both my relief and consternation, he could easily take my weight. *He's as strong as an oak.* The thought caused a stirring of pleasure—at odds with my usual assignations—where I tended to search out those weaker than me. I recomposed myself as swiftly as possible but looking into Runfold's eyes I could tell he was unlikely to miss a nuance.

Thankfully, he busied himself straightening the piece of paper. When I had sufficiently recollected myself—pulling on the mien of a proper English Gentleman—he continued:

"These figures show the amount of profit we made on the Indo-China trade routes by passage. The first column is Portsmouth to Bombay, Bombay to Hong Kong, and then Hong Kong back to Portsmouth."

I looked at the piece of paper. "I see the middle column is by far the highest."

Runfold pulled the piece of paper back and crumpled it into his trouser pocket. "Yes." He sighed. "After your visit this afternoon I decided to see if there was a sound financial basis for a war with China. As you can see, the profits on that one leg are disproportionate. Without the opium trade, there is little reason for the East India Company to continue."

He looked shaken and I could not help but feel the same. I'd known—I was sure—Maximilian Tarrant's power derived from Trade and knew most of this Trade was opium; but seeing how it related to the profits of Her Majesty's Government, I felt as if I'd been run through with an ice-cold poker. This was much greater than just my personal investment.

The sound of Runfold's footsteps drew me out of my reverie. He was pacing the room, his hand in his pocket crumpling the piece of paper.

"You should destroy it." I suggested. "We could get a fire lit in the grate."

He laughed, his spectacles almost falling off the bridge of his nose. He grabbed them and replaced them in his breast pocket and smiled. The laughter lines around his eyes deepened in the candlelight and I could easily see what sort of man he'd become with age. And yet again, I did not feel any of my usual antipathy towards the idea, rather a deep and abiding pleasure at the thought of being around to see it. I shook my head to clear my thoughts. *It's this foreign climate. It's muddling my mind. The chances of us both being here long enough for old-age to overcome us is most unlikely. That of my staying enthralled with him or him with me is even less so.*

"It's summer. It must be ninety degrees. Do you not think they'll consider us somewhat odd if we ask for a fire to be lit?"

I flushed, embarrassed. "Oh." He was right: it was rather stifling. I removed my jacket.

"I'll just . . . ." Runfold pulled his tinderbox from his pocket, struck a spark and set the paper ablaze. He threw it into the grate, but not before the flames touched his fingers. Unconsciously, he put them to his mouth, sucking on the tips.

I must stop this! As the sight of those fingers brought me closer to public humiliation than I'd been in Runfold's office.

When the flames were dying out Runfold stomped on the embers, twisting his foot to grind them into a smooth dust. The smell of smoke filled the room. I could taste paper on the air. A taste that reminded me of Runfold's office, his stacked books.

"That's taken care of, then," I said to cover my confusion. My thoughts were roiling, like those of a debutante during her first season. I had to get myself back in control!

"Do you think you could just forget about it?"

Looking back, I now see that Runfold's voice was timorous, hesitant. But at the time I clung to his cowardice like a lifeline. It provided a focus, which I was so close to losing.

"Forget about it? Sir, have you lost control of your faculties?" His wince brought me no pleasure, but augmented my faltering courage. "Forget about your wretched superior attempting to start a war over his personal pecuniary power?" I pushed the thought of Her Majesty's Government out of the way. "I ask, sir, have you gone insane?"

Runfold sank backwards, resting on the edge of the bed. "There is obviously a market for it here. Would people really use it if it caused them so much harm?"

His naïveté took my breath away. I pulled on my jacket. "Come with me," I said, fully aware he was unlikely to do anything of the sort.

I made my way across the courtyard and out the front door, tossing the doorman a few coins to cover the cost of the room. From the depth of his bow it must have been more than adequate, or perhaps Runfold had paid for the room in advance. Whatever the situation, it was nothing more than a passing thought as I hailed a rickshaw, pushed Runfold in and directed the runner to take us to the mission.

I would like to tell you I remember nothing of the rickshaw ride, that my anger had made my attachment to Runfold pass into the mists of history. But I remember every press of his leg against mine as we jolted along the stinking streets, barely illuminated with their flickering lights. I remember the smell of him—the way it mingled with the offal and ordure—the way the sharp salt of the sea sometimes cut through the murk. I remember the brush of his hair against my cheek as one particularly bad hole jolted the rickshaw almost off its wheels. And more than that, I remember the longing in me warring against my natural inclination to cut the man after showing him what he was trying to sweep under the rug.

* * * * *

We arrived at the mission and I was concerned to see a soft light flickering inside while the door lamp was black and cold. *They're smoking in there!* I pushed the door open, unmindful of the ear-numbing creak as it skittered along the stone floor.

It was as I had feared. The natives were lying on their pallets in a stupor — smiling and emaciated — smelling of rotting flesh and suppurating sores. I believe I heard Runfold gasp, but I paid him no attention, pulling pipes out of lax hands and trying not to inhale the sweet smoke. I picked up parcels of brown tar, cupped them between my hands until I could carry no more. Then unceremoniously and unheeded by the natives lying in a stupor before me, I threw it all down the well.

I leant back against the cross in the centre of the courtyard, breathing deeply and willing myself not to cry. Their powerful addiction spoke to me and still speaks to me now. I equate it with my appreciation, interest, and physical longing for those of my own gender. No matter how debased, no matter how deep the ditch I could stumble into, no matter the risk of death, I was, and am, willing to pursue these urges to the damnation of my soul, my reputation and my family.

Eventually, my thoughts ground to a halt and I remembered that I'd brought Runfold to this diseased hell. I opened my eyes, scouring the courtyard. *No Runfold.* I got to my feet and stumbled through the stupefying fug from room to room, peering past the recumbent natives in their floating dreams. After a quarter hour of searching—much of it repetitive—I finally acknowledged that Runfold had gone.

Chapter Twelve

Thinking it through afterwards, I could not say with the merest modicum of honesty that I ended by being either upset or unsurprised by Lord Runfold's conduct. The man was a peer, had been privileged since birth. He hid himself behind a paper fortress in his office and hid himself behind his spectacles when that was not available. How else could have I expected someone who was so very sheltered to react? He'd not had my experience on the Isle of Dogs. He'd probably not seen much outside the Ton of London.

For the first few days, I was constantly on edge, expecting a summons to the Trade Delegation to proffer an explanation. I half feared he'd run to Tarrant and confessed everything. The days were made no more pleasant by the constant fluttering ingress of Miss Cooke, who was irksomely effusive in her gratitude. Apparently, her uncle's backing had come through and the mission was once more in funds.

Smythe had also taken to following me, halving his sheep-like devotion between Mr. Collins and myself. I could only stare bemused at Collins' complete lack of concern. The bluff old sausage was too kind-hearted — or possibly just too oblivious — to consider Smythe's devotion as anything other than the tenants of friendship. I, on the other hand, knew better, and took once more to retiring to my room and drinking of an evening rather than face Miss Cooke's giggles or Smythe's simpers.

After the first week passed without a summons, the cold steel bands that had strapped themselves about my chest began to ease. If no summons had come to answer for my conduct, it was unlikely they ever would. I could breathe easy.

That Sunday — as was our usual custom — we were all gathered around after Humphries' sermon to the natives. I was making myself more and more of a presence at the mission, ostensibly because I was bound by Humphries' request. While I was ministering to the afflicted, I found it incumbent upon myself to check for hiding places — bedrolls and cubbyholes — in which the natives secreted their opium and assorted paraphernalia. I was astounded that Lin Zexu's guards had not found a trace of opium when they previously searched; either they had only conducted a cursory examination or our parishioners had been warned beforehand. Peering into their inscrutable faces — which oft seemed menacing when focused my way — I felt there was little concern for our well-being. They must have thought that if the white devils' opium is found, on their own heads be it.

Collins was pouring the pre-prandial drinks around the table, Miss Cooke was directing the cook with Humphries looking on paternally, when Smythe sidled over to me.

"I need to talk to you," he said.

This took me aback, for Smythe had not, even with all his proximity, approached me for a direct personal conversation after the previous one in the drawing room. I was intrigued to see the faint lines of fear drawn lightly over his brow. His gaze skittered from object to object, lightly assessing; I was put in mind of those trolling their wares in Hyde Park. The comparison was not an edifying one. I decided to put him out of his misery.

"Certainly, Smythe. I am free for the rest of the day."

He glanced furtively around. "Shall we meet after lunch then, if that suits?"

His obvious anxiety pulled my own to the fore. I kept my voice steady and my face pleasantly schooled as I asked, "May I ask to what this pertains?"

Smythe blushed a deep red, which led me to believe I knew what he was likely to say. I relaxed, my shoulders sagging and my back regaining its usual curve. So when he replied, it hit me like a steam-train.

"I've heard a rather vicious but unsubstantiated

rumour. It pertains to the Undersecretary's secretary at the Ministry of Trade. And you."

Runfold! And me! Good God have mercy. Had someone seen us?

At that point the bell was rung and we were seated. I have no recollection of the food, of who sat to the left and right of me, of what conversation was had. I could have been eating porridge and conversing with a mute for the imprint that meal left in my mind. All my thoughts were focused around Runfold. *What does Smythe know? Is he implicit in some sort of trap? Will Tarrant be breaking in at any minute? Is this why Runfold has been so reticent to contact me?* I felt a quiver of hope at the last thought — maybe whatever had happened with Runfold was still salvageable.

After the cheese, I stood as was my custom, made my apologies to the assembled and walked with a calm and measured tread to my room. I distinctly remember counting the rhythm of my pace, willing it to fall in a natural pattern. I sat on the edge of my bed, my clothing complete and exact. The tantalus taunted me from the dresser but I maintained my self-discipline enough to abstain. Whatever was coming next would require the full use of my faculties.

It seemed an eon until I heard Smythe's double knock on the door. I opened it and indicated my two armchairs. He took a seat, the white fluff coating the back of the seat once more. *I will have to invest in a protective cloth if these are to be regular visits.* I sat opposite him, willing myself to relax back into my chair, my arms open on the rests. I tried to portray an air of mild interest untroubled by the slightest doubt. From the look of pity on Smythe's face, I had failed.

"My thanks for agreeing to see me so promptly." Smythe began, his fingers fidgeting with the hem of his coat. "I believe it to be a most delicate matter."

I watched his fingers travel up to his stock. He twisted and turned it, leaving the greasy remnants of lunch streaked across the poor cloth. "It seemed of some slight importance."

Smythe flushed deeply, and his fiddling sped up, resulting in him almost garrotting himself as he twisted the stock one time too many. "I . . . I don't know how to approach this."

Whether it was the thought of my own possible implication or that of Runfold in some sort of trouble, I plumbed depths of courage I'd not known I possessed. "Come on man!" I said, standing and walking over to him. I pulled his hand down from his stock—trying not to show my displeasure at the greasy texture—and placed it firmly on his knee. "There now. The door is closed. I do not believe we'll be disturbed." I paused for a moment, contemplating how best to continue. "I think we've passed the point in our acquaintance when one feels one should not assume things that one knows through sources other than one's acquaintance." It was a horrible, torturous use of Mother-English but the bombast made Smythe smile and sit up a bit straighter. *Apparently he knows what I meant, even if I'm still somewhat at sea.*

"Vaughan. It has come to my attention . . . . There have been . . . . Oh, balls to it!" Smythe got to his feet and in his passion he assumed an aspect one could only call beautiful. He'd never be handsome, not Smythe with his effeminate looks and greasy locks. But standing in the sunbeam that poured through the window, his hair glistening, his eyes wild with courage, I could see something angelic, something beautiful. In that moment I forgave him his customary lack of grace—his shyness—for he had shown me something few others had seen.

My confusion must have been self evident, for he sat once more. A pervasive calmness had come over him; Smythe was more relaxed than I'd ever seen him.

"Vaughan. There is a rumour passing from lip to lip, in places like the Floating Lotus, that you and Lord Runfold met there last week."

My heart was beating a mile a minute; I now believed I knew what a horse felt like after the steeplechase. I nodded my assent. "That is correct."

"The rumour continues that afterwards you took him to our mission." Smythe's lips were white-tight with disapproval.

I nodded once more. *Who was spreading this? Why would they show their hand so obviously? Or was Smythe just extremely well connected?*

"Tell me, Vaughan, did Lord Runfold and you really come across the parishioners smoking opium?"

I inclined my head again. There was a pause from Smythe, his breathing deep and laboured.

"It is as I feared." He looked at me with a depth of pity I'm relieved to say I've never encountered since. "After he left the mission, Lord Runfold is believed to have gone to Mr. Tarrant's house and confronted him directly about the results of the opium trade."

My jaw dropped. *Runfold. You supreme ass!*

"I see that surprises you as much as it did his colleagues, who I believe were most shocked to see him packing his papers the next morning."

Was he sent back to London? Is he still here? What has Tarrant done? How does Smythe know all this? My mouth was numb; I gestured at Smythe to continue.

"Vaughan, he's in Canton."

I stared at Smythe, askance. His tone was that of a person informing one of bereavement. My puzzlement must have shown, for he continued.

"Have you not been informed? Canton was put under blockade by the Chinese Emperor this morning."

I felt the blood drain to my feet. My head became light and I tilted to one side. I remember trying hard to push myself up, pull myself together, but inexorably I tilted farther and farther — like an unbalanced ship of the line — then slid to the floor.

* * * * *

The acrid smell of *sal volatile* brought me to my senses. A worried Smythe was standing over me. I looked at the door. *Still shut. Thank God!*

"Ah. Yes. Vaughan."

I smiled at him — the first genuine smile he'd ever received from me — and he responded in kind.

"My apologies."

"No, no. Mine. It must have come as somewhat of a shock. I apologise for springing it on you so . . . ."

"No, old chap. I thank you."

He looked at me sadly, as a child who'd given his favourite plaything to another. I levered myself off the floor and got to my feet, smoothing out my clothes.

"I must be off." I began, trying to maintain my balance. "May I ask how you know all this?"

"I have been here two years. People tend to speak unguardedly in front of me. I am not important enough for people to concern themselves. I hear a lot. Just be careful, Vaughan. Now, leave."

There was sorrow touched with pain in Smythe's voice and even through my fug of concern as to Runfold's fate, I knew well enough to reach out and grab Smythe by the arm, pulling him into a half-embrace.

"Thank you, Smythe." I pulled back and saw he was both smiling and holding back strong emotions. I'd humiliated the man enough, so I left the room, closing the door quietly behind me.

* * * * *

The rickshaw dropped me at the door of the Trade Delegation, and I pushed my way past the doorman and up the stairs into Tarrant's office. A small part of me was pleased to note that this time *he'd* not been able to stage the room for my arrival; there were pieces of paper and books strewn across his desk and he was sitting slightly off-centre, which negated the entire effect of his dramatic study.

"Tarrant! What have you done?" I strode over to the desk, slamming my palms onto his paperwork, upsetting his inkbottle and causing the pewter bell to ring once with the impact. I jumped back at the sound.

For the merest blink of the eye, Tarrant scuttled a pace back like a cornered mouse. I could tell the very moment he realised that it was me, unarmed, standing in front of him. A malicious smirk spread like treacle across his face.

"I've done nothing *improper*."

The oleaginous tone of his voice incensed me. I could feel my close-cut nails digging into the palms of my hands; my back-muscles tensed with the urge to haul off and punch him in the face. "I ask you once more, Tarrant, what have you done with Runfold? Where is he?"

"Runfold? How very *familiar*." Tarrant had the temerity to act surprised. "He's in Canton, of course. Poor chap. Stuck out there for the foreseeable. What a pity."

"You pathetic snake!" I pushed his papers to the floor. It was that or hit him. "He's only there because you refused to accept Lin Zexu's proclamation."

"No, Vaughan. You are mistaken. He is only there to prevent him from spreading his calamitous lies about your mission around Hong Kong. We'd not like Lin Zexu to get word of your mission's secret hoard."

"Hoard? They've already inspected the mission and found nothing." I tried to grasp the depths of his perfidy. *He is trying to use Runfold against me. But is he threatening us with exposure? Does he know? Worse, does he have proof?*

"The opium hoard."

"There is no hoard."

"But there will be." Tarrant's face was painted with glee.

I wondered why his forked tail and horns were not

more apparent. This was no man; this was a demon from the depths of Hades mimicking human form. "And if I refuse to comply with your quite shamefully unorthodox request? A missionary does not house contraband at the mission. This should be apparent even to your good self." To this day I still do not have an idea of from where I garnered the courage to ask that question.

"Then Runfold will be left in Canton. Until an even less salubrious post can be requisitioned. Somewhere suitable malarial, or possibly still partially cannibalistic. Somewhere backwards, fomenting on the edge of rebellion."

"He is a peer." I drew out, feeling the world crash down around my ears.

"And that is why he'll be kept on and shunted from lowly post to lowly post. One can't have an unnatural representing Her Majesty at any public level, of course. You, on the other hand—"

"In that case, you know who my brother is. The same logic applies"

"I also know that Baronet Vaughan cares not a whit

what happens to you. He made that most clear by the last mail pouch."

I wanted to retort, wanted to call him on a lie. But I could not delude myself; I knew Maurice would be pleased to see me perish far from home rather than bringing any further stain to the family name. I sank into a visitor's chair.

"What do you want from me?" I whispered.

"Nothing onerous. I want the mission to be used as a staging-post for British opium."

He is asking the impossible. But . . . Runfold. If I do not agree, he will be left to rot in Canton. Even on my short acquaintance with Tarrant, I did not believe he would call Runfold back. *Runfold could end up in the middle of a war!* "And if I accept?"

"Then Runfold will be returned from Canton at the earliest opportunity. All knowledge of this conversation will be wiped clean from my memory. And you'll live to see dear old England once again."

There is no other option. The man in front of me could quite easily destroy my life. But more important to me than that, he could ruin Archie. And for the first time in my God-damned existence, it was the thought of someone other than me that led me to the unpalatable conclusion. "It can't be indefinite. I've had first-hand experience on just how quickly the rumours spread."

"Only until this little unpleasantness is over. I'm sure the Emperor will see reason. And Lin Zexu is not a permanent fixture."

I twisted my lips into a stiff parody of a smile and inclined my head. Tarrant had me by the balls and we both knew it.

"When would you like to commence delivery?" I looked down both to hide my shame and to avoid the gloating smile I heard in his voice.

"This evening." His triumph cut me like tempered steel. "Be at the gates around midnight."

"And if I can't make it."

"That is your issue. But as you've been able to make your way to the Floating Lotus . . . ."

The threat was a silkscreen away from overt. *Damn*

him! Damn it! And damn Runfold for confronting this adder!

I nodded my agreement and Tarrant rang his bell. The servant escorted me none-too-gently out the door.

Chapter Thirteen

The rest of that afternoon and that evening remain a blur. I remember brushing off Smythe's concern, as well as that of Humphries and Collins. I half-remember the buried look of fury on Miss Cooke's face and the bustle of servants in and out of her room. I remember nothing of supper, or of summoning the rickshaw, or of letting Tarrant's men into the mission. I remember where the chests of opium stood, and I remember my gaze passing from the damp corner of the room—where a rat scuttled back and forth with black eyes and glee—to the pallets on which the natives lay, the more aware natives having eyes filled with the diamonds of avarice.

* * * * *

The next two months passed in a miasma of near-paralytic fear. I spent the majority of my time reviewing the conversations with Smythe and Tarrant. I felt my thoughts, my ethics, and my morals deadening from exposure to the black tar and white smoke. I felt them crumpling under my culpability. If I had not indulged in what I'd journeyed here to forget, none of this would have happened. I had protected my own skin and that of a man who shared the same ignoble traits as me above those of the parishioners I had made a God-witnessed oath to protect. I deserved each prick of fear as the days sped onwards. I wondered what Tarrant would have me do next. It seemed unlikely he'd stop with mere courier duties.

In the background of my perception lurked Smythe and Miss Cooke. It was hard not to notice the latter's change in demeanour; it was that of a harlot finding out one has no ready coin. Her eyes crept over me like poisonous leeches and her forked tongue – *it must run in the family* – slowly let slip rumours and pointed remarks against my character. I believed it confused Humphries, for I often saw him looking askance at me. If only he knew the viper he'd clasped to the bosom of his beloved mission. Collins was oblivious; unsurprisingly, as I had begun to think him rather dim. Only the most oblivious imbecile would not realise that *something* was occurring.

    The opium chests were stored in a locked room, one that no one had reason to enter. It was a dank and musty place, strung with cobwebs and with a patina of mould growing up the wall. I even let the natives take their fill of an evening, rather than having them break the door down and have to explain to Humphries. Their depredations were slight compared to the bulk stored and Tarrant had let it be known that this was acceptable. How it rankled to be beholden to that perfidious creature!

    Smythe, on the other hand, was a Godsend. Each time he heard Miss Cooke veering into damaging territory he'd make the most appalling display of being interested in her feminine wiles. At times, it was all I could do not to burst into laughter. Thankfully, her vanity was such she thought it her due, especially when she was bedecked in her frills and finery. She looked no further than Smythe's puppy-dog eyes and adoring glance. Once, when she had dropped a fork and was flustering around the chairs trying to retrieve it, he dropped me a wink and for the first time in months I felt a shining sliver of joy. Even sitting here—the target of suspicion and hatred—there were still the few who would stand behind me. I was sure it was a testament to something good and true, but this only made me feel worse. If Smythe knew of the risk I was running—of just how much jeopardy in which I had placed Humphries, Collins and himself—I doubted he'd be so kind.

* * * * *

Canton was re-opened on the 24th of May: I remember the day vividly, waking up to the sweaty plaster of my nightshirt against my back, the cold-faced ministrations of my fourth valet. The ping of a cufflink as it hit a decanter in the tantalus, and the grain of the floor as I scooped it up. I remember the noxious scent of bacon for breakfast, at odds with the deep perfume of the magnolia, which was one of the few things that could sooth my wretched nose after breathing in opium-adulterated air for half the night.

    I remember seeing the messenger going from English house to English house, my unease growing until he stopped at the residence and told us the blockade was over, that those who'd been held hostage were coming home. I remember the ugly mottled flush that covered Miss Cooke's skin, the look of unconcealed relief on Smythe's face, the jovial grin of Collins, and the assessing eyes of Humphries. I remember stifling my smile, presuming if Tarrant was true to his word then Runfold would soon return.

    The thought of seeing Runfold filled me with quiet pleasure. I knew now our last meeting had ended suddenly, not from cowardice, but because Runfold had been so overcome by the sight that he had to attempt its cessation. I was blinded by relief; it did not occur to me that a two-month siege could have made a mark on the man, that he could well have utilized the hours I spent in shuddering fear in contemplation of his own exposure.

* * * * *

When Runfold's request for a meeting arrived on the Monday night, just before supper, I kept my façade firmly in place. My thoughts were roiling as I attempted an unsuspicious level of joviality throughout dinner.

I took special care with my dress, donning freshly laundered linen, my fingers shaking as I slipped my cufflinks into my shirt. On my arrival at the Floating Lotus, I was ushered once more to a private room and found Runfold pacing nervously. I stood still in the doorway, drinking in the sight of him. He was less stocky than I remembered, the protrusion of his collarbones marring the fall of his jacket. When he turned my way, his eyes were bright and he looked at me with such pleasure, I had to clutch the doorframe to prevent myself from making a scene.

And in that moment, it hit me, precisely what I'd relinquished to be standing there, then. The last unthinking two months piled on top of me and I staggered towards a chair. Runfold was solicitous; he grabbed me by the arm and pulled me down to safety. All I could think was that he smelt so sweet. A wave of grief swept over me—grief for the natives at the mission, grief for Humphries, for the people who trusted me. And lastly, grief for Runfold. I was not the person he thought.

His deep green eyes bore into mine, and I knew I had to tell him the truth. *This man was besieged in Canton because he was so incensed by the workings of his own government. And I betrayed his sacrifice.* The import of this overwhelmed me; I buried my head in my hands.

"What is wrong?" His voice washed back and forth, grating over my frayed nerves. "I thought you'd be pleased to see me. Tarrant mentioned you'd been to the delegation to ask after me. Not wise, I warrant, but—"

I could not stand to hear another word. "Runfold."

The pain in my voice must have cut through his prattle for he sank down on the stool, pain bringing out the deep lines in his face.

"I did not think you'd judge me so severely for trying to stop the trade we both agreed was a stain on Her Majesty's Government."

"No. Runfold. Archie. It's not that. Did Tarrant tell you why I'd come to the mission?"

"He led me to believe it was to enquire after my presence." Archie sounded puzzled.

"That is not a direct untruth. Runfold, can you promise to listen through to the end?" I asked, not wanting a repeat of our last meeting.

Runfold clenched his teeth then bit his bottom lip, thinking my request through. "I promise."

I paid heed to the trepidation in his voice and thought it best to begin while I still had the nerve to do so.

"Runfold, when I heard how you'd confronted Tarrant—that you were in Canton and that there was a blockade—I panicked. I stormed into Tarrant's office. I frightened him for a moment, of that I'm sure, but then—" I broke off, unable to continue.

"Then?" The fact that Runfold's voice was perfectly level gave me hope.

"Then he gave me a choice. I could stick to my principles and condemn you to a low-level career in the outposts of the empire and myself to at best an outcast, at worst an accidental death. My other option was to allow Tarrant to utilise the mission as a staging post for his opium."

There was a long pause, during which I dared not look up. I was certain Runfold was still in the room; I could hear the tap-tap of his fingers against the wall. After several minutes where my nerves twisted tighter and tighter, he spoke.

"As you and I are both here, I will presume you chose the latter."

I screwed my courage to the sticking point. "Yes. Every few nights—over the last two months—I've allowed Tarrant's men into the mission to enable them to store their opium chests. I have also let the natives take their fill of the stocks to cover my tracks and prevent me from having to explain myself to Humphries." *There. It is all out in the open now.* I knew I should feel relief that the secret was exposed, but looking at Runfold's darkened brow all I felt was hollow.

Once more, Runfold paused in tapping contemplation. "So—if I've understood correctly—Tarrant has used rumour and speculation to blackmail you into this position."

I could not raise my gaze from the floor. I saw Archie's shoes as he stood beside me and then knelt down, tilting my head up until I was forced to stare him in the eye. "Edgar, this is entirely my fault. If I'd not run off half-cocked to Tarrant this would not have happened."

I felt my body sag as relief washed over me. *Runfold had not left, he was still here.* I smiled. "I think both of us may be somewhat to blame. I can't say I acted in the most measured manner."

Archie returned my smile and I believed then—however selfishly—I had made the right choice. I could not think of anything I'd not do to keep Archibald, Lord Runfold safe.

"What course of action should we take?" I assayed, realising that if we were caught staring into each other's eyes it would only serve as confirmation of the rumours that were running rife.

Archie smiled. "I would suggest you confess to Humphries and get the opium chests removed at his earliest possible convenience. Then procure yourself a passage out of this godforsaken hole."

"Your only flaw is the presence of Tarrant's men and the deliveries." Despite my words, I was cautiously optimistic. It did appear that Archie had a plan and God knew it had to be better than my two months of paralysis.

"I would strongly suggest Tarrant will be rather busy over the next few days." Archie's smile had evolved into a full grin and he was trembling with excitement.

"May I enquire as to why you believe this?" I asked.

"I'd suggest that his concentration will be extremely narrow in focus, as I intend to challenge him to a duel."

"A duel!" I gasped, feeling the warm air rasp against my throat. "Are you feeling well? Have you lost the last modicum of your sanity?"

"Certainly not."

I wanted to punch Runfold in his smug face. He was only just returned and to risk his life in a duel was beyond the pale. On observing him though, he appeared to be quite confident. Foolhardy as he may be, I could at least pay him the courtesy of hearing him out. I felt it incumbent upon me to point out the obvious flaw in his plan.

"But as the challenger, you'll lack the choice of weapon." Selfish as it was, I felt I should at least try to dissuade him. Duels were a rarity nowadays, and as well as having no assurance he'd come out unhurt, I was none too sure of the legality of such on foreign soil.

"Oh, Tarrant fancies himself a shot. He'll probably choose pistols."

Archie's nonchalance disturbed me. I stood, pacing in a u-shape around the bed, focusing on the dead sounds my shoes made when I walked over the bedside rug.

"And if he chooses swords? Or rapiers?"

Archie coughed, looking like he was suppressing his merriment at my discomfiture. "I have dabbled in both enough to be near-assured of victory against anyone but the most highly trained. And that, Tarrant is most assuredly not."

I wanted to pry further. I wanted to niggle and query until Archie gave up on this idiotic idea. But as a gentleman, I knew full-well that one tends not to be easily swayed after one has expressed the intent of a duel. Let alone someone like Runfold, who was so assured of his prowess. "May I enquire as to the reason will you give for your challenge?"

"He has impugned my reputation. There is no proof of his allegations; we have not performed the required deed which would prevent me from challenging him on moral grounds. So I am free to issue a challenge."

The adroitness of his semantics made me smile. Maybe we'd not performed the requisite act, but it was near enough to require a lawyer to see the difference. However, there was one thing I had to ask before I'd accept his plan.

"I have a proposition for you." I began, cursing my choice of words as his eyes lit up a lascivious green.

"You are incorrigible! You should conserve your strength. What I propose is as follows: I will do as you say *if and only if* you inform me of when and where the duel is being held and then get word to me that you are safe. *And* that you book a passage back to England as well."

Runfold slapped his knee and jumped to his feet. "I'll book it on the same ship."

I seem to be besotted with a complete idiot. I shook my head. "That would be foolhardy. Rumours are running riot thanks to Tarrant and Miss Cooke." Runfold's eyes widened at this and his mouth straightened in disapproval. "The little chit has been passing snide remarks. I presume her uncle let it be known that you're no long suitable matrimonial material."

I laughed as his jaw dropped.

"Yes, there are apparently scandals to which Tarrant will not lend his name. The revelation shocked me as much as it does you."

"Well, at least that is one less complication I have to concern myself with." I could see Runfold try to relax his features but the smile did not reach his eyes.

"There is that. But do stop avoiding the question, Archie. Do you agree to my conditions?"

Runfold put out his hand and we shook on it. I felt the roughness of his palm and wanted to ask what had happened in Canton, why his scholar's hands were so chafed. I sensed this was not the moment—either there would be time after the duel or it would be a pointless exercise.

After a good few pumps, I let go of the last of my inhibitions and pulled him into an embrace. I felt his arms wrap around me as I buried my nose in his hair. His tumescence rubbed against my leg and in defiance of my better judgement I pulled him as close as I could. The feel of him through his clothes both emaciated from his ordeal and sinewy-strong. My thoughts were so riddled with the scent of him I hardly felt his hands reciprocating until the tip of his index finger traced a line down behind my left ear and across my jaw. I pulled away — this was more of a liberty then I'd ever allowed any other of my assignations. But in Runfold's eyes I saw nothing more than pure pleasure at my presence, and what, with hindsight, was a devil-may-care glint, throwing caution to the wind.

I'd never felt so hungry for a soul before, not through my divinity training, or through the Isle or through the mission had the possession of another reached into my very marrow and plucked a cacophonous melody through the middle of my mind. I threw all caution to the wind and shucked my clothes off like a snake's skin, and then proceeded to twist and pull at his garments until he batted me away and proceeded to disrobe in an irksomely methodical manner. Thank God it's warm. The cold would have done nothing for my more personal attributes, I thought, as Runfold folded his stock and neatly positioned his spectacles atop it.

By that time an appreciation of the situation had caused me to assume what I'd hoped was a nonchalant but suitably modest pose. I'd began to regret my hasty disrobing and so was propped against the wall with one hand artfully draped across my member, my fingers idling on the top of my thigh. Apparently I was most mistaken in my choice of position, for the look of mirth that suffused his face as he stood and turned to face me caused my neck to burn. *I give up on this wretched man; I should have let him leave when I had the chance!* I sank onto the bed and put my elbows on my knees, ensuring that Runfold had no purchase for his glee.

This had the edifying result of him losing that wretched smirk and adopting a more serious mien. He came and stood before me, in a state of such pure and innocent nudity that I could barely reconcile it with the man in the peacock waistcoat. My gaze raked over him — and I use the word advisedly for it felt as if they were ploughing through his skin, through the muscle and bone beyond, assessing what damage the depredations of the siege had caused. His complexion was an alabaster white; though I was sure that in daylight he'd appear a greenish grey, the candlelight gave him deep warmth. His face was pointed, and it was obvious he had no need for a Cumberland corset. He looked a sight as compared to that first night in the Floating Lotus, but as my gaze moved towards his face, I caught the green glint of his eyes—both making merry and strangely scared. I paused. *Is he having second thoughts?*

He reached down and pulled my hand up towards his chest, causing me to follow suit. We stood there, mother-naked and staring into each other's eyes. I was at a loss to describe just *why* the moment was so powerful until it came to me. For all my schoolboy fumbles, for all my park-bound assignations, I'd never before taken time to fully appreciate what I was about to do. And with whom.

The power of this feeling rendered me mute. I stood slack-jawed before Runfold, feeling a complete dunce, until he raised his finger to my lips, indicating silence.

Relief suffused my body, and without thinking my hands reached up to brush against his skin, the palms creating a memory map of planes and ridges. A thought blindsided me, and I almost fell over: *This time tomorrow, Runfold could be buried.* My hands seemed to separate from my mind—which was embroiled in memorising the sight and scent of him—and began to run up and down his body like crazed mice searching for the eternal cheese.

I pulled myself back from what felt like the brink of madness to feel Archie pushing me down onto the bed. I luxuriated in the sheets as we indulged in a frenzied orgy of touch and taste. We sampled each other's flesh, our members slip-slided out of each other's mouths. I felt the paroxysm of completion violate me more times than even my most prurient school-boy fantasies had incurred and yet neither my body nor my mind was sated. How I longed to perform the final act, to cleave myself to him and have him cleave to me. I wanted him with the fiery passion of a funeral pyre. It seemed a waste to wait on the morrow, but even my limited knowledge of his Lordship brought the realisation that he'd not strive to win a duel he'd morally lost. So even awash in the miasma of such prurient gratification, I restrained myself from toppling Runfold over into a moral crisis.

To this day, I think it the hardest thing I have ever done.

After our bodies could take no more, and I lay there

staring at the blank ceiling, I felt his arms circle my chest. Not a word was said; though looking back on it now, that moment was worth more than any word could have ever been.

I stood, dressed — hearing him follow suit — and when I was fully in command of both my clothes and my faculties, I looked him straight in the eyes.

"Take care of yourself, Runfold."

I saw his lips move as if he longed to say words best left unspoken. He bit his bottom lip and a look of frustration passed over his face.

"Will you be living in London?" he asked and I was somewhat gladdened to hear the naked import he placed on my answer.

"I believe that I shall. I would suggest that you leave a message at Boodle's; I tend to drop by when I'm in town." I kept my voice light and airy, trying valiantly not to think too much on the chances of such actually occurring.

"Ah. Pall Mall. A ridiculous area, really, but convenient enough." Runfold's voice mimicked my lightness but the tension around his eyes belied his tone.

It was a pleasure to hear someone echo my own private thoughts on the matter. "Runfold. Archie. I should leave now."

"I understand. I will see you in London, Edgar. I promise."

I pressed a kiss to his cheek. "I will be there, Archie. If everything goes to plan, I will be there. I promise you that."

Chapter Fourteen

On getting back to the mission, I sent a servant to summon Humphries from his chamber. I had thought long and hard on the way up the hill and I had decided that just in case Archie decided to challenge Tarrant tonight, I wanted to ensure that the man who'd looked after me since my arrival — who'd attempted to guide and help me — was suitably prepared. And while Archie's plan seemed good on paper, I could think of a few thousand variations that could net us disaster.

Humphries looked most perturbed to be woken in the middle of the night and his scowl grew deeper as I outlined the bare bones of my tale.

"I will be booking a passage home, of course." I ended.

"That would be most appropriate. I do notice you've not mentioned the gross indecency that Tarrant has been accusing you of but I can make the requisite assumptions. One does not live to be my age without knowing a little something about the ways of the world."

His words filled me with trepidation. If he gave even the slightest indication that he too suspected me of unnatural acts I would be destroyed. Humphries must have noted my concern for he continued . . . .

"Do not concern yourself, Vaughan. We're in the Indies. We are a good six thousand miles away from Belgravia. Do you think you're the first missionary who has run here to escape from himself?" Humphries paused and lit his pipe. "What concerns me is that you have endangered the mission and aided and abetted the one trade you were sent here to stamp out."

I opened my mouth to speak, but was cut short.

"A minute, please, Vaughan. I understand the

blackmail, I understand your reasoning, and I feel compassion for your situation. But you were brought here to assume a position of trust over an uneducated native population and you failed in your mission. You will have to atone for this here. But as well you know, your true punishment will await you in the next life."

I was astonished to be getting off so lightly, though the look of resignation on Humphries' face made me think this was not the first time he'd had to have a similar conversation.

"I will do anything you ask, Mr. Humphries."

"While I am dressing, you will summon a rickshaw. Go into the pantry and bring out a tinder box and some cooking fat. We will remove this millstone tonight."

I did as I was bid and then maintained my silence as we made our way to the mission. We piled the chests high in the courtyard and coated them with fat. Humphries handed me the tinderbox and I struck three times until the fat took flame. When the chests were burning brightly — and ignoring the puling cries of our wards — we returned to the residence.

* * * * *

"When will you be able to leave, Mr. Vaughan?"

"I'll look into procuring my passage tomorrow. Just—"

Humphries gimlet eyes bored into me. "What is it now, Mr. Vaughan? You've tried my patience enough this night that I doubt anything you say could confound me."

"May I speak in utmost confidence?" I asked, aware of how my next words would only put a name to the imprecations of which Humphries was aware.

"Certainly, Vaughan. You have my word."

"I would, if possible, like to remain here until the outcome of a duel is known."

To his credit, Humphries did not bat an eyelid.

"When will this duel occur?"

"I hope to know that tomorrow. I would like to be appraised of the outcome before I leave—if possible—sir."

Humphries' face broke into a wintery smile. "I understand. Not that I approve, mind you. Provided you can procure passage the day of the duel, you may remain."

I remember thanking him profusely and praying for good luck to shine on me. I had upheld my part of the bargain; for Runfold to uphold his, I would have to be present in Hong Kong.

* * * * *

A messenger boy arrived the next morning with a scrap of paper. "30th May. Pistols, as previously discussed. Dawn. R." I set the paper on fire and ground the remains underfoot, smiling at the recollection of Runfold doing the same at our first meeting. Even such a small document—if found in my possession—could cause the disruption of our precarious balance.

Still smiling, I made my way to breakfast, and I sat opposite Smythe. He greeted me perfunctorily, and then noting my demeanour, smiled in return. Miss Cooke sat to my left in a pale-green and rose coloured monstrosity, which made her look like either a cheap confection or a flowering shrub.

I was still pondering the matter when a houseboy came in bearing a note for Miss Cooke. She paled as she read it then gave me a look of the most virulent hatred. I cut a bite-sized piece of sausage and raised it to my mouth. *Bliss!*

"You . . . you . . . you!" Miss Cooke had risen to her feet and was pointing a tremulous finger at me. "How very dare you?"

I leant back in my chair, taking great pleasure in her anger. "How dare I enjoy sausage? Quite easily, let me assure you." The double entendre amused me and I could see Smythe desperately stifling a laugh in his napkin.

"How could you influence Lord Runfold to call out my uncle? Archibald is mine!"

At this, I could restrain myself no longer and burst out into hearty peals of laughter. "I have only a passing acquaintance with the gentlemen concerned. However, on this brief acquaintance I can only suggest that Lord Runfold is more than capable of assessing a given situation and making up his own mind and that he must be a saint of most extraordinary virtue not to have called out your wretched uncle sooner." I got to my feet and looked sadly at my half-eaten breakfast. "Now, if you'll excuse me, Miss Cooke, I will be off to book my passage home. I find that *your* climes do not quite agree with me." I paused to let the insult sink in. "Smythe? If I may have a word?" I left the room, pleased to hear Smythe's footsteps patter behind mine.

"I'm sorry for the scene." I began.

"That woman should be committed to Bedlam. Accusing you! During breakfast!"

"I pity her. She's had her expectations raised by that perfidious uncle of hers. Listen, Smythe, could you do me a favour?" I thought to take him into my confidence. Someone would have to clear up the detritus of the opium chests.

"Ask and I will answer." Smythe quipped back, tossing me a shy smile.

"There will be some ashes in the mission courtyard this morning. Would you be so kind as to remove them?"

He rested his hand on my arm and I could feel the gentle twitch of his fingers. "Humphries has already asked me. You did the right thing, confessing everything to him. He may not show it outwardly, but he appreciated being made aware of the issue as soon as it was safe for you to do so."

"I only wish I could have done it sooner." The worlds fell glibly from my tongue; I was surprised to find that I meant them.

"I will be sorry to see you leave."

"And there are things I'm sorry to leave here, Smythe."

"Please, Vaughan, call me Richard."

His gesture of trust discomfited me. "Richard. And do call me Edgar."

"Edgar." Smythe whispered. "Thank you."

"No, thank you. If it was not for your help and knowledge—" I broke off, unsure what to say.

"I know. Go procure your passage. You have a few days here yet, I warrant, and this is not the time for premature goodbyes."

I nodded to him and made my way out to the docks.

Erastes, Chris Smith, Charlie Cochrane, Jordan Taylor – Last Gasp

Surely there must be a berth on a ship sailing back toward England.

Chapter Fifteen

I managed to procure passage for myself on a clipper, which was leaving on the afternoon of the 30th. I would have preferred an evening passage as it would have given me more time to receive word of Archie, but it was my only choice. It was the 30th or a wait of several days, something which I knew Humphries would not countenance.

I called a messenger boy and had him deliver a note to the Trade Delegation. "Passage Booked, 30th a.m. Remember the deal. E." I hoped that it would be enough for Runfold to know I would be present; he would be able to honour our agreement.

The next four days went by in a flurry of purchasing and packing. Even though I was leaving under a cloud, I could not neglect my brother and his wife. It would be assumed that I would purchase enough silks to robe her for at least a season and procure something suitably foreign but useful for him. Quite frankly, it was a chore I could do without, but the presence of Smythe—*Richard*—was a pleasant distraction. At one market stand, while he was admiring the most unsuitable silks for a waistcoat I'd ever seen — *and so I thought about acquiring some for Maurice* — I took receipt of a small jade box and pressed it into his hand.

"I can't." Richard pushed the box back towards me.

"You certainly shall." I wrapped my fist around his and squeezed it shut. "This is a little token of thanks for everything that you have done for me."

I could see him flush and so looked away. Casting my gaze around the stalls, I caught a flash of peacock blue. *It can't be?*

Pulling Richard with me, I made my way towards where Runfold stood, assessing much more suitable silks.

"Runfold!" I called out, mindless of the stares about us. *What should they care? We're the gwailo – they can leave us in peace.* "I did not expect to see you before I sailed!"

Archie turned towards us and smiled. I tried to maintain vague decorum, even if the surrounding people were primarily natives.

"Runfold, this is Richard Smythe. Mr. Smythe, Lord Runfold," I said. I waved my hand towards Richard, who moved forward as if in a trance.

"Mr. Smythe, what a pleasure to make your acquaintance." Archie's eyes were alight with mischief; but a well placed dig with my heel soon put paid to whatever he'd been planning.

"And yours too, your Lordship."

Observing Archie, I could now see that the title really did irk him. "Call me Runfold, I beg. 'Your Lordship' makes me think that my father is looming over my shoulder."

Richard grinned at him. "Certainly, Runfold."

"So, what brings you two bachelors here then? Out enjoying the sights? Purchasing a frock for your lady-loves?"

Archie raised an eyebrow at me and it took a good proportion of my self-restraint not to throttle him.

"I'm purchasing gifts for my brother and sister-in-law, Runfold. As I *leave tomorrow!*"

"Ah yes, familial duty. How tedious."

"And if I may ask, why precisely are you choosing silk on this of all days?" Smythe joined in the general merriment.

"I am also in the tedious position of having to procure familial gifts. It is the curse of the peerage; one can't get away with mere family, no. The dowager aunt three times removed will feel slighted if all the treasures of the Indies are not laid at her door."

I smiled at this. "You fool. I meant with regards to tomorrow's assignation."

Runfold looked comically from side to side. "Hush! Keep your voice down. We're doing our level best not to let this reach the ears of Charles Elliot. He'd be the arbiter of its legality and one of the few things that Tarrant and I agree on is that we would rather not have his input until it is *fait-accompli.*"

"So you're going ahead with—"

"Of course I am. There is no need for any concern."

At this Richard piped up, thankfully breaking the tension. "Good luck, sir. But maybe—if you'd not consider my advice presumptuous—it is not bad to exhibit a little concern. I have found that it concentrates the mind." Richard hopped from foot to foot, nervous after his speech.

"A good plan. I will cultivate some concern." Archie attempted to look suitably grave but he could only manage a few seconds before he burst into laughter.

"Oh, will you behave!" My exasperation had got the better of me. "Just remember our conversation."

"A note sent to you on the ship, then another to Boodle's."

"Yes. Richard?"

"Edgar?"

"Bid the nice Lord Runfold goodbye. He has to prepare, whatever he may think." I failed at keeping the sarcasm out of my tone.

"A pleasure to make your acquaintance, Runfold."

"And I yours, Smythe. If there is ever anything in which I can be of service, do ask."

"And I yours. Good luck for tomorrow."

"Thank you. And if you're ever in London, do look us up."

I looked at Archie askance but he just smiled and turned back to the silks and I decided not to force the dismissal. After a few minutes contemplation I said, "Richard, I do think he meant it."

"Meant it? Who? What?" Richard's voice rose in puzzlement.

"Lord Runfold. About London. And I'd like to second that. Do look me up if you return." I tried to communicate my sincerity.

It appeared that Richard understood, as he said, "I will do so, Edgar. And thank you for my present."

"It's the very least I could do. I did say I would miss some things about Hong Kong." I placed my hand on his shoulder, thinking on how badly I'd misjudged him.

"Edgar?" The tentative tone in his voice brought me to

full alertness.

"Would you like me to sit up with you tonight and see you to the ship on the morrow? I know there is probably no need, but I know that I would prefer the company in your position."

I thought on it only for a second before thanking him heartily and accepting with great relief. I'd been trying not to think on the night, trying not to contemplate the fact that in the morning Runfold could be going to his death.

* * * * *

Richard and I sat up that night playing at cards. I believe he let me win hand after hand in an attempt to get my mind off the dawn. My trunks loomed large in the corner of the room and the flickering light caused me to be less attentive than I usually would be. Without Richard's kindness I would probably have not have won a single hand.

I will not bore you with a description of each and every hand we played or how my nerves became more and more frayed as the dawn drew near. I will not worry you with the way the clock-ticks seemed to be counting down the last seconds of my life and how I both longed for and railed against seeing that first sliver of sun in the sky. How I wished I had had the courage to have asked Runfold to allow me to join him, though I knew it would have only stood as confirmation of Tarrant's imprecations. How that day may well have been the last I'd see Archie and how I wanted to preserve that memory of him—happy, carefree, and extending the hand of welcome to a new person.

The dawn rose, the sun crept higher in the sky and I felt myself perching farther and farther forward in my seat, until I was in danger of tipping the chair face first into the table. There was no word at six, none by seven, and a distinct dearth of information by eight. By the time the clock struck nine, I knew it was time to make my way to the docks. Richard tried to soothe me with tales of messengers getting lost, of intercepts. All I could think of was Archie's handsome face—wreathed in smiles—as I'd last seen it. Though now, there was a bullet through his head.

Epilogue

I'd been aboard the ship for no more than a few minutes — praying for that last message — before it was cast off and the steady thrum of the coal engines increased in volume, propelling us towards old England.

I barricaded myself in my cabin, pulling things out of my trunk and strewing them about the rundown room in the hope that when sea-sickness overwhelmed me I'd be more or less prepared to endure it.

A knock on the door startled me out of my trance-like motions. I was puzzled; we'd only been sailing for an hour or so — it was too late for lunch and too early for tea — and I had already refused the aid of another anonymous valet. I had no urge for anyone to observe me in my distress, no one who could report back on the further peculiarities of the Honourable Edgar Vaughan. I had previously declined a seat at the Captain's table and was damned if I would leave my cabin for anything other than a likely shipwreck.

The knock was repeated and a muffled voice issued through the wood.

"The captain wishes to know if you'll be joining him for supper."

That is enough! I stormed towards the door and wrenched it open, ready to give the wretch a good talking to about the need for proper communication between captain and crew. I stopped, befuddled, and turned cold as ice, refusing to close my eyes, even as I felt my knees collapse under me. *It is Archie. Archie is here.*

He pulled me up to a semi-standing position and escorted me into the chaos of my cabin. I could not stop staring at him—completely unconcerned at my body's inability to respond to basic thought—as he made a space for me on the bed and settled me down, pulling my legs up until I lay completely recumbent.

"I'm sorry, Edgar. I did not think you'd take it like that."

I just kept on staring; I was rendered completely mute.

"Edgar?" His voice turned up at the end, which I took as an indication of his concern. "Edgar. Are you all right? Can you hear me?" He peered deeply into my eyes. "I hope it's not the apoplexy." he muttered.

At that, something seemed to shatter inside me and I burst out into peals of laughter.

Archie looked at me as if I was somewhat touched—as I have no doubt I was at that moment—and then pulled me close until the hiccoughs laughter ceased.

Archie pulled back. "I'm sorry about the note."

"I thought he'd killed you." I tried not to let the horror pervade my voice.

"I told you. I'm the better shot."

My curiosity got the better of me and I rudely asked,

"What happened?"

"I clipped Tarrant. He missed me by a country-mile. All went according to plan until Elliot was informed by one of Tarrant's chums. Elliot set the guards to escort me from the premises. It was all I could do to grab the essentials and beg for a passage on this ship. I decided to lie low until we'd left the port and then come and see you. I was under the assumption that this would meet with your approval."

I was somewhat calmer now, and the anger was beginning to build. "You've seen me. I know you're alive. You imbecile!" I smacked my fist against the wall, denting the board. "Did you not want some time to reconsider before you had to send word to Boodle's about your repatriation?" The words fell from me, and I was astonished to think each of them true. "We're far away from the wagging tongues of Belgravia. Have you thought of what we'll have to do back in London? Just to be near one another?"

Archie sat down by my side and slowly began to unfasten his cuffs. "Let me take this one question at a time. First off, the siege provided me much time to think on this situation. My conclusion then is no different from my conclusion now."

I opened my mouth, but for the first time in many a year, I could not think of a single word to say.

"Let me continue. I realise you're not a particularly nice man. However, I am not a particularly easy person to be around either. If knowing that, you'd prefer for us to meet up in brothels and alleys, I will accede to such."

I shook my head. Once more, Archie had silenced me.

"But if you were willing—if the brother of Baronet Vaughan would consent to taking up the post of my private secretary—I'm sure a more comfortable arrangement could be created."

I looked Archie over. He was beet red and twisting at his open cuffs. His eyes were blood-shot; his legs were trembling. He was the most unprepossessing I'd ever seen him. This decided me.

"Archie, you fool. Did you really think I'd turn that down?" I put my hand over his and held it tight. "We have an understanding. I'll work as your secretary. Few people would question two fellows who met in the Indies and decided to work together on their return to London." I felt quite proud of my ruse until Archie replied.

"We did meet in the Indies, and we are—are we not?"

"Runfold. Of course." I felt a wave hit and my gorge began to rise. I stumbled to my feet and pushed my way out of the cabin, just losing my lunch over the side of the clipper. Archie stood behind me, his hand resting on the small of my back.

"A sea-sick secretary. What have I let myself in for?" He quipped. The smirk in his voice made my stomach heave once more.

"I think you know full-well." I said, between gasps of air.

He moved his hand to my shoulder. "I think I do. I really think I do."

~The End~

About the Author

Chris Smith lurks in the Home Counties with two cats and a very longsuffering fiancé. When not sitting in an office and drawing pretty buildings, Chris Smith can be found glued to a keyboard. She has heard of "fresh air" and "outside" and often ventures forth to investigate, though living in the UK, she is relatively sure that "sunshine" is a myth. You can find her writing journal online at http://c-smith-author.livejournal.com/

Sand

By Charlie Cochrane

"This bloody sand gets everywhere, absolutely bloody everywhere." Charles Cusiter jiggled his feet, attempting to shake the dust of the country from his boots — pretty pointless exercise as the bloody stuff came right back — then brushed down his sleeves with the back of his hand. The air was thick with heat, so thick the skin under his collar felt swollen and clammy, more than it ever became on the hottest of days under an English sky. There seemed to be a pervading smell of camel, even though the nearest one had to be a half-mile away at this precise moment. Why he'd ever agreed to accompany his friend to such a place was beyond him; he'd never been so uncomfortable in his life.

No, he knew exactly why he'd given in. Brute force, excessive charm and a bit of financial pressure, every one of them wielded by Bernard Mottram's mother. The lady in question could make all the sand in Syria vanish with one disapproving look and not even the desert was likely to argue with her. People said even Prime Ministers ran a mile in the opposite direction when Marjorie Mottram came into view.

"*My son is in need of hot weather and mental stimulation, Mr Cusiter.*" Mrs Mottram had made it plain with one look of her gimlet eye that irrespective of whether or not Bernard wanted them, they'd be exactly what he would get. He'd got himself into hot water, appealed to Caesar — or at least to the imperial equivalent in the Mottram household — and overseas he would have to go.

"*He has suffered some disappointments over these last few weeks and needs the opportunity to recuperate.*" Bernard's *disappointments* had been in female form, as his disappointments usually were. This one had been a redhead who'd refused him, then gone off with his so-called best friend. *"Bernard needs someone reliable and sensible to accompany him."* She'd also inferred that if said person let her dear Bernard fall into the hands of any Middle Eastern bints, that person would end up fit only for being mummified himself. Charles had been in no position to refuse; when a man was simply an aspiring writer and his patroness asked him to perform her a favour—and had given him a whacking great lump of cash to oil the wheels—then he could hardly refuse.

"Don't you think it's marvellous, Charles?" Bernard seemed to enjoy every moment of their trip; he loved the warmth and the novelty. Even more, he loved the doe-eyed girls who seemed to be around every Syrian corner, even if he couldn't get his hands on them with his custodian nearby. "Isn't the heat and the smell so invigorating?"

The smell? The only thing Charles smelled was camel; the aroma pervaded absolutely everything, like the bloody sand. They were only a few weeks into the six months of torment Bernard's mother had inflicted on him and he doubted he'd survive. They'd crossed Europe by train, sailed by stages across the Med and then they'd hit the camel train, at which point all pleasure had gone out the window. Or would have, had there had *been* any windows, rather than just tent flaps and sand. Miles and miles of bloody sand.

The intended end of their journey, an archaeological dig located miles from anywhere, received contact with the outside world only when someone managed to wander up the camel route. Charles found consolation in the rumour it was a well set up foundation, excavating archaeological sites with care and dedication, rather than just robbing tombs. The foundation apparently provided a base for students to visit—as long as they had sufficient funds to pay for a placement—to broaden their knowledge and get their hands dirty.

And it catered to tourists, of the more discerning and wealthy type, who would be treated to some time in the camp. The usual itinerary included a tour of the latest digs, being allowed to clean some of the less important artefacts and a mock Bedouin feast or two. A popular combination, especially when the accommodation provided struck just the right balance between local primitive and western luxurious.

Charles just prayed the camp would be free of women, and, more importantly, free of camels.

* * * * *

Our guests seem rather late." Andrew Parks owned Dahmalia camp. While he had his heart well and truly set among the Seleucid Empire, he wasn't so immersed in dusty tombs to be averse to making some money on the side, and looking after his visitors formed part of that. He looked out from the rooftop, scanning the horizon.

"There have been storms south of here, Dr Parks. They will come when they come." Yaseem, Andrew's steward, smiled inscrutably.

"They will indeed." Bringing their payment with them. Visitors were a necessary evil, keeping Andrew's expedition well supplied, allowing him to indulge his enthusiasm for artefacts and hieroglyphs to the maximum. He had a handsome legacy from a maiden aunt for whom he was the favourite nephew, but some extra funds never went amiss. "I hope they'll bring the English newspapers."

Having guests brought the added blessing of helping him keep in some sort of contact with the world he'd left behind. He loved the digs, the desert, the life that bore very little resemblance to London, but he couldn't turn his back entirely on the land of his birth. Especially when he'd left it under inauspicious circumstances.

As far as the high society of London was concerned, Andrew had been sent off '*to further his studies and make something of himself*'. His mother had told all and sundry how he'd be taking over a recently established dig, which a close family friend had been in charge of, one who'd lately succumbed to what she called *an unfortunate disease*. The description hid, literally, a multitude of sins. The endeavour had been presented as a natural progression in her son's career, his having graduated with '*a marvellous first in*

Archaeology and Anthropology', followed up with a shining doctorate researching Roman client kings.

    The reality was different, of course, except for the academic record; that, at least, remained unblemished. Andrew had become a bit too fond of the youngest son of one of the local county families and both sets of parents had conspired to part the young men before scandal and disaster fell upon them all, despatching Robert to the United States to study at Yale and Andrew in the opposite direction. About as far apart, in terms of miles and ease of communication, as the families could engineer.

    "Do you miss your 'green and pleasant' land, sir?" The humorous edge in his steward's voice wasn't lost on Andrew.

    "I do, Yaseem, sometimes. Although when I smell the desert air . . . ." He need say no more. He'd become enchanted beyond all measure with this country, settling down rapidly in his new habitat. In a strange way he felt like he'd come home, and Robert, for whom his enthusiasm had been waning, became a vague, pleasant memory. And despite what his father had anticipated, Andrew hadn't once sought solace with the local boys, no matter how doe-eyed or loose limbed they'd been.

"I believe men either love or loathe our land, Dr Parks. The desert is like a woman; she captures your heart or she leaves you cold."

"She certainly captured mine." She'd been the only love Andrew had found in the time he'd been in the east. No handsome sheik had come sailing up the Euphrates or riding over the sands on the back of a camel, a fact which left him free to concentrate on making his dig one of the most respected in Syria. "I see a cloud of dust, Yaseem. Perhaps our guests won't keep us waiting much longer."

* * * * *

The sheer scale of the operation at Dahmalia always astounded visitors, forcing even Charles to break his sullen silence. "This isn't just a camp. There seem to be proper buildings here, rather than the tents I was expecting."

Their guide nodded. "Indeed, this is a most comfortable site, although not just for visitors. The excavations have been going on here for several years, and both Dr Parks and his predecessor have demanded the staff be well treated. He wants everyone to be comfortable — workers, students and guests — or else the first two can't be productive and the last might take home bad reports. Then there would be no more visitors."

"Well, I just hope there are some girls about." Bernard lowered his voice, addressing Charles alone. "I know they'll all be terribly blue stocking but a man can't be picky."

Charles smiled ruefully. Bernard must have suffered dreadfully since leaving England; there had been a few nice young things in the offing when they'd been travelling by train, but Charles had made sure his charge steered well clear of them. Once on the boat, his vice-like grip on the man's morals had loosened, as all the females aboard had been at least fifty. Bernard had been reduced to staring out at the islands, no doubt trying to imagine what graceful examples of femininity were tripping sinuously among the village streets or preparing sweetmeats for their loved ones. Now there were women to be seen, but none seemed to get within touching distance. Being able to look, yet not touch, sent him crazy — which wasn't really what Mrs Mottram had intended.

Camels and women — a combination liable to plague any man. Charles hoped the camp would prove to be an entirely male affair and didn't hesitate to tell his travelling companion so. "I bet they have as few women as possible on site because they only ever cause trouble; you should know that fact better than most. Six months without women, that's what the doctor — or rather your mother — ordered. And I'm the chump who has to see that's what you get."

They rode into the encampment without speaking further, Charles wanting to be alone with his thoughts. Bernard's constantly chattering presence was starting to wear him out, but he'd had Hobson's choice. All journey long it had been wearisome; he'd needed at least three pairs of eyes to make sure Bernard wasn't straying and while he'd found some respite on the boat — none of the ladies there were likely to lead Bernard astray — once they'd been put ashore again, he'd had to renew his vigilance. Charles desperately hoped his prediction about the camp would prove true and they could spend their stay with no females in sight, except those depicted on some mural. He rode into the camp with all his fingers and toes crossed.

Dr Parks wasn't there to greet them, being — as his steward explained — called away to be on a rope, down a hole, trying to find out whether they'd discovered a treasure cache or just some rubbish pit. Yaseem implored the two visitors to make themselves at home, addressing them with such attentiveness, Charles wondered whether the man knew Mrs Mottram had given an enormous douceur to the operation that employed him. He guessed this money would ensure they'd have pretty well free run of the place as long as they kept to the rules, both those governing the site and the one that would have come as a stipulation with the money. No women in the vicinity of Bernard.

Yaseem led the two guests on an extensive tour, delighted at how impressed they were at the spaciousness of their private apartments. Charles grew more optimistic with every passing moment, although poor Bernard's spirits were evidently becoming equally depressed at the lack of any female substances. They lunched on watermelons and flatbreads, the contrast of cool and sweet with warm and salty being better than the sanitised fare they'd been treated to on the boat. Charles felt that as long as he wasn't made to eat sheep's eyes at some point over the next few months, he might just enjoy himself.

*****

The men slept through the heat of the afternoon, the natural order of things being to break up the day with a siesta and take advantage of the cooler times, morning and evening, for working. Today had been particularly sweltering and Andrew Parks had returned from his cave exploration all of a sweat. He'd towelled down as best he could then taken a nap, something he usually avoided during the day unless he felt intensely tired or overheated.

Sleeping in the daylight muddled his brain and he wanted to be at his most astute to meet Mrs Mottram's son. Andrew may have been comfortably off and the expedition pretty well provided for, but not to the point where money had ceased to talk. And now it was saying, "*Put on your best face; these guests (or their patroness) have paid over the odds so they need to be looked after.*"

He prepared to play the genial host, no matter how often the exercise had ended up boring him in the past. Visitors to Damahlia camp were always treated to a mock Persian banquet the first night, eating under the stars around a campfire. It smacked of penny dreadfuls, the faux desert rather than the real, but the paying guests appreciated it, especially the ladies. Although if any of them harboured hopes that their resident 'sheik' would whisk them off to his tent, they were always disappointed. Andrew had no great desire to be taking any females off to his room.

He wasn't really looking forward to meeting this pair of guests. Yaseem's astute description that '*one talks too much and the other not enough*' had hardly filled Andrew with confidence and their first encounter, for cocktails before dinner, seemed to confirm his worst fears. Bernard Mottram—a man whom Andrew's sister would have described as being handsome in a floppy, silly-ass sort of way—seemed to chatter endlessly. Somehow the man always managed to come invariably around to the same point: women, the allure of them, and the lack of any in the camp.

Andrew's sister, had she been present, would have declared that Charles Cusiter couldn't be called handsome at all, but then would surreptitiously have looked at him for the rest of the evening. The man was certainly slow to speak, although the few things he chose to say were always to the point and Andrew found himself fascinated. Slim as a reed, Charles's dark hair framed a face with the most piercing green eyes Andrew had ever seen, and, on the rare occasions he smiled, his face lit up. His skin appeared clear and smooth, although the hair on his chin seemed to be losing its fight with his razor, making Andrew wonder whether he should offer his manservant's services to provide both the men with a decent shave. It felt a distinct indulgence to be employing a decent barber when you were out in the middle of nowhere but the sensation of being really well-shaved and trimmed added greatly to one's feeling of wellbeing.

And, Andrew reflected, Charles would look much nicer with a smooth chin.

By the time they'd reached the conclusion of the long, slow meal—taken out under a myriad of stars—and were savouring little cakes dripping with honey and adorned with nuts, Charles had become almost talkative. And Andrew was imagining what it would feel like to have that dark head in his lap and to run his fingers through the close cut, wavy locks. He tried hard not to let his glance linger too long on Charles's face or hair or hands, all the parts he found so incredibly attractive.

With dinner finished, the guests began to yawn, making their apologies for being so impolite and for having to take to their beds. Andrew lingered by the fire, watching the pictures in the guttering flames, as he had when just a boy and all the world had been in front of him, awash with potential. Many of those possibilities had been left behind, links severed and old friends despatched to the far side of the world. Now something amazing had happened; the most striking man he'd ever met had walked into the camp and charmed him. Andrew held no great hopes that any magnetism he felt might be returned, although Charles's presence was at least something to make the next few months unusually pleasant.

He retired, to lie on his bed and struggle to keep awake. The sensible thing to do would have been to give into sleep, but he wanted to etch the evening in his memory, filing everything Charles had said or done safely away in a store of remembrance, where they couldn't wither or fade.

*****

The next week established a routine that became increasingly satisfying to all concerned. Bertram had soon shown he'd no inclination to be lowered into caves or enter tombs, but turned out to have an unexpected interest in, and flair for, the cleaning and preserving of artefacts. Andrew plonked him down among the small team in charge of preservation and Bernard found himself welcomed with open arms. It soon became obvious he was using his newfound talent as a channel for the energies usually directed towards the fair sex, but what did that matter? The ladies' loss was Seleucid coinage's gain.

Charles preferred to be active, accompanying Andrew—by some sort of unspoken agreement that had arisen between them—to whatever part of the venture he was visiting. No one commented on this; it wasn't unknown for 'the boss' to let some knowledgeable and sensible visitor accompany him on his daily business, especially one who showed a genuine and intelligent interest in the work of the camp.

When he'd arrived, Charles admitted to no knowledge of ancient times and empires, his own interest being the recent history of warfare, but he'd seemed to drink in all the information given to him with an unquenchable thirst. His questions had been to the point, he'd never tried to hide his ignorance and Andrew had enjoyed having such a sharp pupil. Having such a handsome pupil, one who made the hairs stand up on the back of Andrew's neck every time he smiled, was really just an exquisite bonus.

Still, Andrew hadn't raised his hopes, even when some carefully careless questioning over dinner evening after evening failed to reveal the existence of a girlfriend or wife in Charles's life. That mightn't mean a thing. He had no hint of effeminacy about him, but that too didn't necessarily signify anything; Andrew's rugged looks made other men look epicene. There'd been no real clues to latch onto either way and Charles's sexual inclinations remained as unreadable as some new version of the Rosetta stone in which all three languages were unknown.

"Are you enjoying yourself, Charles?" Andrew reached for the coffee pot, which Yaseem had brought them once the meal had finished. Their eighth day in the camp and it felt like they'd been there forever.

"I am. Much—I must admit—to my surprise." Charles settled into his chair, the dinner things now cleared from the table and the pair of them alone, Bernard having gone off for a lesson in dating coins, one he'd approached with unexpected relish.

"Have we that bad a reputation?" Andrew poured his guest a cup of coffee.

"No." Charles spoke quickly and then seemed to relax, taking the cup to cradle it fondly in his hands. "I'd dreaded coming to Damahlia—all that bloody sand en route and the stink of the camels. Now I'm here, it's like a pearl in the desert, a real oasis of calm and peace. And the archaeology isn't as boring as I'd anticipated."

"Thank you so much for your generous endorsement." Andrew bowed theatrically.

"I'm sorry, I wasn't being sarcastic, but I've never been one for shards and inscriptions. It's a great surprise to find them interesting."

"There are not a lot of camels around the camp, either. I suspect that adds to the allure." Andrew placed the pot between them.

"That, and the lack of women. Not having to be constantly hovering over Bernard has allowed me to relax."

They drank in silence, Charles draining his cup and then taking a second coffee, sweet and very strong. This one he sipped. "I can start to enjoy myself for the first time since we left England, what seems like years ago."

"You must have been a magnet to all the ladies, you two travelling all the way here unchaperoned." Andrew edged the conversation nearer the point where clarification might be found.

"Bernard's the one for the girls, not me."

"So I've heard. I have to be entirely frank and say his mother forewarned me about his tendencies. She even made me do an inventory of all the females who might be found near the camp, ages and all." Andrew grinned. "I promise you, it's not one word of a lie. I've noticed that on the rare occasions one of them does grace our halls — and that's in the form of the laundry ladies who are to a woman almost toothless and most of them older than Mrs Mottram — his eyes follow them with a hungry look. Has he always been like this?"

"As long as I've known him. An absolute sucker for a pretty face or a sob story. And terribly naïve, or at least he always used to be. I remember him kissing one girl in the shrubbery at Kew and her swearing to him a fortnight later that the act had got her pregnant. I think that's when his mother had to tell him the facts of life, and send the girl off with a flea in her ear, or at least a letter from their solicitor." Charles smiled. "Which is the modern equivalent."

"And did telling him the facts of life make matters any better?" Andrew sat back, stretching his legs under the table.

"Infinitely worse. He was mortified anyone should do such things, especially his own mother in the begetting of him, but then he discovered such things might actually be well worth trying." Charles sipped the last of his coffee. He shook his head over all the scrapes Bernard had managed to get himself into down the years. "He'd be better off in a chastity belt."

"Yet it's not as if he's handsome, is it? Or would you say he's the sort the ladies swoon over, like Irving or Du Maurier?" Andrew phrased the question cautiously; they were steering into the sort of waters he was anxious to explore yet he didn't want to lose his true course.

"I think he has a fatal combination of seeming innocence, a pleasant manner and a bank balance the size of the great pyramid of Cheops. I suspect women can detect the last item a mile away and come running." Charles ran his hands through his hair, the curls framing his handsome face. "He'd be a very nice catch and his mother is well aware of that fact. She's keeping him clear of any inconvenient hooks until some plain heiress turns up she'd like to ally the Mottrams with."

"Mothers are like that. Mine has given up with me although she got my older brother down the aisle with a suitable candidate. Filly from the right stable and all that." Andrew twirled his cup thoughtfully, trying not to look at Charles's face, especially when he spoke about his mother abandoning her matrimonial efforts.

"I don't think my mother would ever think of trying. She's far too interested in her good works than to waste time trying to fob me off with the right girl." Charles smiled fondly. "That sounds very harsh; she's no Mrs Jellaby. She just never intended to impose her wishes on me and has told me a hundred times to plough my own furrow. And so I do. . . ."

Andrew looked up sharply, hoping to catch some momentary tell-tale sign on his guest's face, but it was too half-shadowed from the lamp to show any delicate emotion. "We're lucky to be in a position to do so, then. Not every man—or woman—can remain true to their dreams and aspirations."

Charles nodded, his dark hair lit by the guttering flames and full of subtle tones and highlights. Andrew had to clasp the coffee cup as tightly as he could so he wouldn't be tempted to reach out and stroke those locks. He couldn't assume anything, not this early, even from the charily phrased words. If he made a wrong move now he'd be rejected; worse still, he'd run the risk of exposure to public shame and scandal.

"It's not been easy. There's the financial side of things for a start. That's why I have to take little commissions like looking after Bernard to keep me solvent while I get on with my writing."

Andrew wondered if there were other things that hadn't been easy, but Charles didn't seem to want to add to his statement. "Long may those commissions continue. I love books—well written, erudite books sprinkled with esoteric references that only a few people get. Are yours like that? If so, I'd like to read them."

Charles considered. "I suppose you would say they match that description, although I've only had one published so far. The Times lauded my efforts to the heavens as did one or two rather academic tomes. The more popular press either ignored it or said it was heartily highbrow. Damned with faint praise." He suddenly turned and looked Andrew straight in the eye.

Andrew took in a swift breath. That piercing gaze seemed to break down all barriers in search of honesty.

"Would you really like to read it? I have a copy with me. And before you think that's vanity, let me say it's just practicality. I'd hate to repeat myself and I can't always remember offhand what descriptions I've used. I need to refer back . . . ." He trailed off, evidently not wishing to become a bore.

"I really would like to read it. Even if it's the slushiest romance. I'll give you my honest opinion on it."

"I would value that, if you promise to be honest. I'm afraid one's friends tend to be either sycophantic or scathing, depending on whether they want to butter you up or do you down. If you can be objective it might help me find my way more clearly with my latest offerings." Charles drained the last dregs of his coffee. "I'll fetch it now, if I may."

"Please do. I have a longing to read something new." Andrew watched his guest leave the room, admiring the cut of his clothes, the grace of his movements. Charles gave very little away about his character in his spoken words; perhaps his written ones would speak more clearly.

* * * * *

The next day — one in a series of days that had passed pleasantly for all concerned — Charles decided that Andrew's interest in him had to be more than friendly. Maybe the book he lent him had been the catalyst; Andrew had said he found the first few chapters were 'very well written, very interesting'. Perhaps he'd picked out the tiny clues the author had scattered throughout the text regarding the real explanation behind his hero's unhappiness, the reasons he'd volunteered for the mission in Peshawar, which could only end up in his death. Charles had made nothing obvious; he wasn't stupid enough to take that risk, but if you knew the code, the little signs . . . . Maybe Andrew could read it as plainly as he could read cuneiform.

They'd spent the morning out on site looking at potsherds, just the sort of thing you could find in any domestic midden, but which seemed to bear, for Andrew, as much hidden meaning as Charles had put into his book. Andrew had held up a finely polished piece of handle for Charles to examine and they'd drawn very close to each other, bare forearms touching. Sweat broke out where their skin met, whether due to the stifling heat or the close proximity of a pair of bodies beginning to recognise and explore their attraction to each other, Charles couldn't tell. He risked one small glance straight into Andrew's sea-grey eyes, a glance that left little doubt; this was magnetism, whether you'd call it animal or spiritual, on both their parts. Charles hadn't felt such a strong attraction in years.

There'd been a young man, two years before, who'd produced the same sort of wild emotions in Charles's normally pragmatic breast. He'd inspired a character in the novel Charles was working on at present, when time away from keeping an eye on Bernard allowed. The relationship had ended in tragedy and Charles had spent much of the time since then moping around and trying to get Jerry's face out of his mind. Eventually the pain of being left behind had waned from a burning ache to a smouldering discomfort. If he stayed around Andrew Parks much longer the pain might die out entirely.

How long until they'd get the chance to be alone together again, away from the all-seeing eyes of servants or conservators? Maybe if he gave some clear acknowledgement that he'd noticed his host's interest and returned it in full, then they could engineer a valid excuse to be alone in Andrew's rooms. Shame he'd been told it wasn't safe anymore to be out alone at the digs after dark; in the pitch black and starlit silver of the Egyptian night they could say what they meant, without fear. Still, this was Andrew's camp and Charles had no doubt the man could arrange to do whatever he wanted within its walls.

"Andrew, can I . . . ." Charles began but the sound of one of the foremen calling out that he might have made a valuable discovery split the air, drawing Andrew away from potsherds and him.

"Later, Charles. We can discuss it later, I promise."

And with a smile Andrew set off in pursuit of new treasures, leaving Charles rueful at having been a couple of minutes too late in speaking. He took refuge in studying the potsherds again.

They took lunch in the tent where finds were initially sorted; there, the men grabbed both some food and some welcome shade. Charles found that Andrew hadn't returned — they said he was still out, probably halfway down a shaft into a newly located tomb — and would be back when he could. Charles sat and ate, deliberating on everything that had happened since they'd arrived at the camp. The contentment he'd found here hadn't just been the surprised pleasure of enjoying the archaeology; learning the local names for all the constellations had been incredibly romantic, especially by firelight, with Andrew at his side. He'd even become rather sentimental over the pair of hobbies that haunted the vicinity of the main set of buildings. Charles had never had much time for birds — or any other creature — before, inherently mistrusting nature and finding her a touch barbaric, but the local animals had proved interesting, especially when they weren't camels.

As Charles sat and ate, watching the life of the camp go on around him, he saw a young local lad passing by with a bundle of wood to be transported through the site. The boy suddenly gave a shrill cry, dropping his burden and flinging something from him, something small and dark that landed near Charles's leg. Whatever had been thrown had been affronted at both its unexpected flight and the hard contact with flesh. The scorpion rapidly took its brief revenge. Perhaps Mother Nature knew how Charles felt about her beasts of burden and had become determined to take her vengeance on him, proving that she really was red in tooth and claw, or rather sting and telson. He cried out in pain, immediately drawing everyone's attention, not least because none of them expected such a show of emotion.

"What's happening?" Andrew appeared out of nowhere, pushing his way through the small knot of onlookers that had gathered around.

"The boy had this in his load." One of the conservators pointed at the small, possibly deadly creature, now smashed into an almost unidentifiable heap. The curve of the tail remained recognisable.

"Sorry about this, Charles." Andrew drew his knife and efficiently cut out a piece of flesh, clearing all the area surrounding the vicious red mark disfiguring Charles's leg. "Think it's a scorpion sting, old man. Needed to attend to it as soon as I could." He regarded Charles with grave concern, his usually happy face clouded with worry.

Charles knew from his friend's expression that things were serious. He'd barely registered the soreness of the incision at first, too shocked to understand fully what was going on. But now, the knife having done its work, a wave of real pain hit him and he began to feel faint, his perception of events around him fading and returning as in a dream. He remained vaguely aware that they'd called for the resident doctor and that someone was preparing a makeshift stretcher, to take him back to the camp. Andrew's face—he could see that most clearly above all else—looked full of fear and even through the pain Charles sensed his friend trying very hard to hide his concern. Just how bad was this bloody bite going to turn out to be?

*****

Dr Peterson had served Damahlia camp for two years and had only seen two such stings. He attended briskly to Charles's wound, seemed satisfied everything that could be done to get the poison from it had been done, and accompanied the man back to his quarters, talking to Andrew *sotto voce* while he weighed up the prognosis. "So was it a fat-tailed scorpion?"

"That I don't know." Andrew shrugged. "The men reacted as you'd expect and stamped the creature to smithereens before we could identify it. It might have been a fat-tailed, or it could equally have been something a lot more innocuous." Andrew desperately hoped the latter was true and that Charles would suffer nothing worse than some local discomfort and feeling a bit sick. The strength of his feelings didn't surprise him; he couldn't bear the thought of anything happening to any guest and this one in particular.

"Only time will tell. He's shivering already, but that might just be shock, especially if he knows anything about these creatures and what they might do to an unsuspecting victim." Dr Peterson allowed the stretcher to get several paces ahead. "Best to keep him in the dark for the moment. Sometimes it's the thought that death might be on its way that ends up killing the victim, rather than the toxicity of the sting. I've seen someone get bitten by a corn snake and pass away from sheer terror."

"Take him to my rooms," Andrew announced to the stretcher bearers. "Young Oakley's already confined to the ward; we don't wish to disturb him." Oakley had been victim of a bout of food poisoning, having unwisely consumed something of dubious origin while visiting the nearest town. Andrew didn't want his guest to be looked after in what were still the rather unpleasant environs of the sick bay, or at least that's how he'd rationalise his decision to anyone who asked him. The reality? He wanted to have

Charles where he could keep an eye on him and where they could be alone. If Charles died, Andrew might end up in an embarrassing emotional state and he wanted to be able to make a fool of himself without the world gawking at him.

Peterson agreed immediately, advising Andrew he would have suggested something similar, at least confining Charles to his own room so that if he had to be eased into the next world then it could be in privacy. In Andrew's quarters, the patient would be much more comfortable and an observation could be kept on him without disturbing or alarming the rest of the camp. They reached the rooms at last, put Charles onto the bed and stripped him of his outer clothing, despite all protestations to the contrary.

"I'll be fine; I can take care of myself." Charles's appearance — pallid face and sweat breaking on his brow — belied his words. He made a feeble attempt to swat the doctor's hands away then lay back, apparently exhausted at the effort.

"Don't be an ass." Andrew busied himself with getting Charles's boot off, an innocent enough task. He'd leave the man's shorts to the doctor. "My old nanny would be telling you that you're *not* fine and couldn't take care of a balloon on a stick. Be a good chap and just let us get you comfortable. The doctor has a job to do and we mustn't get in his way." He caught Peterson's eye and received a nod of agreement.

"Dr Parks is right. The best thing you can do is be cooperative and not get agitated. I'm going to rig up a drip and get some liquid into you. You can thank your host for having such a range of medical facilities here — very advanced." As he spoke, Peterson's assistants arrived with the equipment required and the bedroom began to resemble a hospital ward.

Andrew kept his gaze averted from needle and tubes; he had a strong stomach for such things normally but on this occasion he didn't want to watch the piercing of skin or emission of blood. With every moment his desperate affection for his guest grew, feeding both the concern he mightn't survive the night and Andrew's determination he wouldn't show his own anxiety. Even if Charles was now falling in and out of consciousness, Andrew would be keeping up a brave front.

Peterson took the first watch over the patient, once Charles's wound had been dressed, the saline was flowing and he'd ensured the man lay as comfortably as possible. Andrew settled in to wait, busying himself with finding Bernard and assuring him his friend wasn't about to drop down dead, although he didn't necessarily share that confidence. He made sure to leave Bernard in good hands, kept well entertained and well out of the way of anything concerning his friend. It was no accident that the person left to entertain him was brawny enough to guarantee he didn't go walkabout in search of stray females.

Andrew didn't try to sleep, even though logic dictated he should attempt to get some shut eye in anticipation of a long night ahead. Rather than pursue a vain exercise, he tried to spend some time with his work, although that proved highly unproductive, as well. In the end he couldn't resist coming over to his rooms and sending Peterson away to take some rest.

Andrew placed his favourite chair by the bed, made a pot of coffee and settled down for his vigil with a book that he looked at but didn't see. He railed at God and his angels, begging them to deliver this man from whatever poison ailed him. Surely the universe would not be so supremely unjust as to bring him someone to fall in love with, only to snatch the man away again before they'd had the chance to explore whether they both felt the same.

Peterson's departing words had been optimistic about the chances of the offending creature being one of the less harmful species. "Or else Mr Cusiter would be much worse by now," had become a little theme Andrew let play in his head again and again as he watched Charles turn fitfully in his sleep. Maybe the man was suffering an idiosyncratic reaction and by morning he'd be well. Of that, Peterson had been ninety percent confident — although the remaining ten percent concerned Andrew. He gently wiped the perspiration from Charles's brow and talked quietly, trying to call him back from wherever he'd gone, be it slumber or unconsciousness. Charles murmured as he turned in the bed; Andrew could persuade himself he heard *his* name being repeated.

Don't raise your hopes, despite what you thought you read into that book. This 'Andrew' might be a brother or another friend, or even the family hound, although he suspected Charles would have confided such a coincidence. Perhaps he'd misheard and the name was Andrea, in which case he'd no hopes at all. Andrew tried not to think — he mopped Charles's brow and concentrated on keeping awake.

He succeeded in the first but not in the second; he awoke to the early dawn, feeling cold and stiff. His head rested on Charles's bed — Andrew's bed, surrendered for the night or for as long as needs be — facing the patient, who slept peacefully, his face much less pale. Charles's hand rested on the back of Andrew's head, feeling like it had been put there deliberately. Even in slumber it had a purpose to it, as if the protected had become the protector. The steadiness and strength in the touch, even in sleep, even in illness, promised loyalty and valour. And to be in such direct contact was itself a joy.

In the end, the discomfort in his neck and shoulders forced him to move, leaving the comfort of the touch. Charles seemed to sense his hand no longer lay where he intended it to be and stirred. Andrew waited, intent not to rush headlong and risk spoiling things; why ruin his chances through being precipitate? But Charles continued to rouse, and once Andrew assured himself the man was fully awake — and trying weakly to smile — he ventured a word. "Feeling any better? At least you look human now."

"I don't feel it. But at least I think I'll live — wasn't so sure last night." Charles smiled again, shyly. He glanced at Andrew, but his gaze quickly dropped away and he studied the sheet. "I'm sorry to have been such a nuisance. I'd been told enough times to avoid those wretched creatures."

"Well you didn't do it deliberately, I assume? I mean, you'd have been stupid going out and looking for the little beast." Andrew smiled, not least at the wonderful English stoicism on display. The man had potentially been at death's door and here he was apologising, as if he was to blame and shouldn't have been so inconsiderate as to nearly die.

"I'll make sure I don't cross paths with another one."

Charles yawned and stretched, a sight Andrew found surprisingly alluring, not least because he only wore his vest and drawers.

"Thank you — and Dr Peterson — for looking after me so well."

"I would say it was our pleasure, only it wasn't, but I hope you get my meaning. The least we could do." Andrew's heart began to pound. "Can I get you a bit of breakfast? The doctor would want you to drink, at the least."

"A little coffee would be fine — very sweet, if you could — and I'll see if that stays down. Not ready for food yet, I'm afraid." Charles risked another direct glance, slightly more confidently.

"I dare say you're not." Andrew placed his hand on Charles's forehead and was pleased to find it dry and cool. He wondered whether his guest felt the same little ripples of excitement at the contact as he felt. "I dare say that by the end of the day your appetite will be back. Your fever appears to have broken." He kept his fingers on his friend's brow slightly longer than was strictly necessary and then reluctantly removed them. "I'd better see about that coffee; I could do with some myself."

Charles smiled again. He hadn't seemed to be a great one for showing his emotions before, probably due to the strain of making sure Bernard didn't stray, and smiles had rarely been in evidence. "Andrew, you will come and keep me company while I drink it, won't you?"

"Of course I will, if you want, so long as it doesn't fatigue you to talk."

"I'll be fine, although I know you must be tired. You seemed worn out last night."

Andrew grinned. "Ah, you caught me in dereliction of my duty, did you? Not going to arrange for a court martial, I trust?" He recalled the wonderful feeling of waking with Charles's hand on his head and was afraid his voice might falter unless he made light of things.

"I'd hardly call it dereliction—you must have been shattered." Charles studied the sheet again.

"That's all right, old man." Andrew decided to take a small risk. "Not an unpleasant sensation to wake with your hand on my head. Comforting, you know—to think you were feeling better." He added the last piece to give them both a way out still; if Charles felt the same, if he knew the way of things, then he could make the next miniscule move. If he didn't—well, they were still within the bounds of respectability.

Charles nodded and seemed about to say something when Yaseem knocked at the door, bearing the pot of coffee they both so badly needed. A clear demonstration of a servant who knows his master's needs, even if his timing was dreadful. Dr Peterson followed in his wake, insisting Charles be put through his paces before he could agree to declare the worst was over and they could abandon the hour-by-hour watch. They'd all but finished the coffee before Andrew and Charles had any time to be alone and then the time for the day's business to start came horribly near to hand.

"I'll have to be about my duties, I'm afraid. Yaseem will make sure you have all you want. I'll ask him to pop in during the day and see you're comfortable. Whistle if you need him in between." Andrew patted his friend's shoulder. "And don't go doing what you shouldn't. You had a lucky time of it yesterday and you don't want to go tempting fate."

"Do you always look on the bright side?" Charles rolled his eyes and screwed his mouth up into a grin.

"I'm just being practical about things. You'll get up and wander around and then faint somewhere and it'll cause all sorts of unnecessary work for us." Andrew suddenly felt unusually serious. "I mean it. You have to look after yourself. Bernard will keep and so will the camp." He smiled again and headed about his duties, guilty at leaving Charles alone, but given that the man had been officially declared to be 'on the mend', how could he engineer spending the day at his bedside? Especially without arousing the suspicion, and not a little resentment, from those who'd have to shoulder the extra burden of work.

* * * * *

Andrew popped in and brought Charles some watermelon for lunch, along with a little piece of cake that resembled baklava. He seemed pleased to find Charles interested in his food and perched on the side of the bed to eat his own rations.

"You look almost human now," Andrew said. "I think we'll see you back on the dig in no time, so long as Peterson is happy you're still making progress. He can be a bit of a fusspot at times, but his heart's in the right place."

"You're lucky to have such a competent man out here. Everyone speaks highly of him."

Andrew smiled ruefully. "There's a bit of a story there, I'm afraid. He lost a patient when he was back in England. No one blamed him, but he blamed himself and he wanted to get away from things for a while. *A while* has lasted rather a long time, which is to our advantage, if not his."

"What happened? Did he perform an operation that went wrong?" Charles had known of such cases. They were often hushed up if the surgeon happened to be well connected and the hapless victim without influence.

"No. He had a rather well-to-do patient who suffered from coronary disease. His Lordship had a heart attack, but afterwards seemed well on the road to recovery. Only then he took a sudden turn for the worse. He died within the hour, irrespective of what Peterson had done to save him. It's not uncommon, as I understand it . . . a bleak night after a false dawn." Andrew shrugged. "As I said, our doctor is the only one who lays the blame at his own door."

"And doesn't he want to go back?"

"One day. I think he's fallen in love with this country—quite a contrast to Surrey and none the worse for that—and almost needs to work it out of his system." Andrew smiled, making Charles's heart race worse than the scorpion had done. "People do fall in love with Egypt, you know."

"Perhaps it's the pull of the exotic, or because they feel less constricted here than back at their London bank or wherever they've run away from, even if it's just for a few weeks." Charles turned his gaze from his host. Not the place to reveal the depth of his feelings yet, in the man's bed, in broad daylight. "I'd be bewitched by the place if I stayed long enough. Anyone would."

"No." Andrew shook his head. "Not everyone. You're open minded enough to embrace the things that are different from home, others aren't. It makes me wild, the way people come out here and expect Damahlia to be like Leatherhead or Worthing. What's the point of travelling if all you want is the same as you have at home, except with different stars overhead?"

Charles shook his head at the folly of such narrow minded behaviour.

"Do you know, one of the two most difficult problems I have to deal with here is women who complain about the quality of the tea and the fact there isn't a local equivalent of Fortnum and Mason's they can send out to at the drop of a hat." Andrew picked up another slice of watermelon, turning it in his hands. "Look at this—it's more wonderful than the finest jewels and most of the old biddies turn their noses up at it."

"Then they have no taste." Charles took the slice offered him and bit into it with relish, the cool succulence refreshing his throat and taking away the last lingering tastes of illness and fear. "And you said that was just one of the two most difficult problems. What's the other?"

"Ah." Andrew blushed, his handsome face suffused with embarrassment. "That would be the visitors who see fit to fall in love not with Egypt but with their host. I suspect it's not any particular attraction of mine but the air of this place. The young ladies seem to feel it's steeped in romance and probably mistake me for a character from a romantic novel. It's a shame to have to disappoint them."

"And do you always disappoint them?" Charles had to force out the words. Andrew seemed to be directly challenging him to say *he'd* gone the same way as the young ladies, falling for the romance of the desert and the allure of his host.

"The ladies, yes. I steer a path well clear of them and if that doesn't work I confess to having a love at home for whom I pine day and night and to whom I would return except that she's married." Andrew grinned, rose, reached over and tousled his guest's hair. "And that usually does the trick—they go and cry on Peterson's shoulder if they're still up for a bit of romance, so it works out conveniently all 'round. And now, I'm afraid, I've a pair of intriguing potsherds to mull over for an hour or two with one of my more intelligent students. I'll be back for dinner."

"I don't think I'll be up to joining the rest of the party."

"Wouldn't think of it. You'll eat here off a tray and I'll keep you company. I'll send Bernard over for a short visit—he's straining at the leash, poor chap, convinced you're at death's door and we're hiding it and he's going to get the blame from his mother. Don't let him wear you out."

"I won't." Charles watched Andrew's golden head as it turned the angle of the door, knowing there was only one way he'd like to be worn out in Damahlia camp and poor Bernard didn't fit into that scheme of things at all.

* * * * *

Bernard visited, seemed happy enough to find his friend wasn't already trussed up in a coffin, said a quick good-bye and tootled off for dinner and a game of bridge. Charles dozed for a while, tired by even such a short visit and aware, for the first time, just how much the encounter with the scorpion had taken out of him. He awoke to the sound of Andrew hissing to his servant to be quiet and not rouse their guest.

"I'm sorry to disturb you — we could have kept this warm." Andrew indicated a covered platter under which there must have lain a host of goodies, judging from the incredible smell wafting from the general direction of the plates.

"No, don't apologise. I was waking already." Charles sat up. "And I could do with my dinner."

Andrew came over, studied his guest carefully, evidently making sure in his own mind that Charles wasn't dissembling. "Dinner it is, then. The lamb is said to be excellent, or so my chef assures me." He uncovered the plates, exposing a bed of saffron rice, topped with tender lamb and fruits. "I'm sorry, invalids first." He offered the plate.

"I'll ignore that remark. Invalid always sounds to me like a derogatory term and I'm feeling almost a new man now, after my sleep." Charles took the plate and began to tuck into the rice. "This really is very good."

They ate pretty well in silence, appetites restored despite their tiredness, and when the plates were almost as bare as the desert wastes that stretched out to the east of the dig, they at last put them to one side.

"Would you like one of these?" Andrew produced some small confections, honeyed and adorned with nuts, as sweet as a first kiss.

Charles shook his head. "They're delightful, but I'll leave them for now. To be honest" — He grinned — "At the risk of sounding like those guests you decry, the one thing I miss is a good old-fashioned pudding. I even dreamed about treacle sponge this afternoon."

Andrew beamed. This latest revelation — a confession about dreams of food that conjured up visions of England and childhood, the nursery and innocent joy — filled his heart with nostalgia for the home he'd thought he no longer needed. But, while no amount of jam roly-poly would draw him back there at the moment, the man lying on his bed just might. "I'll see if my chef can oblige, although whether it would resemble the real thing, I couldn't say."

Charles carefully smoothed the crumbs of food off the sheet. "I can live without pudding, at least for a while. More important priorities, like finding some lead-lined boots to wear about the place. I have no intention of going through *that* experience again."

"You'd be very unlucky if you did." Andrew carefully tidied up any remains of the meal, clearing the bed of everything but his guest and himself. Ideas were springing up in his mind and he needed a clear field to work them through. "We all get the odd stings but generally the beasties avoid the company of man. That particular form of lightning really does rarely strike twice, believe me."

Charles looked up, a boyish, guileless expression on his face. "I'd believe anything you told me." He studied the sheets again, in search of nonexistent crumbs.

Andrew gently laid his hand on his guest's. "And I you. Even if you said the sky here is pink, the Jordan is full of Guinness and the pharaohs all spoke Geordie."

"For an intelligent man you really are remarkably silly at times." Charles clasped Andrew's hand. "Oh, bugger this wretched sand. It's even got in between your fingers, and my poor toes are itching with it."

"I can truly say I've never met anyone who attracts the desert like you do. When Dr Peterson and I undressed you last night I thought you'd brought half a dune in here with you." Andrew — unwillingly — let go of Charles's hand and shuffled along to the end of the bed. He pulled back the thin coverlet. "You're right; those feet are full of the stuff. I'll give them a good cleaning and make you feel better. Not ticklish, are we?" he asked over his shoulder, as he went to fetch a wash bowl and towel.

"Not especially, and I'd be grateful for the relief. When I'm better I'd like to go bathing in that little river again."

"The one where Bernard made such a to-do over the possibility of crocodiles? That can be arranged, and perhaps we could just go ourselves this time. I'm sure Mr Mottram won't want to risk another potential encounter, not after the tales the men have been telling him in the camp." Andrew gently cleaned between each of Charles's toes, like a mother might with a baby. The feet were long and lean, but the toes were elegant and he'd never had such an interesting way to begin a flirtation.

"Are there really crocodiles there, then? And did they have someone's leg off?"

"Not so far as I know of in that particular stream, and the leg is a pure flight of fancy. But poor Bernard is so very gullible it seems a shame not to try to put one over on him." Andrew finished drying his guest's feet, laid down the bowl, then sat on the bed. "There, feel better now?"

"Much, thank you. That bloody sand penetrates every crevice." They exchanged a look that broke down the last barrier; both now knew exactly where they stood. Or lay.

"Does it?" Andrew grinned. "Does it really?"

"Oh yes." Charles ran a finger along Andrew's arm, from wrist to shoulder. "Every single one. Test the thesis if you don't believe it."

"I'll have to. Completely." He shuffled down the bed again, fingering Charles's toes. "Well we know these were full of it, so . . . ." He ran his hand along his guest's calf, finding the curve at the back of his knee. "Some sand here. Not much, but enough to count." He carried on up, hand creeping under the thin cover and across Charles's hip, finding the material of his drawers unmistakably taut. "Must be some more around here." Andrew slipped his hand between drawers and skin, inching his fingers gently between Charles's legs. "Oh yes, plenty of sand here. Amazing how it can penetrate so totally."

"Not the nicest thing to penetrate down there." Charles's voice had deepened, his refined tones suddenly hoarse. "I can think of a better."

"So can I." Andrew's fingers moved between, around, over, along. Hot flesh under hot hands responded to his touch. "But maybe we shouldn't try it tonight, not after that sting. If you were taken ill, however would we explain it to Dr Peterson?" He chuckled, softly.

"Now there's a real incentive to get better." Charles reached for Andrew's shoulder, caressing the strong muscles. "I'm well enough for other things, though."

"I can see that for myself." Andrew gently loosened his friend's silk drawers, sliding them down and exposing his magnificent body. "I'll resist saying it's ironic you should hate camels when you're built like one. And I'm not talking about your legs, either." He got to work again, stroking and squeezing, fingers roaming all over the soft skin between

Charles's legs, then briefly feeling inside him, stretching and teasing.

"Oh." Charles had been prepared to face death, the day before, and now the prospect was here again, if only in the *petit mort* form.

"I'm sorry." Andrew took his hand away, the look of concern darkening his sun-kissed face. "Did I go a bit too far?"

"No, it's just"—Charles motioned for Andrew to move closer—"if you carry on like that I'm going to come and I don't want to, not yet." He pushed his fingers into Andrew's tawny hair, pulling his face closer and stealing their first kiss. "Hmm. I was frightened you'd taste of sand, like everything else seems to."

"I don't taste of camel either." Andrew proved his assertion with a series of long, languid kisses, tongue gently probing Charles's mouth, strong muscle on silken flesh. "I think"—he took another deep kiss—"we should lock the door. We've been interrupted enough recently."

"So we have. Anyone would think your team here didn't want two people to be alone together." Charles watched his host—or should he start to think of him as his lover, now?—slide the bolt across, the action and its associations making his pulse race. If it weren't for the state of his calf, they'd be doing the same thing, uniting bolt and hole; they'd certainly be doing it once his leg got better, unless tonight ended in some sort of disaster.

Too precipitate? Perhaps. He'd only known Andrew a matter of days and he'd never tumbled into anyone's bed on so short an acquaintance, not any of the three occasions so far he'd actually tumbled into a shared bed. Even he and Jerry had performed a winding courtship, a labyrinthine journey from tentative exploration of feelings to a hot Mediterranean night spent in Charles's bed, unsleeping. There'd been plenty of practice sliding the key into the lock that night.

Charles's thoughts began to race on, leaping into the minutes that lay ahead. The chance of climax, however achieved, seemed intoxicating after so long a time of abstinence. He was certain now that sex with Andrew wouldn't be some inexperienced fumbling, hurried and clumsy; it would be slow and expert and wonderful.

"You seem miles away." Andrew stripped off his shirt—such a beautiful sight—and sat on the bed, easing off his own drawers.

"I was thinking about the risk of spoiling things with haste." Charles ran his hand down the creamy ladder of his lover's spine, gently caressing the processes of each vertebra. Like caressing a marble statue . . . Antinous or Alexander . . . in all his splendour and perfection of body. Only Andrew really did seem perfect, rather than being some sculptor's ideal. "I'm concerned I might be rushing you."

"Rushing me?" Andrew leaned into the touch, rolling his shoulders in relaxation. "I'd have had you in my bed as soon as you came into the camp. Seize the day or lose it, that's what I believe."

"That's what Bernard says, too. Should that worry me?" Charles pulled Andrew back, leaning towards him for more kisses. They were the best cure for a wound that had begun to smart again. "He's terribly good at chasing anything in a skirt but once he catches a woman he has no idea what's going on and they take advantage of him."

"Not something that would ever happen to you." Andrew grinned, turning in his lover's grasp until he could straddle his leg—the good one. He was as hard Charles was, as seemingly ready to come. "What's best here, then, if we aren't to spoil that dressing and bring down the wrath of Dr Peterson? Mouth? Hand? Good old fashioned abrasion?"

"Hand, please." Charles tousled his lover's hair. "Only I'll sort you out first, because I'm not sure I'd have the energy *afterwards*."

"Are you absolutely sure you're well enough?" There may have been a hint of reticence in Andrew's voice but the eager way his fingers were drumming a tattoo on Charles's chest, a tattoo which rapidly paraded southwards, belied it.

"I'll have to be well enough. Look at the state of us—something's got to be done about it." They were both beyond the rescue of even the coldest of showers. Excited, desperate, ready to spill. He drew Andrew up for another kiss then took him in hand, eager to finish the job. Before long, Andrew buried his face buried in Charles's chest, restraining his rapture to a series of low moans; the mud walls here weren't that thick or soundproof. Charles lay back, waiting for his lover to compose himself and get to work.

Beginning with a series of kisses, mouth on mouth, mouth on neck, mouth on chest and stomach, Andrew showed a gentle dexterity in his lovemaking that Charles had never known before. As if he applied all the practice he'd had with handling delicate artefacts to his bedroom technique. No roughness, no force, just art and experience. Charles achieved as rapturous a climax as he could have hoped for, given the circumstances of heat and injury and lack of familiarity with each other's likes and dislikes. If this was just the start of their lovemaking together, then he'd anticipate the next few months with excitement.

Andrew kept his hand in place while the last ripples coursed through Charles's flesh, then he kissed his shoulder. "Welcome to Damahlia, Mr Cusiter."

"Thank you, Dr Parks. Now it's not just the desert that has my heart." Charles's energy level surprised him; maybe there was the chance of an encore rather than just the anticipated drift into sleep. He wanted Andrew mounting him, to be pinned down by strong arms and legs even if he wasn't up to penetration. He tugged at his lover, trying to manoeuvre him into place. "Come on, get on top of me. We can pretend we've just done it, get used to the feeling . . . ."

"I'm not going to object." Andrew inched onto him, pressing and rubbing en route, till he sat astride his lover.

"No, lie on top of me, please." Charles pulled Andrew's head towards him, pushing his own chest up so their bodies met. "That's so good, I—bloody hell."

"I'm sorry, I'm so sorry." Andrew rolled off, carefully moving his leg from where it had accidentally pressed on Charles's wound.

"Not your fault." The sharp pain shortened Charles's breath. "Mine for being overly ambitious. Come here. Please." He gingerly drew his lover closer, so they lay together in a sticky, sweaty heap, unsure of what to say.

Afraid they'd broken the spell. Charles, aware of the tension in Andrew's shoulders, spoke first. "Despite the fact that my leg feels like someone's branded it, it's a long time since I've been so happy." He twisted his fingers in his lover's hair. "It's been very nice. And what is so funny?"

Andrew suppressed his laughter. "I keep thinking of all those wonderful lines people have used to speak to their lights of love. *If I could write the beauty of your eyes. Live with me and be my love and we will all the pleasures prove.* Stuff like that. Me, the 'sheik', and you, the writer, and all we can manage is: *It's been very nice.* We're a disgrace to the traditions of romance." He reached his hand up to stroke Charles's cheek.

"Stuff and nonsense. Just because we don't talk like Romeo and Juliet doesn't mean we don't feel the way they do. I feel star-crossed at the moment." Charles closed his eyes and released a huge, shuddering sigh. "Exhausted but star-crossed."

"Do you really mean that, too? I think you might be getting mixed up there. Starry eyed, perhaps?" Andrew wriggled until he was cheek to cheek with Charles, his hot breath caressing Charles's face. "It's as well this isn't a tent—a sheik would be a lot more accomplished and debonair and wouldn't have whacked your leg. I'm afraid sex with me will always border on the clumsy."

"It'll border on the garrulous, as well. You're almost as bad as Bernard." Charles turned his face, until their lips met. "I'm so very glad you're here with me. It's a long time since I felt like this and the object of that affection was drowned while bathing off Naxos. I believed I might never love again, but I'm pleased to be proved wrong."

"I'm sorry for your loss—for the fact it made you sad, that is. I can't bear to think of you bereaved and unhappy." Andrew kissed him again then sat up. "Still, I think I should find that minx who led your friend Bernard astray and buy her a fur coat. She did us both a huge favour."

Andrew rolled off the bed to replenish the water in the bowl . . . the bowl that had seen the start of all the mischief.

"You need not leave Damahlia when your friend does, Charles. See Bernard safely home then return, if you want. You could write your book here and we could call you my protégé for decorum's sake."

"Would that work?" Charles smiled at the possibility.

"We send artefacts all over the place under secure shipment, so a manuscript or two shouldn't be too hard to add to the load. And we won't be staying here forever—I want to get as much stuff excavated as I can, before...."

"Before what?"

"Before the scorpion turns and stings us all." Andrew shrugged. He cleaned himself off before refilling the bowl and returning to the bed. "Do you want me to clean you?"

"No, thank you; you'll be looking for sand again and I'm not sure I have the energy left." Charles took the flannel and moistened it carefully. "As to your suggestion, I could give it a try, returning here while we're still made welcome. But if you grow tired of me, you would say so? I'd never wish to be a burden."

"You'll never be a burden, Charles, of that I'm certain. Now please let me help you; you look all in." Andrew grinned, administering the bed bath quickly and efficiently. When he finished, he patted Charles's good leg. "Sleep and get well for me. You're going to be no use unless you get regain your strength."

Charles lay back, releasing a deep, satisfied sigh. He smoothed down the sheets and found scattered grains, the gritty sensation between his fingers raising a smile. "Bloody sand — gets everywhere . . . ."

~The End~

About the Author

Charlie Cochrane writes gay fiction, predominantly historical romances/mysteries, but with an increasing number of forays into the modern day. She's even been known to write about gay werewolves – highly respectable ones. Her ideal day would be a morning walking along a beach, an afternoon spent watching rugby, and a church service in the evening, with her husband and daughters tagging along, naturally. She loves reading, theatre, good food, and watching sport.

Charlie was named Author of the Year 2009 by the review site Speak Its Name. Learn more about Charlie online at www.charliecochrane.co.uk

The Ninth Language
By Jordan Taylor

Mitsrii lay full-length on the ground, head turned to one side, ear pressed into the moss. His eyes closed as he held his breath. The earth beneath him breathed with the gentle hum and movement of a pulse. Silence, like a fog, hung over him, while in the same moment tiny sounds threatened to deafen the peace—blowing, twisting, growing, stretching, running, singing life rushed over him like the waves of a vast river.

Quietly, and with little effort, he inched forward on his stomach to see over the ridge. The shallow valley below was alive with buzzing insects and twittering birds. Late spring sun blazed down on endless wild flowers, turning the field into a sunset of colors.

Vibrations through the moss beneath his chest grew more distinct. He looked down and to his right, straining to see around the solid bend. A moment later, a family of moose, ten or twelve strong, including calves, galloped from around the corner and charged through the field. His gaze did not follow them but remained on the bend. An instant after the last moose had cleared the turn, a wolf appeared. Mitsrii pressed forward, farther on the hill, to watch the animals, a rush of exhilaration and pride sweeping through him.

After the first wolf, came four others, ever closing on a straggling moose whose nose ran with mucus and whose eyes were clouded and oozing. The wolves ran with almost magical speed and elegance. Guard hairs along their shoulders rippled in the sunlight, muscles contracting then bursting out with the whip-like snap of a bow. Mitsrii sensed the pressure of their paws into earth, felt the cool air surging in and out of their lungs, understood their intensity, their longing to succeed. He saw their chase as an expression of life at its most intimate—when one is desperate to remain alive.

"There're the bastards!"

A human voice, from behind and well to his left, made him jerk his head around to look, grabbing for his rifle in the same moment.

A man in a flannel shirt and dark pants stood on the ridge higher up the hillside. Two other men stepped up beside the first. The one who had spoken now pointed eagerly toward the herd. The other two leveled rifles into the valley. They continued to speak, excited, babbling words like a raven calling his family to a fresh kill.

Mitsrii looked away. Burning hatred, like sulfur, surged into his throat at the sight of the three men. They would shoot into the herd, disrupting the wolf hunt and randomly take mothers of calves and still pregnant cows in their lust for more meat than they could ever haul back to their tents or cabins before flies infested the bodies.

Sickened, Mitsrii crawled backward, rifle in hand, before standing. He turned away as the first shot rang out. His moose hide moccasins made no sound as he retraced the path he had taken earlier to await the wolves.

Another shot. The men yelled in anger. A hint of a smile touched Mitsrii's lips. Then the echo of a third shot ripped over the hill and through the valley. An instant after the explosion, Mitsrii froze at the yelp of a terrified wolf, his body tensing with fear and anger. Surely, it was a mistake. These men wanted nothing with wolves. They would not eat them. They did not tan hides themselves. In a few fast bounds he was back to the spot where he had watched the chase.

The moose were racing away, north, up the valley. The wolf pack had scattered, two turned back the way they had come. They ran so fast their legs blurred. Another skidded about, looking back at a fourth, who was struggling to her feet with blood beginning to mat over the fur of her hip. The fifth wolf fled south, toward the hill where the men waited, laughing and whooping and slapping one another on the back.

The young wolf's eyes were glazed with fear, blinded by panic, running at random, his tail tucked and his mouth wide as he fled from a terror he could not comprehend. Tears flooded Mitsrii's eyes.

Another ear-shattering crack rang out. The young wolf was thrown over backwards, flipping through the air before landing on his side. There he writhed, struggling, unable to stand. No sound escaped him as he thrashed at the ground, claws gouging out great chunks of earth, his blood staining the blue wildflowers red.

In a flash, Mitsrii lifted the rifle to his shoulder. He aimed with the precision of an eagle setting its sights on a fish. The bullet struck the young wolf at the base of the skull. His head dropped. His body relaxed.

"What the hell?" From the hill to his left, Mitsrii heard the yells as he spun to face the men. Rifle still at his shoulder, he leveled the sight at the nearest man. There was an instantaneous uproar as the men scattered—but Mitsrii had pulled the trigger. The second bullet struck the nearest

man in the forehead, sending him flying back, crashing to the ground, dropping out of Mitsrii's sight.

Two remaining men descended the bank, jumping rocks and crashing through scrubby brush to reach him. One held a rifle, which he tried leveling at Mitsrii. Both yelled in wrathful excitement as they approached, though their words held no meaning. Mitsrii drew a bead on the man with the rifle. As he pulled the trigger, the man tripped, sprawling forward at the foot of the bank, the bullet smashing into a dirt hummock just above his back. The other man lunged, crashing into Mitsrii with his full weight and forward momentum. Mitsrii brought up his knee as he fell, driving it into the man's stomach while crashing the barrel of his rifle into the man's face. Mitsrii was on his feet almost before he finished falling. He twisted and leapt back like a cat, using his feet and legs alone, his hands still gripping the rifle.

The tripped man had regained his footing while Mitsrii fought off the other. Mitsrii raised his rifle to block a swing from him. At the same time he felt his feet knocked from underneath him as the man lying on the ground kicked him hard across both ankles. The two men were still yelling, screaming like cornered lynxes. Mitsrii made no sound as he hit the ground on his side and twisted, once more trying to right himself. He looked up just as the butt of a rifle smashed into his head, knocking him over onto his back. Lights popped like lightning in front of his eyes as a searing pain shot through his skull. He tried to roll back to his side but was struck by the hardwood rifle butt again and again on his exploding head until the popping lights burst apart into a thousand sparks. In a final flash, they were gone.

* * * * *

It was almost nightfall — past midnight. The cabin smelled of pipe smoke, wood, sweat, ink, whisky . . . and dog. A red dog with long, fragile looking limbs, hanging ears, and light bones, which lay by the desk near the door. Her fur was not fur, but hair. Her muscles were as delicate as the soft, long-haired ears which drooped past her jaw.

Men moved around her, pacing and arguing,

gesturing at one another with angry thrusts of their hands. They were just as soft as the dog. Just as lacking in any skill or instinct for survival here — where winter days were lit only by the moon and stars, and summer nights clung to the sun unceasingly, never allowing her to fall below the horizon. But the men, like the dog, did not know this. Unlike the dog, they prided themselves in their firm belief to the contrary.

Mitsrii sat on a bench against the back wall with his hands tied behind him, watching them. The two men in red and black uniforms spoke with the most authority and the softest tones. Of the other four men in the room, two yelled and stormed around, one twisted his hat in his hands, watching the yellers, and the fourth stood beside the door. This man shook his head, thick mustache shifting as he mumbled inaudible words.

One of the uniformed men, standing next to the dog and desk, spoke to the quiet man, who then left the cabin. The angry men shouted more at this, but the man in uniform only pointed to a row of three chairs lined along the front wall of the cabin. He said two or three words. Instead of sitting, the other whipped around, and stormed away from the desk.

Several minutes later, the man with the bristling mustache returned. Behind him, a younger man stepped across the threshold. He was clean shaven and wore a parka disproportionally heavy for the mild night chill. All the other men turned to look at the two.

The uniformed man by the desk stepped forward, speaking. The younger man walked with him toward Mitsrii. He said something in return, nodded, and then moved forward to stand in front of Mitsrii.

"Jënezhu yä dìntth'ëk ?" he asked.

Mitsrii looked up, staring at him, narrowing his eyes.

The young man nodded, as if Mitsrii had answered him with something he wanted to hear. Then he went on, still speaking in Hän, "My name is Karlson. Mr. Stanton and Mr. Eugene"—he indicated the two men behind him, the ones from the hill—"say that you killed their partner. Is that right?"

Mitsrii stared, his expression unchanging.

The uniformed man stepped forward to speak to Karlson. Karlson shook his head, then glared at Mitsrii.

"Do you want to be killed?" he asked in Hän.

Mitsrii only gazed at him.

Karlson went on. "That is what they want and what is going to happen unless you have a really good reason for what you did."

Mitsrii cocked his head to the side very slightly, as if hearing something far away. "What reason do white men need for killing? I know why they brought me here instead of shooting me on the hill — to make an example of me, to make me suffer. There's nothing to discuss."

"They may have wanted that, but they did not know Sergeant Reyes believes in getting all the facts before taking the word of two known drunks. He wants to hear your side, so I suggest you start talking. Did you kill a man who was with these two earlier today?"

Mitsrii watched him in silence. The pulse beating in his swollen brow was nauseating. The room seemed to rotate slowly around him.

"I shot him in the head from no more than thirty yards," he said at last. "I assume he's dead. I didn't look at him afterward."

"Why did you shoot him?"

The uniformed man behind Karlson said something. Karlson looked around for a moment to answer him. Then he looked back at Mitsrii.

"What did you tell him?" Mitsrii asked, forcing himself not to wince at the increased pain from speaking.

"I told him you said yes, you did kill the man. Now tell me why."

"It doesn't matter." Mitsrii leaned back, careful not to let his head touch the wall behind him.

"Yes, it does. Was he trying to kill you?"

"No. He didn't know I was there. I surprised him."

"Why?"

Mitsrii sat motionless.

"Do you want to save your own life? Sergeant Reyes is a reasonable man. He wants to know what happened."

"I shot him because I'm a raving, savage, bloodthirsty animal who eats raw meat by the light of the moon and clothes my body in the still hot and bleeding skins of my enemies."

Karlson stared at him.

"Well?" Mitsrii said. "Why don't you tell them what I said? Wait, why bother? They already know."

Karlson continued to watch him for a moment then turned to look at the uniformed man behind him. They spoke for a few minutes. Halfway through the discussion, one of the men from the hill, as well as the slightly older man standing beside him, both stepped forward and began yelling again. This time at Karlson rather than the sergeant. The yelling went on for some time on all sides. The other uniformed man stepped forward. Only the man with the hat in his hands and the man who had brought Karlson remained quiet.

Mitsrii felt as though he was trapped in a packing crate. His heart raced. But it raced from the pressure of walls and ceiling, and the cord cutting into his wrists, not from any apprehension toward the men around him.

The older man stopped yelling. He turned to look at Mitsrii. His eyes glittered in the low light with a flinty hatred. The man had dark hair with streaks of gray. His mustache also showed flecks of gray. He spoke as his gaze bore into Mitsrii. His voice was deep and sharp as a porcupine's quills.

Karlson turned to look at the man with the streaked hair, then at Mitsrii. "They want me to ask you something," Karlson said in Hän.

Mitsrii looked at him, waiting.

"So . . . say something."

"You haven't asked a question."

Karlson shook his head. "Just act like I did, okay? And say something. What is your name?"

"Why would a white man care what a beast calls itself?"

"Fine," Karlson said. "Good enough." He turned back to the sergeant.

Karlson pointed toward Mitsrii, then to the cabin wall

as if to indicate something far away to the north. After more minutes of argument, the sergeant held up his hand and the others fell silent. He spoke several words, causing the two shouting men to start again. But the sergeant made himself heard, at last pointing to the door. The other uniformed man stepped forward, shifting the two men toward the door. The man with the hat in his hands jumped up and followed. Eyes still cold flames, the man with the streaked hair turned to look at Mitsrii. Then, all three were gone.

The sergeant spoke to the second uniformed man then to Karlson.

Karlson spoke again in Hän. "This man is going to escort you out of Dawson. We do not want Stanton and Eugene and Riley causing trouble for you so it will be best to get you out of town with one of the Northwest Police."

Mitsrii looked at him for a long moment before he spoke. "Why?"

"I just told you why. The sergeant thinks—"

"Why are they letting me go?"

"They think you . . . did not mean to kill that man."

"That's a lie."

"Would you rather tell the truth and die, or lie and survive?"

"Tell the truth."

"But you would not tell it to me. So I told them a story for you and you are free to go."

"You shouldn't have lied for me."

"You are welcome."

* * * * *

Mitsrii awoke next morning to find his head throbbing and burning like an infected wound. The sun was just up. Flies and mosquitoes buzzed about him. He looked around before remembering his rifle had not been returned. A series of images flickered through his mind — the rifle smashing into his face — waking to find his hands tied — forced at gunpoint to walk to Dawson with his captors — the police cabin — Karlson, who spoke Hän. Not just spoke it enough to say, "*How much?*" for a bundle of beaver skins, but spoke it fluently. With a thick accent but otherwise without error.

Mitsrii had not gone far after his escort left him the night before. His head had seemed as if it would split apart and he could not get his bearings enough to go on in the dark. Now he looked around to find north. An image of the valley flashed across his mind's eye. The body of the young wolf. The pain in his eyes. The cry from the female when she was hit.

He walked steadily, uphill and down, looking only ahead, or at the invisible path before him. Around him loomed jagged peaks and snow capped tips of mountains whose shapes he had known since birth. The sun was well in the sky when he reached the hills and the sharp but short drop-offs leading to the foot of the valley.

Midstride, he stopped and dropped onto his belly like a lynx spotting a hare. Less than a hundred yards away, a small procession moved southwest, heading for Dawson. Two men walked with a horse. A large, bundled object stretched across the horse's back.

Mitsrii wondered how much had been left of the dead man. The weight on the horse looked substantial so perhaps the foxes and wolverines had not gotten to him yet. Regretting only that the body had served the world no purpose, Mitsrii slipped along once more. Following the same path the moose and wolves had run the day before, he came into the valley, moving like a shadow — this time, watching for men.

The body of the female who had been hit in the hind leg was nowhere to be seen. Perhaps she had made it to her den and her pups before she died. Mitsrii clenched his fists and closed his eyes. When he opened them, he bent to pick up a smooth stone half the size of his fist, then moved on once again until he came to the open valley. From a distance, he spotted the she-wolf's son from the previous year lay where he had fallen the day before.

Mitsrii walked on, through the valley alive with bees and thousands upon thousands of wild flowers. When he reached the wolf, he dropped to his knees. The ravens had found him, pulling meat from under the hide, and, in places, tearing the skin open to reach their food. The thick, gray fur of his ruff moved gently in the breeze, much like the flowers did. His mouth hung open, the lips pulled back in a permanent snarl of terror. A single blue flower grew up between his open jaws so he appeared to be holding it in his teeth.

Mitsrii set the stone at the wolf's head, placed a hand on the ruff and closed his eyes. He remained still for a long time. Pain, like his own life-force peeling away from his soul, made his breath come short. He had known the animal since he first toddled from the den at six weeks old with his mother pushing him insistently back. Mitsrii had seen his first hunt with the pack and watched him grow for a year.

When Mitsrii at last opened his eyes, he touched the stone. It was warm, almost hot to his fingers. He took a deep breath and got to his feet. The next moment, he whirled to look up at the hillside where he had seen the hunt the previous day.

A man sat on the hill, watching him, making no effort to hide or dodge from sight. He held no rifle and seemed interested only in observing. A burning, intense anger surged through Mitsrii at the sight of the man. Mitsrii clenched his fists at his sides and walked away, back through the valley toward the trail he had followed in.

He was past the bend in the hills when he heard running feet sliding on loose rocks some distance off. He did not look around.

"Wait!" The man spoke Hän.

Mitsrii walked on.

"Wait a minute, please." Karlson's voice sounded closer, panting, out of breath.

After a moment, the footfalls sounded at Mitsrii's back as the man ran up behind him. Mitsrii ignored him and kept walking.

"Is this why you killed that man? Because of the wolf?"

Mitsrii made no response.

"I am sorry. I would like to talk to you about it if you would. About what happened. I came to Dawson to work for the Canadian government. I am a linguist. They want people like me to—"

Mitsrii spun to face him, fists still clenched at his sides. "*Destroy us.*"

"What? No. They want people like me for translators. To study cultures like—"

Mitsrii turned away again, walking quickly and northeast now.

"I saved your life back there. Does that mean anything to you?"

Mitsrii did not turn around. "I killed one white man already yesterday. Does that mean anything to you?"

"I want to be your friend. I want to help you."

"If you want to help me, you will go away and never come near my family's home again."

"I would like to meet your family. Very much."

"They don't wish to meet you."

"You do not understand how important it is for us to work together."

Mitsrii walked on without speaking.

"Are you going to Moosehide?" Karlson panted as he

jogged to keep up with Mitsrii's strides.

Mitsrii's teeth were clenched so tight his head burned with sharper pain. His grandmother's grandmother, and on, going back hundreds of years, had lived on the river banks at Tr'ochëk, what others called Dawson City. But they had been in the way. In the way of men who sought to brutalize and rape their land, or build over it until all was hidden from sight. Chief Isaac had realized he needed to protect his people. He worked with the Canadian government to orchestrate the relocation to Moosehide. But not all clans had gone the same way.

Karlson was still speaking, though Mitsrii had not answered his last question. Now he asked, "May I come with you?"

"You may," Mitsrii said. "You will be killed as soon as you're sighted."

"That would cut short my report. Could you ask them to not kill me?"

"I could. I could also ask fox to stop hunting mouse, but I wouldn't. It's how he survives."

"Killing me would not help your people survive. It would be more harmful for you to kill me than helpful."

"Mouse would say the same thing. That wouldn't make it true."

"You don't understand how important this is. For *you*. Not just for me."

Mitsrii spun around to face him so suddenly his shoulder smashed into Karlson's, knocking the man off his feet. Mitsrii stood over him, jaw clenched as Karlson scrambled backward.

"That's the second time you've told me what I don't understand. Now tell me, how do you know I don't understand? How do you know what I know and think and feel?"

"I-I do not," Karlson stammered, still sitting on the ground. "Sorry. I did not mean—"

"Didn't mean to know everything there is to know in the world? Didn't mean to understand everything and see every point of view with perfect clarity? Didn't mean to possess an inner awareness so great it is difficult for even you to believe what a wonderful creature you are? *Why didn't you mean to? How could you not have meant to?*"

Karlson stared at him, mouth hanging open.

"*Well?*" Mitsrii snapped. "*Answer me.*"

Karlson slowly turned over onto his hip, then pushed himself up on his feet. He brushed off his pants, looked at Mitsrii, then took a deep breath.

"My name is Troy Gregory Karlson. I am a citizen of the United States. The Canadian government is looking for linguists to help communicate with native people around the gold claims because of the stampede. I wanted to help. I speak eight languages including Gwich'in and Northern Tutchone. I know nothing about you and your people. I am looking for an ambassador who would be willing to teach me."

Mitsrii looked at the man for a moment in silence then said, "There's nothing for you to see of my people. Soon Hän will be gone from here. Those who are not dead from your diseases will flee from your greed that desecrates our home with your mills and explosives. Moosehide will only be a temporary home."

As Mitsrii started away again, he could hear the man walking behind him. "If you follow me, you will be killed," Mitsrii said.

The footsteps stopped.

Mitsrii walked on alone.

* * * * *

Mitsrii bent his body low as he crouched on the forest trail, moving from shade patch to shade patch, eyes forward and feet making no sound. A squirrel jumped to a new limb above his head, but he did not blink or look. Sliding behind a spruce, he pressed himself among its branches and remained so still he may have been mistaken for a part of the tree.

He watched the three men walking, thirty yards away. Two Tagish tradesmen and Troy Gregory Karlson. Mitsrii's vision was sharp and clear, the swelling and bruising on his head and face were gone. All his senses were keenly awake and keyed, like stretched wires, to an almost painful pitch. A fly landed on his cheek, but he did not move until the men were far enough ahead their backs were to him. Only then did he slink on, like a living ghost, through the shade of the forest.

The sun sat low on the horizon when Karlson and his guides stopped to make their camp. They had been traveling for two days, following a winding, often invisible path, and were fifty miles north and east of Dawson.

Mitsrii climbed a tree, scouting out the camp as the men made a small fire, ate their supper, then crawled into their blankets. All was still as the sun dropped just below the mountain peaks in the distance. Then, moving as quietly as Mitsrii, the Tagish men crept out of their bedding and packed away their blankets and the rest of their gear — ax, rifles, cooking pots, coffee, beans, and salmon. They shouldered their bags and walked away, back along the trail they had arrived on.

Karlson slept on beneath the lavender-pale night sky of early summer. The sun would soon be climbing back above the mountains without ever dropping lower than it was now. When the air warmed enough that biting mosquitoes began alighting on his exposed face, Karlson awoke. Mitsrii, who had dozed through the night in the tree, watched as Karlson slapped a mosquito and then rolled over. He looked around, sat upright, rubbed his eyes, and then looked around again.

He called out, his voice tense with worry. There was no answer.

Karlson scrambled to his feet, pulling his pants and shirt on over his underclothes, rolling his blankets, then flinging pack and blankets haphazardly together on his back.

The sun had crested the mountains, sending a warm golden glow through the sparse forest. Karlson again called out for his guides as he started off — heading straight for Mitsrii's tree. He tripped as he looked around and brushed at mosquitoes, ever calling, ever catching himself and stumbling on.

Mitsrii eased his body forward on the tree limb then

dropped to the forest floor. He landed not four feet in front of Karlson. The man let out a yell, as if a grizzly had slashed him across the face, at the same time jumping into the air and backwards. He spun his arms franticly as he fell, still yelling when he hit the ground.

Mitsrii stood watching him. A moment later, the sheer panic in Karlson's eyes changed to recognition. Mitsrii did not understand the stream of words Karlson let out as he rolled, gasping, onto his hands and knees before clambering to his feet. He was shaking as he brushed himself off, still speaking in English.

Karlson looked up, met Mitsrii's stare, and shook his head. "Sorry," he said in Hän. "I did not mean — you scared me."

"I'm aware of that," Mitsrii said.

Karlson started laughing. He took a step back, leaning into the birch tree he found at his side, laughing and shaking his head. "Yes, I guess you noticed."

"It wasn't my intention to frighten you."

"Then I would hate for you to try. You would give me

a . . . what do you call it when your heart gives out?"

"Death."

"That was not the word I wanted, but yes, that is usually what happens."

"It wasn't my intention to cause you death either," Mitsrii said, raising one eyebrow. "But that was the intention of your Tagish guides."

"What do you mean?" Karlson's face became serious. "What are you doing here? I was coming out here to meet with other tribes. I woke up and my guides were gone. Do you know what happened?"

"I mean that they left you to die here. I am here because I followed you from Dawson. Yes, I know what happened."

"You followed us? Why?"

"Because I knew why you were being led out here."

"Were you spying on us in Dawson?"

"I don't enter Dawson unless forced."

Karlson looked away.

"Anyone could tell where they were taking you,"

Mitsrii said. "I didn't have to spy to figure that out."

"Do you know where these tribes are yourself?"

"What tribes?"

"The ones they were taking me to. They said there were Gwich'in villages up here. I am going to Moosehide as well, but after I get back to Dawson."

"They were not taking you to any village. They were leading you on to leave you. They think it's entertaining. You had already paid them, I'm sure."

"They would not do that. I told them why I was here. They were interested."

Mitsrii stared.

"They were. They said they wanted to help."

"They helped themselves to whatever you bargained with, led you on a wild path until you had no hope of finding your way back to town, then left you. They intended to from the start."

"Then why are you here? Are you part of the game?"

"I don't work with Tagish." Mitsrii's voice was a snarl.

"Why then?"

"To take you back to your town."

"Why?"

Mitsrii cocked his head, both surprised and annoyed. "I'm in your debt."

"You are? I mean, yes, you are, but I did not realize you . . . cared. Or that you were spying on me."

"I wasn't. I saw you leave Dawson."

"You wasted your time. I do not want to go back. I want to meet the tribes out here."

"No, you don't."

"Yes, I do. I wish to make contact with some native villages and learn what I can about the people."

"They may kill you if you meet them."

"I do not think they would. I met other Hän from Moosehide in Dawson. They have all been much more pleasant to me than you are, and you have not killed me."

"That doesn't rule out the possibility."

Karlson laughed again. Mitsrii wondered if he was a little insane; the man laughed at the strangest things.

He turned away from Karlson and began walking

carefully through the forest. "Come."

"Is that south?"

"Yes." Mitsrii glanced back.

Karlson was squinting in the direction of the sun. "I already told you, I do not want to go back. Take me to one of the northern villages. That would be more than repayment for anything you owe me."

"No." Mitsrii stopped to face at him.

"Why not?"

Mitsrii frowned. "Do you hear poorly or do you not listen out of conceit for your own opinion?"

"I was listening. You said they might kill me. Why would they do that? They will not kill me because they will understand I am only there to talk."

"You talk too much. It would be to their advantage if you were dead."

"Now really, does that not seem unreasonable to you? How could me being dead help anyone?"

"If you were dead you wouldn't be able to blast our land apart, or murder our brothers, or take our children to be raised in your schools, or give us your plagues, or kill our game."

"I am not doing any of those things to you."

Mitsrii stared at him for a long time. Finally, Karlson looked away. Mitsrii turned and began walking south once more. Karlson followed.

The sun was well up in the sky before either of them spoke again. Mitsrii had stopped by a stream to drink and offer Karlson a slice of dried meat — which the man took gratefully. Several feet apart on the pebbly ground by the stream, they sat and ate. Mitsrii watched Karlson as he smiled at a squirrel chattering in their direction from the trunk of an aspen across the stream. He seemed unreasonably happy at the sight — as though the squirrel were his own personal pet. Karlson's brown hair fell across his forehead, almost matching the squirrel's reddish brown coat. His green eyes matched the spring birch leaves the little animal clung to. He had two days of stubble on his otherwise smooth face.

Karlson turned his head and their eyes met. "What is

it?" he asked, still smiling.

"Why do you look at the squirrel as though it is your bride?"

Karlson chuckled. "It is cute."

"Cute? Don't you understand what she is saying to you?"

"Saying? Well, it is chattering its head off. I guess it says 'Look at me. This is my tree.'"

"You speak eight languages, but you cannot decipher the simplest ones?"

"I never heard of squirrel language." Karlson smiled.

Mitsrii looked away as he stood, gritting his teeth.

Karlson clambered noisily to his feet behind him. "Sorry, I did not mean to offend you."

"Your presence here offends me."

"That is a whole different thing," Karlson muttered. He followed Mitsrii along the bank for fifty yards in silence before he said, "I am sorry about the wolf."

Mitsrii felt his shoulders stiffen. "You can't be sorry about something you don't understand."

"I understand that it meant something to you. I understand that you killed a man because he shot it. And I am sorry about that."

Mitsrii said nothing for a moment, biting his tongue, not wanting to speak at all. Then a rush of words surged up through him and out of his mouth without his lips being able to stop them. "He was not the worst loss. He was only a yearling. A hunter in the pack. The mother was also killed. Their bullet smashed the bones in both her hips but she still drug her body back to her den and her pups before she died. They shoot to wound, to torture. Or else they are very bad at aiming."

"I guess the pups died too . . . ?" Karlson said hesitantly from behind him.

"They were no longer dependent on their mother. That's the only reason she was out on the hunt at all. The rest of the pack will raise them."

"Really? They do not eat them with the mother gone? Will the father not kill them if he finds them?"

Mitsrii closed his eyes for several paces. At last he

said, "Don't keep speaking to me or I will also leave you out here — and you will die."

Karlson did not speak another word as the trail took them steadily downhill. Insects buzzed and birds flitted about them in the blazing sunlight. Aspens and willows were vibrant with moist, green life. Pines and spruce sent forth familiar odors, which had lain dead throughout the long, dark winter and now seemed determined to make up for it. Grouse darted into underbrush very near to their feet. The distant sound of a working woodpecker reached their ears more than once. Squirrels leaped among branches. A flash of brown hinted at a hare that had been there a moment before. All around the two men the Earth seemed to sing, almost bursting at the seams, as if aware how little time she had before the ice returned.

Late in the afternoon, thick, dark clouds rolled in from the south and blotted out the sun. Karlson's heavy boots clunked and shifted rock and earth under him while he stepped at random on small sticks and twigs, snapping them each time. He panted as they climbed one slope after another. The sound of his breathing was close to driving Mitsrii mad. He found himself so irritated by the constant noises, he wanted to stop and hit Karlson.

"Do you think it will rain?" Karlson asked after hours of not speaking.

Mitsrii did not answer.

"Are you still angry with me about the wolves?" Karlson asked.

Still, Mitsrii said nothing.

"I grew up in Minnesota." Karlson went on as though he had been invited to. "That is a northern state in the United States. Where I grew up, there were always ranchers out trying to kill wolves. They used to say wolves were the devil on Earth. They told us kids that a wolf would swallow us whole as soon as look at us. When we heard their howls at night we were terrified. When a man went out and shot a wolf, or caught one in a trap, it was a great thing. Everyone was happy. They told us wolves were the most cruel and cold-blooded killers ever to stalk the Earth. They killed and ate anything they got near, including each other half the time.

"You think I am an ignorant brute for thinking a father wolf would kill his offspring, but no one has ever told me otherwise. The men who shot those wolves you cared about do not know otherwise either. Killing a wolf is no different to them than killing a devil—a service to the world."

Mitsrii felt the first drops of rain on his face as he walked, now down a hill.

"If you think a wolf's life is equal to a man's, then I want to know about it. I want to learn everything I can about your people."

Mitsrii led them far to the west where he knew there was a network of caves in the rocky cliff face over a wide creek, which eventually joined the Yukon River. They were both soaked to the skin, and the rain had become a torrent, by the time they reached the creek.

Karlson had asked him several times where they were going and if they could find somewhere to get out of the rain. Not once did Mitsrii answer. As they walked near the bank of the swift creek, Karlson started forward toward the rock formations. Mitsrii reached out and grabbed his elbow, jerking him back so forcefully he staggered and almost fell.

"What?" Karlson shouted over the sound of the rain and the creek.

Mitsrii answered with a single word. "Bear."

Karlson froze then looked around. "Where?"

Mitsrii shook his head. He released the other man's arm and walked forward alone. He climbed an outcropping of rock and made his way around and over the uneven surface as he checked inside the shallow caves formed in the rocks. When he found one nearly large enough to stand in and several feet deep, he stepped back to wave Karlson over.

"Are there bears?"

"Not now. They've been here. Can't you smell them?"

"No."

Some time later, Mitsrii had collected the little dry wood he could find under the shelter of rocks. It was only enough for a short-lived fire that they built near the cave mouth, just in from the rain so the smoke could escape. Both men remained silent as they made the fire and Karlson tried several times to start it with his lighter before success. They worked to get as dry as possible before they lost the flames. Karlson held his shirt in one hand and his blanket in the other, kneeling almost inside the fire as he tried to dry his pants. He glanced up at Mitsrii as he pulled the supple caribou skin shirt off over his head.

"Is there some reason you will not tell me your name?"

Mitsrii looked down at him. "Is there some reason you want to know it?"

"I want to know what to call you."

"Why do you need to call me anything?"

"You know what? I think you are just about the most difficult person to talk to that I have ever met."

"Then why do you keep trying to talk to me?"

"I would like to get to know you."

"Yes, your job. You must have to report about me? Like studying a wild beast? This must be fascinating for you."

Karlson's gaze darted to Mitsrii's bare chest, then back to the fire. "Not for my job. I would like to get to know you even if I was not here with any job." Karlson looked up again and his eyes flashed angrily for a moment as they met Mitsrii's. "Why are you taking all this out on me? I did not do anything to you. Nothing. I am not here for gold. Or to force you out of your home. Or hurt your people. Or kill your game. In my life, I have never killed anything bigger than a spider. Explain to me what I did that is so offensive to you."

Mitsrii sat cross-legged in front of the fire, holding his shirt. For a few seconds, he met Karlson's gaze, then shrugged. "You are trespassing, just like the rest of your kind, in my home."

Karlson stared at him. "Sorry. I did not mean to trespass. What would be the proper custom if you wanted to travel in another tribe's land? What would you do?"

"I would ask permission."

Karlson burst out laughing.

Mitsrii frowned at him. "You think it's amusing that

your people have never heard of asking permission?"

"No," Karlson said, looking up and still grinning. "But I think it is amusing that none of us ever think to." He composed himself but continued to smile as he looked across the fire at Mitsrii. "So, whatever-your-name-is, may I . . . visit your land? I mean you no harm and I mean your home no harm. I am just here to . . . get to know you a little."

Mitsrii looked at him for several seconds with Karlson smiling back. At last he said, "Mitsrii. My name is Mitsrii."

The smile on Karlson's face faded into a look of serious intensity. "I am very glad to meet you, Mitsrii. My name is Troy."

Mitsrii frowned. "Karlson."

Karlson made a face. "Do not call me that. It is not my first name. Call me Troy."

"Troy." Mitsrii was careful with the foreign pronunciation.

"Yes, like the city in—" He stopped and shrugged. "Never mind."

"Troy is the village where you come from?"

"No. The biggest city near where I am from is Minneapolis. You would hate it. Full of people and really loud. It is not at all like being out here."

"Like Dawson?"

The other man laughed. "Not even like that. Imagine if Dawson went on and on and on. So loud you could not hear your own thoughts. That is what it is like. I was up north in the country though, growing up. I did not live in Minneapolis. Then I went to school in Chicago. Talk about big and loud."

"Soon that's what we'll be here," Mitsrii said quietly. "Big and loud, without end."

"No, no it will not. This country is huge. Men cannot possibly build over all of it. There is a lot of talk about the new century coming. 1898 and only two years to a new decade. A lot of talk about all the 'progress' we have made. All the progress we will keep making. But I think . . . ." He met Mitsrii's gaze. "I think this right here is progress."

* * * * *

Troy awoke with his muscles so stiff and sore he felt as though he had been sleeping on granite. He pressed his hand into the ground beneath him, felt the cold stone, then jerked wider awake and looked around. Everything from the day before rushed back to him. The sun was shining into the cave mouth. Black bits of ash showed where the fire had been the night before. But something was missing.

"Not again." Troy rolled to his painful side and struggled to his feet. He was shaking from cold, still damp all over from the night before. His blanket, shirt, pants, socks, underclothes, everything, was still wet—or at least damp. Wishing he had his parka, he shivered his way to the front of the cave and looked out.

Mitsrii was nowhere to be seen.

"So much for that," Troy said aloud as he kicked moodily at the ash with his toe. "What's it take to keep a native guide around here?"

Maybe he could find some dry wood and get another fire going. The thought of starting out walking again, or doing anything in his current condition, was unappealing. But so was looking for firewood.

His stomach growled. Mitsrii had given him another piece of his dried meat the night before, but that was it.

"Stupid. I've got to be the world's stupidest, most gullible bastard. Think now we're real close. Now he told me his name. Now I'll have no problems. All's swell." He kicked at the ash again. "Stupid, stupid, stupid."

"You shouldn't do that."

Troy jumped, slipping on the stone and falling back against the cave wall, hitting his head before sliding down it to the floor.

Mitsrii stood in the cave opening, watching him. He held a large bundle of firewood under one arm and two trout hanging by their gills on the fingers of his other hand.

Troy swore as he clutched his head, rolling onto his side and curling into a fetal position. "Bastard, bastard, bastard. What the hell? Why do you keep doing that to me? Gonna kill me."

He looked up to see Mitsrii still watching him. His

face was impassive. His dark eyes looked jet black as he was silhouetted in the cave-mouth.

"Sorry," Troy said in Hän, as he realized he had been speaking English. Why did he always end up apologizing after this man terrified him? He glared up at Mitsrii. "Why do you do that?"

"What did I do?"

"Sneak up on me all the time."

"I have never snuck up on you."

"You did!"

"I did not. I was making no effort to be silent when I walked up here. If I wished to be quiet, why would I have spoken to you?"

"To scare me to death?"

"You're not dead."

Troy gritted his teeth as he rolled to his hands and knees. He slipped back into English for a moment as he swore at the pain.

Mitsrii set the fish down on a rock outside the cave then went about building the fire. Troy sat leaning against the rock wall, clutching his head as he glared. When the kindling was ready, Troy lit it with his lighter while Mitsrii slid each of the fish onto a long stick, mouth first. He handed one stick to Troy without saying anything then held his own almost within the flames.

"How did you catch these?" Troy asked, looking up from his own fish.

Mitsrii did not answer.

Troy rubbed his head again.

Mitsrii looked at him. "Are you hurt?"

"What do you think?" Troy snapped.

"I think . . . I think you are exaggerating your injury to invoke sympathy."

Troy stared at him for a moment, letting the slightly unfamiliar words translate in his mind. "Why would I do that?"

Mitsrii shrugged. "You are self-pitying and fragile, like other white men."

"Fragile? You think smashing your head into a solid rock wall and being aware of the pain is fragile?"

Mitsrii held up his left hand. Part of each of the two last fingers were missing. "Bitten off by a bear," he said.

"And I bet you did not flinch," Troy said scathingly.

Mitsrii gazed at his fish. "I killed the bear."

"So you think I should have killed you for making me hit my head?"

"I didn't make you hit your head. Your own fear made you hit your head. And no, I do not think you should kill me. Nor do I think you capable of it. You have no weapon and no courage. But I do think you should take action against what is causing you hurt. If you can't take action against it, or refuse to take action against it, you should move on."

"You think I am a coward?" Troy asked.

Mitsrii raised his eyebrows. "It's not what I think that matters."

"I never thought I was a coward. You were the one who just said I do not have any courage."

"You're afraid of me and I have done nothing to harm you."

"You think that rock wall was not harmful?"

"You did that to yourself."

Troy shook his head.

Mitsrii withdrew his fish from the fire and held it for a moment in the open air, then began peeling off the flesh with his fingers. Troy kept his in the flames until the skin was crackling and blackened in areas. Though his hunger seemed hardly sated from the single trout, he felt immeasurably better after it. His head was clearer and the ache had subsided. He crawled out of the cave with Mitsrii beside him. They threw the remains in the river for other fish to consume, and washed the grease from their skin before returning to the cave to dry the rest of their clothing.

Troy watched Mitsrii pulling off his moccasins and holding them by the fire with the insides turned toward the heat. He pulled off his own shirt and undershirt, then boots, socks and pants, trying to hold everything up to the flames at the same time.

"Sorry I snapped at you before," Troy said, watching the fire.

Mitsrii looked up at him. Troy felt unexpectedly uncomfortable beneath his steady gaze. As though his body was under a microscope.

"You were right." Troy felt heat creep up his neck and into his face. "I should not have blamed you. It was not your fault."

"I know."

Troy laughed. He looked again and was so startled to see Mitsrii smiling at him that he almost dropped his blanket in the fire. He had a strong, smooth jaw-line and high cheekbones, which were accentuated by the smile. Troy felt a rush of exhilaration looking into his eyes.

"So," Troy said. "Will you introduce me to some Gwich'in today?"

"No."

Troy sighed as he pushed his boots closer to the fire. "Because you are so concerned that they could kill me?" He glanced up, smiling.

"Hmm . . . ." Mitsrii added the last few sticks to the fire. He did not speak again for several seconds, gaze fixed on the flames. Then he asked, "What did you tell them about me that night?"

Troy looked away. "Nothing."

"You spoke a very long time to say nothing."

Troy glanced back at him. "I told them you were on a sacred 'becoming a warrior' quest. That to do it you had to kill an animal and bring it back to your village. But when you go on the quest you smoke a pipe that makes you have all kinds of strange visions. When you saw the men on the hill you were hallucinating and thought they were wild animals you were hunting. So you never meant to kill a man and never would have done such a thing if you were not on the quest."

"You told them all that?"

"It was … detailed."

"And they believed you?"

"Of course they believed me. Well, I do not think Stanton or Riley, the dead man's brother, believed me. But the sergeant did."

"They think Hän do such things?"

"I guess so. It seemed to make sense to them."

"And you are here in order to educate their government about my people?"

"It saved your life. I did not know what else to do. You would not tell me what happened."

"If I had told you what happened, would you have told them that story?"

"That the man shot a wolf so you killed him? Probably not."

"And if I had told you he shot two friends of mine . . . would you have told them that?"

Troy looked down at his now dry socks.

Mitsrii pulled his moccasins on and Troy stood to get dressed and roll up his blanket.

The sun was high in the sky by the time they started out. Troy could not tell which direction they traveled. He did not ask. He felt a subtle, but still present, hostility emanating from the man who walked before him along their unseen trail. He noticed, as they walked, how softly Mitsrii stepped, without watching where he placed his feet. Each step landed with great care while he moved briskly.

Troy glanced at his own heavy boots. He set one foot down with great care, then the other, then another step, moving as softly as he could. He found that he could walk along quietly when he tried, but he soon fell so far behind Mitsrii that he had to run to catch up, crashing through brush and breaking sticks as he did.

They had walked for perhaps two hours without speaking when Mitsrii stopped so suddenly Troy ran into him.

"Sorry —"

"Shh!" Mitsrii's command came out as a hiss. He was looking up and to their left.

A wooded ridge towered above them. Troy thought it looked too steep to ascend easily, but a moment later Mitsrii did just that. He dropped to his knees at the crest, one hand on a birch tree. A smile leaped across his face and he looked back at Troy and waved for him to follow.

Troy started but Mitsrii whispered, "*Quiet.*"

Troy glared at him. Slowly, and as quietly as he

could, he scrambled up the ledge until he too could see what lay beyond the top of the embankment.

He gasped and Mitsrii grabbed his arm, preventing him from hurrying back down the hill. A mature grizzly bear shuffled past less than forty feet away. Behind her bounced a cub.

Troy's heartbeat hammered in his throat as he watched them. The size of the animal was incredible. Bigger than three men, the bear seemed to own the forest with her walk — take the entire place in and claim it as her own. The cub tackled her foot then rolled over in a summersault as he shot past, having misjudged his own speed. The mother turned her head to watch him without breaking stride. Her muscles rippled like a separate living thing surged under her vast, bristling coat. Slowly, with the ease of confidence, the two bears moved away until they disappeared among the spruce trees.

Mitsrii released Troy's arm and slid back to the trail they had been following. Troy inched down the slope behind him. At the bottom, he tried to brush himself off. His hands were shaking so badly he gave up.

Mitsrii was watching him. He was smiling.

Troy felt a rush of burning anger at him that only increased the shaking in his hands. "What the hell—!" He started, then caught himself and switched languages. "Why did you do that? That animal could have killed us!"

Mitsrii shook his head. "She wasn't interested in us."

"She could have been!" Troy pointed a shaking finger toward Mitsrii's left hand. "Do you ever think about that? Does it bother you that one of those animals ripped off your fingers?"

Mitsrii shrugged. "He was defending his territory. I was careless. No animal will hurt you if you understand it and respect its space. They will hurt you to protect themselves, or their young, or their land. Or for food. An animal will not randomly attack you for no reason."

"Just because it has never happened to you does not mean it never happens."

"Why would an animal, who is not feeling threatened and isn't hungry, attack you?"

"I do not want to find out. What if just the sight of us made her feel threatened?"

Mitsrii cocked his head to the side, watching Troy. He stepped forward to take Troy's trembling right hand in both of his and press it against an aspen beside them on the trail. Troy stared at him, feeling too shaken to resist. Closing his eyes, Mitsrii pressed his hand against the back of Troy's. Unlike Troy's, Mitsrii's hand felt warm and very steady.

"Can you feel it breathing?" Mitsrii asked.

Troy did not answer.

"It will calm you," Mitsrii said. "This tree is as old as your grandfather. She has seen a great deal in her time."

"How exactly does it see anything?" Troy asked, watching Mitsrii's face and closed eyes.

Mitsrii smiled. "All living things have souls. When I say 'see' I mean an awareness. She is aware of what is around her. Just as aware as you or I."

"You believe this tree has a soul?"

"Yes."

"What makes you think so?"

"What makes you think the sun is warm?"

"That is hardly the same thing. You can feel the sun. You can tell it is warm."

"You can feel the tree's soul also. Close your eyes."

Mitsrii had not opened his own eyes to know that Troy still had his open. Troy obeyed irritably as he wondered what this had to do with bears.

"What do you feel?" Mitsrii asked.

"Bark?" Troy said uncertainly. "A tree? An aspen?"

"What else?"

Troy thought of the feel of the fingers pressing against the back of his own hand. There was a callus at the bottom of Mitsrii's palm, which Troy felt against the back of his own wrist. The man's skin felt warm, yet cool at the same time. Infinitely comforting, like a good meal and warm bed after a long day's work. Mitsrii's skin was dry. Troy was aware of sweat on his palm against the tree. He could feel the pulse beating in Mitsrii's thumb . . . .

Troy jumped away as though given an electric shock, eyes snapping open and almost tripping over his own feet.

Breathing hard, his heart rate was accelerated once more. He could not think. He could not catch his breath. His pulse seemed to pound strong and fast in his ears.

Mitsrii was watching him. Troy found himself unable to meet the other man's eyes. He glanced up the trail, wanting to say something but unable to think of any words. He could not remember what language he had been speaking.

Mitsrii said, "Nänjit dähònch'e ?"

Troy looked at him. What in the world was that supposed to mean? A high-pitched buzzing filled his brain. Troy shook his head. "I don't—sorry . . . just . . . ," he muttered in English. He should be able to understand, yet . . . . Troy started down the path once more.

Behind him, Mitsrii asked something else. The cogs and wheels of Troy's brain were sliding sluggishly back into place. Mitsrii had asked how he was. Now he was asking if Troy felt all right.

"Uh . . . ąhą," Troy said, alarmed by how hard he had to struggle to come up with the affirmative. *Get a hold of yourself.* He dug his fingertips into his palms, looking fixedly ahead at the path.

Mitsrii said nothing more as he passed Troy and took over the lead on the climbing trail. Not taking his eyes from the uneven ground, Troy slowed his pace to let Mitsrii get farther ahead.

* * * * *

It was late afternoon before Troy looked around at the scenery and the man ahead of him. Mitsrii had stopped on the forest trail.

"Is something wrong?" Troy asked in Hän — the knowledge of how to do so having returned to him over the silent hours of travel. His voice came out hoarse. He cleared his throat.

"Come up here beside me," Mitsrii said.

Troy did not move. He was standing twenty feet back along the trail. "Why?"

Mitsrii frowned as though he had not understood the

question. Troy started to ask again, wondering if his accent had garbled the word too much to be understood — but Mitsrii cut him off. "For your safety."

"My safety?"

"Yes. If you walk into the village on your own, you may be in danger."

"The village?" Troy's heart leapt. "You brought me to a village?"

"No. I brought you to a forest."

Troy studied Mitsrii's face then he shook his head and walked forward. "Is there anything I should know before we get there? Anything I should do?"

"Do? Like what?"

"In my culture men would shake hands with each other and take their hats off to women."

"You don't have a hat."

"Only an example."

Mitsrii shook his head. "Just let me explain about you to them. You will not be harmed."

Shoulder to shoulder, they went on down the path,

soon stepping out into an open clearing on the bank of another creek. Troy stared. There was no great village bustle. No running children or squaws chasing after them. No noble warriors guarding the outskirts of the village. No rows and rows of ridge pole lodges or stretched hides tanning in the sun.

There were five or six lodges. Two children played by the creek's edge with a pile of stones. A few skinny dogs sniffed around as if for food. Some adults, men and women, moving about. The scene was quiet other than the sound of the flowing water.

Mitsrii glanced at Troy and Troy quickly closed his mouth. They walked together toward the village that was not a village. One dog barked. The others rushed forward.

"*Quiet,*" Mitsrii said. Silence fell as the dogs sniffed around his legs. They seemed much more interested in sniffing at Troy than they were with Mitsrii. Two jumped away from him, hackles raised.

Troy looked at Mitsrii. "This is your village?"

Mitsrii nodded.

"I thought you went to Moosehide. I thought all Häns around here had been relocated to Moosehide when the miners came."

Mitsrii's eyes flashed, though he said nothing.

The barks of the dogs had brought the rest of the camp out to see them. The children jumped up from their play. Men and women approached. The nearest man reached for something leaning against the ridge pole lodge closest to him and, in the next second, Troy found a rifle aimed into his face from twenty yards away. His stomach leaped, weightless. He wanted to reach out and grab Mitsrii's arm but did not.

Mitsrii held up his hand. "He's here at my invitation."

"Why's that?" The man pointing the rifle snarled, not lowering the weapon.

The children had stopped in their tracks. The others also stood still, watching in silence. Four men and three women, in all.

"He is my friend," Mitsrii said.

Troy resisted the urge to look at him.

"He saved my life." Mitsrii glanced around at them as he spoke. "He speaks our language and he wanted to meet you."

There was some softening of expressions and Troy felt the tension level lower, though the rifle remained raised. Despite Mitsrii's warnings, Troy felt startled by the hostility of the villagers. He had found most dealings with natives in and around Dawson to be unremarkable, and the people, if not friendly, had never been aggressive either.

One of the men, not the one holding the rifle, said, "He's bringing the white man's plague back to us. Get him away from here."

"Yes," a woman said. "Please, Mitsrii. We've lost so many." Her eyes filled with tears as she spoke.

Troy glanced around the tiny village and felt a sudden rush of sick horror that had nothing to do with his own predicament.

"*No.*" Mitsrii spoke with conviction, the single word like an order. "He carries no sickness. He is our guest."

The man who had spoken shook his head in obvious

irritation. But the rest of the group seemed to be considering the matter closed. One of the women turned away to a cooking fire she had been tending a moment before. The man with the rifle lowered it, though slowly.

Troy took in a deep breath and held it for a moment. "How many were in your group before the plague came? When you still lived on the Yukon River?"

Mitsrii did not return his gaze. "Over forty."

Troy looked away. He had heard that Indians had no resistance to outside diseases. That was all. Nothing about the this kind of devastation.

Two men greeted Mitsrii and Mitsrii introduced them to Troy, who nodded and told them he was grateful to be able to see their village and speak with them. Then the women offered Mitsrii and Troy both cooked salmon and some leafy plant with a bitter taste he did not recognize. He was ravenous after days of little food and endless walking and ate everything they put before him.

They seemed amazed by his skill with their language and had many questions for him about what white men were doing. Why did they care so deeply for yellow rocks? Why did they blow up the land? Why did they kill animals without reason? Why did they want to take Hän children away to be taught in their own schools? Troy found himself faltering, unsure of answers to many of their questions. They did not seem angry, only genuinely confused, which made him feel worse. By the time he was done eating, he wished Mitsrii had not brought him. He could feel Mitsrii's gaze but avoided returning it.

The children stared at Troy with wide eyes while they hid behind Mitsrii.

"Are they yours?" Troy asked Mitsrii.

Mitsrii shook his head. "Their father was my brother. Both their parents are dead."

"I am sorry."

"For what?"

"For your loss."

Mitsrii looked uncertain and Troy knew he was not using the words right. Apologizing for a death did not make sense to Mitsrii. Unless Troy himself had caused the death and was apologizing for his actions.

Troy shook his head. "I feel bad that you have lost so much from the sickness."

Mitsrii nodded. "You shouldn't feel bad. You didn't bring it about."

"I thought all white—" Troy stopped abruptly. "Never mind."

Mitsrii looked at him.

One of the women stepped up to them with more fish. She seemed delighted by how much he was eating. After thanking her, Troy glanced at Mitsrii, who was holding a piece of salmon out to a black and white dog.

"Are . . . do you?" Troy struggled for the correct word as he looked across the fire toward the women, then back at Mitsrii.

Mitsrii followed his gaze. "No. There are only three women left, and seven men."

"Seven? Where are the other two?"

"Hunting."

Another woman approached him. "Would you like to

see the blankets?" They had already discussed things the Hän made.

Troy nodded. "Thank you."

He followed her to one of the lodges. She was little more than a girl, fifteen at the oldest. She seemed almost to glow with her eagerness as she showed him her treasures. Troy guessed she did not get many visitors. The lodge was the size of a large canvas tent, constructed of long poles forming an A-frame, with animal skins covering the poles.

Troy had to bend doubled to enter, then found he could not straighten up much more even once inside. He knelt as the young woman also dropped to her knees by what was clearly a bed. She ran her hand along a colorful blanket. It was incredibly detailed, with a vast interchanging color palate. More beautiful than any quilt he had ever seen, the blanket seemed almost alive with its complexity and vivid hues.

"It is wonderful. Did you make this?" he asked.

She ducked her head as her face flushed. She turned to a wooden box on the floor and pulled out another, smaller blanket. It looked very old and worn but was no less stunning.

"My grandmother made this. She taught me."

"She was a very good teacher," he said, glancing back at the bed.

She looked away, smiling so hard she pressed her lips together to try and stop it.

"And the baskets?" he asked. There was a row of them by the entrance, all different sizes.

She nodded as she folded the blanket back into the box. "My mother made those."

He picked one up at her invitation, studying the delicate yet strong work of the weave. It was made of birchbark strips so thin and fine the thing he held hardly resembled a basket, but rather a solid box with no lid. A lump came into his throat as he set the basket back on the ground. The people who had made these things were dead. He turned to look at the young woman behind him, smiling at him. He wanted to hug her and apologize over and over. Instead, he nodded and said, "Thank you very much for showing me these things. They are all beautiful."

She gave him a dazzling smile before they left the lodge together. Troy looked around for Mitsrii as soon as they emerged. He saw him in the same spot by the fire. He was talking with one of the other men. The same one who had been aiming a rifle into Troy's face not long ago. Troy approached slowly. Mitsrii looked up at him and smiled. Troy was startled. He wondered for a moment if he had a chunk of that leafy plant stuck in his teeth. But he had his mouth closed. What was it about his appearance Mitsrii found amusing? Or was it amusement? The smile was not a laughing one but a sincere one. As though he was pleased to see Troy, rather than that he found the sight of him comical. Troy frowned. That couldn't be right.

"What's wrong?" Mitsrii asked, his smile faltering.

"Nothing. Should we be going?"

"Going?"

"Back to Dawson."

"I didn't realize you wanted to be back tonight."

"I am not trying to rush back. I thought you wanted to

get me back. You kept saying that." He added the last with an accusatory note he could not quite hold back.

Mitsrii gazed up at him. "You can stay with us tonight and I'll take you back in the morning. We are half a day from Dawson."

Troy wondered what "us" meant. Where exactly would he be sleeping? But he did not ask.

Two young hunters returned to the village a short while later. Another moment of tension spiked then ebbed, while Mitsrii explained Troy's presence to them. Troy spent the remainder of the evening learning as much as he could about what these people did. How they lived and what they made. What tools they used and how they hunted. Some remained cool to him, but mostly they were accommodating. One of the hunters explained at length how he made his arrows. Troy was startled to realize they still used bow and arrows. But he did not question.

For half an hour, he watched one of the women weaving a birchbark basket, mesmerized by every movement of her fingers. She sang while she worked, her voice rising and falling in rhythm with her weaving as her song spoke of the phases of the moon and migrations of caribou and geese. When her song finished, a man told a story of his shaman grandmother who foretold weather two weeks away and always knew if a hunt had been successful before the hunters returned home.

The sun had been perched at the edge of the world for at least an hour when Troy closed his eyes in exhaustion. A hand touched his shoulder and he gave a start. Mitsrii's laugh drifted softly beside his ear.

"You did not frighten me." Troy glared at him. "Just tired."

"Go to bed," Mitsrii said.

Troy followed him to one of the lodges. When he ducked inside, Mitsrii did not follow, but left him alone. Troy wondered if he would have the place to himself. The interior held a bow, arrows, a rifle, blankets, furs, and various other items. Troy gazed at the rifle as he settled on the hard bed, which rested on the ground. Why did Mitsrii not carry a rifle? He had one with him the day he'd shot the man on the hilltop. Troy yawned, making a mental note to ask him. Troy's own rifle had been taken by his would-be guides.

He rubbed his eyes and pulled his shirt off over his head. With boots, socks, and pants removed, he stacked them on the floor at the foot of the bed then slid back to the top so he could pull the colorful blanket over himself. A full stomach, combined with four days of travel with little sleep, left him so tired he did not have time to wonder any longer about sleeping arrangements.

He awoke some time later, aware of heavy breathing beside him. He knew it was Mitsrii without having to think about it. The inside of the lodge was dim. Perhaps the sun was now below the edge of a mountain peak. Making the time two in the morning . . . or perhaps three?

Why was his heart racing as though he'd just seen another grizzly? He closed his eyes, willing himself back to sleep. And to think about the sun. Or the time. Or trains. Trains had always fascinated him. He pictured a steam engine in his mind. Huge and powerful, gleaming in the light of that damned endless sun. Why couldn't he relax? Trains, *trains*, what did he know about trains? He knew all kinds of things about trains. Things about steam and . . . and . . . what else?

Think of something else. French. He could speak such good French, he could pass for a native to anyone not paying too close attention. But French was easy. He'd practically picked up French in his sleep. Dutch was easy too. The Indian languages, now those had been a challenge. So different, so intriguing. So . . . worthwhile.

Troy's eyes open in the same instant he turned his head. Mitsrii lay beside him in the gloomy tent-like lodge, with his back toward Troy. The urge to press his hand against the back, or even run a hand around to the other man's chest, pulling the two of them close together, made Troy feel as though some external force was trying to bend him to action. His heart beat fast in his throat, making his breath come short. Sweat broke out on his brow. He twisted away, rolling onto his side to face the poles of the wall. He wanted to get up and run. It did not matter where, just run — anything physical — and away from here. He clutched the edge of the blanket with both hands, gritting his teeth together with his eyes closed tight, as if waiting for a wave of nausea to pass.

The sleep that had found him so easily before was slow in returning. He lay awake for another hour or more, staring at the poles until the outside light began to increase. At last, his own exhaustion forced stillness over his racing mind. He fell asleep still gripping the blanket.

* * * * *

When Troy awoke again, he was alone in the lodge. The sun hit the outside, heating the inside and making his mouth feel as dry as the baking hide wall. He could hear the children running and laughing and could smell cooking fires.

He had just pulled on his clothes and boots when Mitsrii ducked through the doorway. Troy was once more startled to see the other man was smiling at him. He tried a weak smile in return but heat returned to his face, and he ended up looking away.

Mitsrii handed Troy a small wooden box. "I thought you might want this. Then come have breakfast and we'll start out."

Troy nodded mutely. He opened the box to see a straight razor, brush, and tiny mirror. He looked up. "Where did you get this?"

Mitsrii, who had turned to leave, looked back at him. He cocked his head to the side. "I killed the man who used to own it."

Troy glanced at the box, then back at him.

Mitsrii chuckled. "My people have been trading with white men for many, many years. Long before men crowded their way into our land for gold." He glanced at the rifle, propped by the front of the lodge. "Did you think we made those ourselves while we tanned hides?"

"So that was a joke? You made a joke?" Troy laughed. He felt giddy and his palms were damp with sweat. He shook his head, trying to clear it.

"It belonged to the husband of my mother's sister," Mitsrii said.

"He . . . was a white man?"

"Yes."

"Is that . . . accepted by your people?"

Mitsrii glanced out the opening toward the village. His smile had grown sad. "Perhaps not so much now as it was then." He stepped outside, leaving Troy gazing at the little box.

Half an hour later Troy was finishing his meal— a piece of hot salmon and a handful of the best strawberries he had ever eaten—with the women and some of the men. He felt refreshed and more able to focus after walking downstream to wash and shave as well as he could. The razor had been so sharp it went a long way to clearing his mind just to hold it near his throat.

One of the women sat to his left, stitching a soft hide moccasin for one of the children, chatting away about her own mother teaching her to tan skins. He listened fixedly, as enthralled by her work as he had been by the weaving.

Once more, Mitsrii's hand was on his shoulder. He turned. Mitsrii had a rifle slug across his back.

"Time to go," he said. "Time for you to learn a new language."

Troy stared at him. The electric current he felt surging from Mitsrii's hand, through his own shoulder and down his back left him momentarily silent, unable to get his throat working. After a pause, he nodded.

As they prepared to leave, the young woman who had shown him her blankets and baskets ran out of her lodge with a blanket in her arms. It was small, mostly red and blue, neatly folded. She held it out for him, eyes bright as she smiled.

"This is for you, Troy Karlson," she said. "Safe journey home."

The two other women stood behind her, nodding and smiling.

"I could never take that—" Troy started. Out of the corner of his eye he noticed Mitsrii shooting him a glare. He reached out for the blanket. "Thank you. Thank you so much. You are very kind."

"Thank you for visiting us, Troy Karlson."

He smiled and thanked the rest of them for sharing their stories and food with him. Then Mitsrii turned and walked away downriver. Troy followed.

"Mitsrii?"

"Hmm?"

"Do you ever wave?"

"Wave? Like water?"

"No, wave goodbye with your hand."

Mitsrii looked sideways at him as they walked. Troy demonstrated a wave of his hand. Mitsrii frowned. "What does it mean?"

"It means goodbye. I used to wave to my mother every morning when I walked to school."

Mitsrii shook his head. "You should not look back when you walk away from someone you love."

"Why?"

"You should only be looking forward."

"Where I come from, waving . . . shows you care

about someone. You wish you did not have to leave them. It is like saying goodbye, only from a distance." Troy could tell he was not selling the idea to Mitsrii. He sighed and said, "Why do you have a rifle now?"

"We will be near dangerous predators today."

"Dangerous predators? What did you call that bear yesterday?"

"Mother, teacher, protector." Mitsrii looked at him again.

Troy did not meet his gaze. They walked east until the sun was well overhead. Troy was becoming more and more aware they were not heading for Dawson, which lay to the south, but he made no comment. They dropped into a scrubby forest before midday. Mitsrii's steps grew slow and cautious. Troy imitated him as well as he could. He heard the soft canine sounds of whining and yipping a moment later and knew where they were going.

The wolf den was tucked beneath a tangle of two fallen trees with their numerous limbs twisted together for added shelter. Scattered through the clearing in front of the den were four adult gray wolves, all curled in sleep, except for one. He had his head up as three puppies leaped about him, licking his face, biting at his toes, springing back then in again. He kept turning his head as though bothered by flies, mouth open and ears down to the sides in a relaxed position.

Mitsrii sat down softly at the side of a tree and seemed almost to merge with it. He was gazing toward the wolf den with the rapt expression of someone seeing a miracle unfold before him—unsmiling, yet emanating contentment.

"Sit down. Tell me what they're saying."

Troy sat, realizing only after he did so, he was unafraid of the wolves. The ground sloped gradually away and down toward the pack, sixty or seventy feet away. He leaned forward to watch them, his elbows on his crossed knees.

"Is that the father?" Troy whispered.

"No. That's their brother and the lowest of the pack."

"Why does he not snap at them? He looks like they are keeping him from sleep."

"He would never hurt them. Young are precious to every member of the pack."

Another adult, much larger than the one with the pups, lifted his head and sniffed the breeze. His ears twisted this way and that as his nostrils quivered.

Troy looked sideways at Mitsrii. "You tell me what they are saying. I would like to start learning that new language you promised."

Mitsrii did not answer while the large wolf first sat up on his haunches, then stood and stretched. The other three adults turned their heads to look at him. Then, one by one, they got to their feet and walked toward him.

"See how they carry their bodies?" Mitsrii asked. "They keep lower than him in respect. Their ears and tails stay down to tell him they look up to him. While he is calm, they are calm. While he is alarmed, they are alarmed."

"Would they attack us if they knew we were here?" Troy asked. "Or run and hide?"

Mitsrii shook his head. "They know we're here."

"What? Not one has looked our way. We are

downwind of them."

"They know. Look at the ears of the leader."

Troy looked. The huge, gray wolf stood sideways to the two men, head up and ears up. Allowing his family to lick his lower jaw and grovel before him as if he were an emperor. The far ear faced forward. The near one twisted in the direction of Mitsrii and Troy.

"He is listening to us?" Troy asked.

"He's saying 'I know you're there, but you do not worry me. I will stay alert in case you do anything you shouldn't though'."

"He is saying all that?"

"Yes."

"With one ear?"

"Yes."

Leaning back so he was sitting upright, Troy turned to look at Mitsrii. When Mitsrii returned the gaze, their faces were only a few inches apart. Troy saw in a flash, like a sudden ray of sun breaking through clouds, his own hand reaching up to touch Mitsrii's face and to pull them together.

His whole body felt charged with heat and pounding blood, which surged through his vanes like a million tiny locomotives, leaving him feeling dazed and light-headed.

The vision disappeared as he realized Mitsrii's expression had changed. He looked concerned, was frowning slightly.

"Troy? Are you all right? Are you listening?"

"Yes," Troy said quickly. He looked back toward the wolves. His name. The sound of his own name falling from Mitsrii's lips made him dizzy. He pulled the colorful blanket off of his shoulder, where he had been carrying it, and laid it across his lap as he uncrossed his legs.

Mitsrii was looking at the wolves but glanced at Troy again. "Are you cold?"

"No."

Mitsrii waited. Troy said nothing else. Mitsrii returned his attention to the wolves.

They stayed at their vantage overlooking the wolf den for nearly an hour while the pack moved about, played, and "spoke" to each other. Three of the four adults had gone, sliding away at a smooth, gliding trot, leaving the low-ranking male to babysit the pups before Mitsrii and Troy stood to leave. Troy moved as quietly as he could away from the den. He was unable to keep his eyes on the trail for watching Mitsrii walking in front of him. When Mitsrii stopped and turned in one motion to shush his noisy twig snapping, Troy nearly walked into him. He brought himself up short, fighting not to go on ahead and act as though the contact had been a mistake.

His eyes stayed fixed on Mitsrii's shoulders shifting under the supple leather shirt as they made their way out of the wolves' forest, heading west. He could not touch those shoulders. Could not even try it. Never. What would Mitsrii think of him? What did Mitsrii's culture think of such a thing? Troy had no idea. He did not know a word in the Hän language for what he was thinking and feeling. He did not know if there was none, or if he had simply never learned it.

His mind flitted to the wolf family. They had been so gentle with each other. So loving. Using their bodies to communicate in incredibly complex ways that Mitsrii understood. Every movement, every ear turn and tail twitch and eye shift. He read them as clearly as if they were speaking aloud. Did he read Troy as well? Did he understand what Troy was feeling for him? Last night, when Troy returned to the fire, Mitsrii had looked up and smiled to see him. Not smiled about something he said or did, or something someone else had done. Just to see *him*.

Troy's pulse quickened as he took in the shining black hair that fell past Mitsrii's shoulders. He wished he could feel it between his fingers. A reckless rush of emotion swept through him and he darted forward. He had to say something—do something. He did not know what, but he had to act. He felt as though his body were about to rip itself apart.

His eyes were fixed on Mitsrii's hair as he threw himself forward for some speech or action he had not predetermined. His right foot came down hard on open air. His center of gravity was thrown off in an instant as he launched sideways and down through a wooded ravine. Earth was sky and sky was Earth as he spun over and over, sticks and branches tearing at him, his own arms flailing to stop him without success. His shoulder crashed against the trunk of a birch tree. His back slammed into a fir, spinning him around so his feet faced down the slope, knocking all the breath from his body. And still he slid and rolled on until the slope leveled out and he rolled to a stop, fighting to inhale, spitting and gagging the dirt out of his mouth, clutching his chest as he gasped.

He had nearly caught his breath and was trying to sit up and assess the damage when Mitsrii stepped up next to him and knelt. Troy did not look at him, knowing his own face was burning. He was acutely aware of the carelessness and stupidity of what he had just done. The path they had been following was wide enough for two horses to walk abreast.

Mitsrii said nothing for a moment, watching Troy brush off dirt and spit it from his mouth as he sat upright. Then he said, "This was a faster trail than the one we were taking, but I could have shown you how to come down better."

Troy glanced up sharply at him. Miatsrii's expression was blank. Troy looked away, clenching his fists. He tried to struggle to his feet, but he had not recovered his breath. His ribs ached, his head spun, and he ended up sitting back.

"Are you hurt?" Mitsrii asked, still kneeling beside him.

"No." He hated having to sit there being patronized and talked down to like a toddler who tripped and fell into a ditch after being warned about going too near.

Mitsrii reached out to touch his arm.

Troy jerked away. "*I am fine.*"

Mitsrii lowered his hand. Troy pulled his shirt off over his head and shook the dirt off. He used the inside of it to wipe the rest of the dirt and debris from his face and hair. He shook the shirt out again before pulling it back on, feeling ready for another try at getting to his feet.

Stupid, he thought, *incredibly stupid.* He rolled away from Mitsrii to push himself to his knees. He used a tree for support as he stood. Mitsrii stepped quickly to his side, taking his elbow in one hand to help him.

"Stop it!" Troy shouted, recoiling. "Why do you treat me like a child? I made one mistake. I am fine. *Fine.*"

"If you've made only one mistake, you've lived a remarkable life," Mitsrii said.

Troy turned his head to look into the serious, dark eyes and found their faces very close. He moved forward, lifting his hands at the same moment to grab Mitsrii's head. He pressed his mouth against the mouth of the other man so forcefully Mitsrii stepped back in order to keep his balance. Troy opened his mouth to push his tongue against Mitsrii's lips and between his teeth until he felt Mitsrii's tongue against his own. The unyielding reality of teeth made the kiss painful, yet all the more intensely satisfying. Arousal flared through his body so fast and powerful he felt as though he would climax right then. But he wanted more — needed more, with a fierce desperation like a drowning man fighting toward the surface of a lake.

He had to get his own pants down — was nearly in a panic to — but he was just as panicked by the thought of releasing Mitsrii. What if that broke the spell? What if Mitsrii would not let Troy touch him again? Then Troy felt something incredible: Mitsrii's hands touching him, running down his stomach to his belt. A rushing sound like a waterfall filled Troy's ears, blotting out all sound, bird and insect and rustle of leaves.

By the time Mitsrii had the belt buckle undone, all of Troy's fears vanished. He dropped his hands to Mitsrii's waist, pulling franticly at a tied cord, feeling both their erections through their pants, aware he himself was wet with pre-cum. Troy moved with the blind speed of someone at the losing end of a life and death relay as he undid the knot. He was so hard it was painful, or perhaps it was only his own desperation giving him the illusion of pain.

The sensation of Mitsrii's hand on him made him for an instant feel that he might pass out. When he reciprocated the gesture, Mitsrii pushed him back against the tree he had leaned on a moment earlier, forcing their bodies together while Troy moaned into his mouth. Troy reached one hand up to wrap around Mitsrii's neck, pulling them as close as possible. With his other hand he tried to encircle both their cocks, but could only cover Mitsrii's hand with his own.

He wanted this to be forever — wanted the feelings to last and last — leaving him in unending bliss. Yet his arousal was pitched so high to begin with, he could last only seconds before he released. He had not known there was such power and pleasure in his own body as he thrust forward into Mitsrii's hand and groin. He gasped and swore in English against Mitsrii's throat as waves of ecstasy took him outside himself.

The world drifted very slowly back into focus. So slow, it seemed almost to move backwards. Birds hopped from limb to limb in the wrong direction. The sun went the wrong way in the sky. Leaves fell upwards, from ground to tree.

Troy lay on his back on the forest floor, watching the leaves of an aspen wave gently in the breeze. Sunlight caught them, making them sparkle with light and dark while they danced and shifted and seemed to laugh. Troy chuckled at them. They were so beautiful — everything was beautiful — the tree, the sun, the color of the leaves, the forest, the birds, the world.

"Troy?"

He turned his head to look at Mitsrii, standing over him. He had just walked back down the slope, having gone up it to gather Troy's sleeping blanket and the one given to him in the village, which had both left him in the fall.

"We should be moving on," Mitsrii said. "You need to go home."

It took a long time for the words to make sense in Troy's mind. "Home" seemed unfamiliar for a moment and he had to think about it.

"To Dawson?"

"Yes."

Troy smiled. "I do not want to go back."

Mitsrii frowned at him and walked away, shaking out the blankets.

Troy rolled over and scrambled to his feet, rushing to catch him. "Mitsrii, wait. I mean it. Why should I go back there?"

"That's where you belong." Mitsrii did not look

around.

"I am not sure I do."

"What about your work for the government?"

"What about it? I can still do it. Could I come back to your village with you? If you teach me the trail, I can go in to Dawson to make my reports."

Mitsrii shook his head. "In another day or two my village won't be there anymore."

"*What?*" Troy felt his muscles tense in shock, his happiness fading away like rain into soft ground. "What do you mean *not be there?*"

"We're leaving this land. We can't stay here anymore. While some of us still live, we're going as far from your towns as we can. My brother and sister and parents, and their brothers and sisters, and all their children, are dead. Those left in the village are strong enough to travel. We've known for a long time we would be moving on."

"Why had you not told me you were leaving?"

Mitsrii looked at him. "I hadn't realized I needed to."

*****

Mitsrii stood on a hill north of the mining camps, gazing out at an endless landscape of mud and trenches, cabins and tents, huge piles of dug up earth, thin wooden structures like elevated, manmade snakes winding among it all. Men swarmed through the black mud and creeks like ants, picks or pans in hand, stretching for miles and miles, farther than he could see.

Mitsrii felt Troy's eyes on him and quickly turned away from the scene, a muscle working in his jaw.

"I am so sorry," Troy said softly.

Why did he offer apologies when he had done nothing wrong? Mitsrii handed him the blanket he had been carrying.

"Come into town with me," Troy said. "Please."

Mitsrii shook his head.

"No one will pay any attention to you. You will not be home until the middle of the night if you start back now."

Mitsrii looked north. What could he say to this man

who seemed both to understand him and yet, to be woefully ignorant? He turned to face Troy, looking into his eyes, and knew how Troy felt when he was always apologizing. Troy must have seen the regret mirrored in Mitsrii's eyes because he dropped his own gaze to the ground between them.

"I will miss you," Troy whispered.

Mitsrii lifted his hand to Troy's face and tilted his chin back with two fingers. Their gazes met once more.

"I'll miss you too. I'm glad I met you, Troy."

Troy closed his eyes. "Please come with me. You can stay the night before you have to go back. I have a room at the Green Tree Hotel. No one—" he stopped abruptly and swallowed.

Mitsrii lowered his hand. "Goodbye."

Troy nodded as though unable to speak, then turned and walked toward the mudflats. Mitsrii watched him for a long time before raising his own hand and waving. Troy did not look back.

Mitsrii sat at the top of the hill looking out through

the wildflower valley. Only a few bones were left of the young wolf. He sat without moving until the sun was low, feeling as though someone had died all over again. This time without the aid of a plague or bullet, but no less gone. His body ached and he found it difficult to get his breath, as though he had fallen from a great height.

* * * * *

Troy lay awake in the darkness of his hotel room, images of the last few days racing through his mind. He felt as though he had been struck a mortal blow. He had learned so much. Had so much he could report. But he did not care anymore. They wanted information on the Indians in the same way they wanted information on the wild animals of the Yukon. Troy had leaped at the chance because it sounded like an adventure, not because he had even the slightest idea of what he was getting into. To the people he worked for, he was a biologist, not an ambassador. It had not bothered him before. It could not bother him, since he had given the matter no thought. Now everything had changed. The world had changed.

The hours crawled by without him feeling any closer to sleep or any less stricken. He had never felt like this about anyone in his life and could not stop thinking of his own loss.

There were footsteps in the hall, then a tentative knock at the door. "Mr. Karlson?" a woman's voice called out softly. She was one of the assistants working for the proprietor, "Arkansas" Jim Hall, a Bonanza king who had only recently put the finishing touches on this handsome, two-story hotel.

Troy closed his eyes, wishing she would go away. Not tonight. He could not go out and translate for someone tonight. There was another soft tap. He sighed and rolled off the bed, still dressed from the day, with the exception of his boots. The room was nearly dark since the Green Tree featured the luxury of heavy, dark curtains to block out the midnight sun. Troy switched on the single electric light before opening the door.

"Good evening, Miss Scott."

"Mr. Karlson, I'm terribly sorry to bother you, but there's an Indian downstairs. He knows your name, but not a word of English—"

Troy rushed past her, into the hall and down the steps, pulse racing. He could see into the lobby from the landing and stopped. Mitsrii stood at the bottom of the steps, looking up at him. Troy's mind reeled. He could not get his breath. Miss Scott stood behind him, watching. He was terrified she would be able to see through his reaction.

"Yes," Troy said in English, turning to the slender woman who now stood at his elbow. "Thank you very much. I know him." He beckoned to Mitsrii. "We have . . . much to . . . discuss."

"Would you two like a drink?" Miss Scott asked.

"No. Thank you. We're . . . uh, fine."

She nodded. "Very well. Just give a shout if you need anything."

"Of course." Troy walked as fast as he could back up the stairs and down the hall without running. He knew

Mitsrii was behind him, though the other man's footfalls made no sound on the wooden floor. What if something had happened? Was Mitsrii here for him, or had he come back for some other reason? Did he need help? Did he need to talk to Troy about something important?

Troy stepped into his room. As soon as Mitsrii moved across the threshold, Troy shut and locked the door, moving forward against the other man, kissing him. He held Mitsrii's face with both hands before sliding his fingers around to the back of his neck as he lowered his head to press his mouth against Mitsrii's neck.

"Why did you come here?" Troy whispered against Mitsrii's skin, barely remembering to speak Hän.

"I couldn't keep walking away from you," Mitsrii said.

Troy pulled away to stare into his eyes.

Mitsrii was smiling at him, but the smile faded as he returned Troy's gaze. "What's wrong?"

Troy shook his head. "That may be the nicest thing anyone has ever said to me."

Mitsrii leaned forward to kiss him.

Troy tried not to think this was his last night with Mitsrii as they lay together on the small bed. They were gentle as they kissed each other and caressed one another's bodies. This time, they both wanted to move slowly, so slowly they would never stop being together.

After hovering above the horizon throughout the midnight hours, the sun had begun the journey upward through the sky when Troy found himself drifting unwillingly into sleep. He pressed his head against Mitsrii's bare chest as Mitsrii's arms pulled him close. He could hear Mitsrii's heartbeat and the breath filling and leaving his lungs.

A tangle of thoughts and feelings warred within him. So many, he could not process all of them. He had to speak them, had to talk to Mitsrii about them. But he could not find his voice. He, who knew words in a way few other people in the world did, could not find the ones he needed—not in any language. At last, after almost starting to speak several times, Troy closed his eyes. A single tear ran down his face.

When he awoke, it was to feel Mitsrii's fingers delicately brushing through his hair.

Troy whispered, "Please . . . do not leave."

Mitsrii kissed his forehead.

"I want to come with you."

"No," Mitsrii said. "Your life is here. What about your work? I don't know where my family will go, but you might not be very welcome by others on our way."

"Then you stay here."

"In Dawson?" His tone held disgust.

"We could build a cabin—live out in the hills together."

"I won't leave my family. They need me. They need every hunter they have if we are to have any chance at survival."

Some time later, Mitsrii told him it was time to go. The morning rushed past in the blink of an eye. A moment later, Troy found himself walking out of the Green Tree's front door with Mitsrii. In another half second, they were on the other side of the mining camps and a mile from town.

Troy looked down at his muddy boots as he walked along beside Mitsrii. Neither of them spoke. It was midday when they passed the outskirts of the camps and the countryside became truly wild. They stopped on the south side of one of the many streams running toward the Yukon River and looked at each other.

"Stay," Troy whispered.

"I can't."

"Please."

Mitsrii looked into his eyes and Troy saw his own grief reflected in them.

A man chuckled behind him and someone spoke in English, "Now isn't that just the sweetest thing?"

Troy spun around. Three men were walking toward them. The oldest, whose dark hair and mustache were streaked in gray, aimed a revolver at Mitsrii.

"Saying your last farewells to your Indian pal?" The man asked Troy. "You should, 'cause in a minute you're going to be out of time, and he's going to be in hell where he belongs."

Troy started forward. In a flash, the revolver was aimed at him instead.

"You want to go there with him? That can be arranged."

"You wouldn't dare," Troy snarled.

The other two men laughed.

The first one smiled. "Wouldn't I? You don't think I would kill the man who made sure the sergeant let my brother's murderer walk free? You think I would hesitate to kill you both and throw your bodies in the river?"

"You've got too much to lose, Riley. How much did you two haul in this spring on your claim? Fifty thousand? A hundred? You think the Northwest Police will let you walk out of here with that after you've murdered two people?"

"*People?*" Riley's voice rose to a shout. "Two *people?* You think the wild animal beside you is a person?" Riley turned his head and spat at Mitsrii.

Troy threw himself at Riley, hardly aware of the gun shot ringing in his ear or of the chaos erupting around him.

He had to hurt this man, had to make him suffer. He did not care what else happened. There was another explosion near his face. Troy seized Riley's right hand in both of his, twisting at the fingers as hard as he could to get the weapon out of the other man's grasp.

Another shot rang out, but not from the gun he was fighting for. Riley's fist came up and smashed into the side of Troy's jaw, knocking him sideways. With a final jerk, Troy pulled the gun free. He spun, aiming it for the source of the last shot. Stanton was standing only five feet from him, his own revolver aimed at Mitsrii, who had just thrown the third man to the ground. Troy sighted for the man's arm. He pulled the trigger as he was punched in the head by Riley. The bullet hit the revolver itself and the weapon flew out of Stanton's hand. Troy did not see what happened next, having been thrown to the ground from the force of the blow.

He jerked the revolver up as Riley lunged for him, smashing metal into Riley's nose. Riley fell back, clutching his face as Mitsrii grabbed Troy's arms from behind, pulling him to his feet. Troy was shaking violently from head to toe as he pointed the revolver into Riley's blood-streaked face.

"Go," he said in a strangled voice. "Now, or I'll kill you."

Riley carefully got to his feet, lifting his hands to shoulder height, his eyes blazed with hatred. Stanton was already retreating, walking backward as to watch them. Eugene was apparently unconscious. Then, as quickly as they had come, they were gone, Riley and Stanton hurrying back up the hill they had just descended, toward the camps.

Still shaking, Troy turned to face Mitsrii. "You have to go," he said in Hän.

Mitsrii was looking at Troy's arm. "You're hurt."

Troy glanced down. Blood had soaked through his sleeve over an area of several inches, just above his elbow. He was stunned to see it.

"No. I am fine. I had not even realized . . . . Go."

Mitsrii reached for the arm. "We should stop the bleeding."

"No!" Troy jerked the arm away. "Go! They could be

back after you with more men and rifles at any minute. I will not let them kill you."

"You need to—"

"*Go. Now.*"

Mitsrii looked at him. "You're not a coward, Troy."

Troy let out a short laugh that was half sob. "Please, go home and help your family. Go as far from here as you can."

Mitsrii leaned toward him, kissed Troy on the forehead, then turned and stepped across the stream. On the other side, he broke into a swift, effortless run, his feet making no sound on the mossy earth.

*****

Mitsrii paused at the top of a hill to look back and assure himself the two children were keeping up. One was so small she was being carried much of the time. The other was large enough to have his own tiny pack and carry his share like the rest of them—including the dogs, who all wore packs on their backs filled with thirty to forty pounds of tools and blankets apiece.

Mitsrii waited until the little boy and girl were past him, then the woman behind them. He stood on the trail for a long time, looking down it as though he would see more stragglers, though he knew there were none. One of the dogs stood beside him. His brother's dog, a large, black and white animal with a thick ruff and long, straight, strong legs. She was both the best sled dog and best pack dog of the group. Mitsrii reached down to touch her head and the dog looked up at him. He did not pat or stroke her, only touched her head, then moved on with the dog walking by his side.

They made camp later that evening, under a bright sun in an open valley. They fed themselves and the dogs then rolled out sleeping skins.

Mitsrii sat on a slope, well above the camp, with the black and white dog lying at his feet. He felt so intensely alone he wanted to weep. But he sat and gazed at the camp, fixing his mind on what had to be done over the next few days — mentally mapping the trails they needed to take and the game they needed to find in the course of their travel to keep them all alive. The dog lifted her head and Mitsrii's heart leaped. With a sudden flood of excitement, he looked in the direction the dog was looking. A tiny bird had landed on the slope fifty feet away.

Mitsrii turned back to gaze down into the valley. He closed his eyes and took several slow breaths.

When he at last got up and walked down to join the others, the dog followed him. He felt a rush of annoyance at her closeness. He turned to face her, glaring into her eyes. She froze, averting her gaze. He walked on to his blankets, wishing he had not stopped her.

Mitsrii lay on his back, watching cloud shapes in a brilliant blue sky. The dog, now lying on her stomach twenty feet from him, lifted her head, looking toward the hills and the trails they had arrived on. Mitsrii avoided glancing at her, though he saw the movement out of the corner of his eye. She stood, and he heard her growl. The other dogs were alert now, all standing, all looking. Mitsrii, along with two of the other men, sat up to look in the direction all the dogs now faced.

A man walked toward them from the foot of the hills, coming out of the trail they had taken. He was indistinct; a tiny figure in the far distance. Mitsrii threw back the blanket from over his lap. He ran, barefoot, across the valley so fast the ground beneath him was blurred.

He could see Troy watching him as he approached, though Troy did not run forward himself. He limped and one arm was in a sling. He appeared exhausted as he moved forward in the fastest walk he could manage.

It seemed to take a season to reach him—an eternity. Then Mitsrii was right in front of him, pulling him into a crushing hug. When he turned his head to kiss Troy, Troy pushed him away.

"They can see us."

"They can't tell what we're doing." Mitsrii was panting. "Too far away. How did you find us?"

"I have been trailing you." Troy made a face. "As well as I could. I believe I took the long way. Twisted my ankle falling down another ridge."

"Why did you come? What about your work?"

"I went to Moosehide. Chief Isaac has tried to protect your songs and traditions by sending them for others to keep in the west. I took his story, and yours, to Sergeant Reyes. He will pass along my report. I gave him the blanket. I . . . ." Troy trailed off, biting his lip. "I do not know if anything will be done. They need to know how much damage they are doing. I just . . . do not think the government is going to do anything to help. But Sergeant Reyes is a good man."

Troy's expression was so pained, Mitsrii knew he was not saying everything he really thought about what the white men and their government would or would not do based on his report.

"It's not your fault," Mitsrii said, and Troy looked away. "Thank you." Mitsrii reached up to touch his cheek.

"I have a favor to ask you," Troy said. "I believe you are once again in my debt." He nodded to his own injured arm.

Mitsrii cocked his head and smiled. "What is it you

want?"

"Take me with you. I will do anything you say — hide anytime we run into tribes that might be . . . unfriendly toward me — pretend to be your prisoner — help you if you do have to deal with white men. Please — "

Mitsrii shook his head, and Troy stopped. "You don't understand how difficult this life is, Troy."

Troy grabbed one of Mitsrii's wrists with his good hand. "You taught me my ninth language. I want to learn more. I want you to be my teacher. I do not want to live without you. Please."

Mitsrii held Troy's gaze, seeing and understanding the man's desperation and his love. The low sun threw one side of his face into shadow. Evening birds twittered around them. At last, Mitsrii hugged him then turned his head to kiss him. Without speaking, Mitsrii looked again into those eyes.

Troy's whole face was now alight with joy and excitement. "Thank you."

Mitsrii smiled.

Side by side, they returned to the waiting camp.

~The End~

About the Author

Jordan Taylor lives in the Pacific Northwest with several pets; dividing time between training dogs, collecting canine movie memorabilia, reading classic and modern literature, and writing. Learn more about Jordan online at http://www.jordantaylorbooks.com/